To help you remember that you read this book, you may put
your initials in a box below. Please do not write on the book
pages. Thank you.

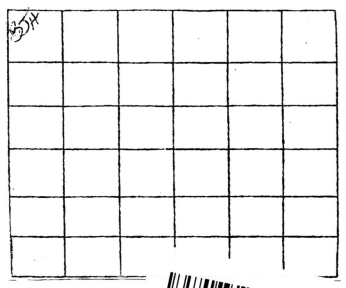

D1446190

TIME TO SHARE

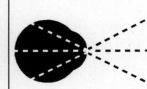

This Large Print Book carries the
Seal of Approval of N.A.V.H.

TIME TO SHARE

JO ANN BROWN

THORNDIKE PRESS
A part of Gale, Cengage Learning

GALE
CENGAGE Learning

Detroit • New York • San Francisco • New Haven, Conn • Waterville, Maine • London

GALE
CENGAGE Learning™

LIBRARY OF CONGRESS CATALOGING-IN-PUBLICATION DATA

Brown, Jo Ann.
    Time to share / by Jo Ann Brown.
        p. cm. — (Thorndike Press large print Christian mystery)
    (Patchwork mysteries)
    ISBN-13: 978-1-4104-4061-7 (hardcover)
    ISBN-10: 1-4104-4061-3 (hardcover)
    1. Quilts—Fiction. 2. Theft—Fiction. 3. Conduct of life—Fiction. 4.
Large type books. I. Title.
PS3602.R714T56 2011
813'.6—dc22   2011028316

Published in 2011 by arrangement with Guideposts a Church Corporation.

Printed in Mexico
1 2 3 4 5 6 7 15 14 13 12 11

For Bill,
with whom I always
share the best times

CHAPTER ONE

Clouds slid away from the peak of Mount Greylock just as Sarah Hart and her twin granddaughters, Audrey and Amy, reached the summit. The valley below, squeezed between the Berkshires to the south and the Green Mountains to the north, was a patchwork of emerald fields and gray rooftops.

"Just in time," Sarah said. "I don't think I know any more 'mountain' songs we can sing."

As her granddaughters laughed, Sarah looked up at the Veterans War Memorial Tower set on the mountain's highest point. The white granite monument, over ninety feet tall, had been invisible only seconds before, but as they emerged from among the bent and gnarled trees edging the open area at the summit, it was awash in sunshine.

"It looks like a giant pepper mill," Amy said with a twelve-year-old's perception.

Like her twin, Audrey, she was wearing blue jeans, a Red Sox cap, and a white T-shirt with HAWTHORNE MIDDLE SCHOOL in bright red letters across the front.

"More like a pawn on a chessboard," Audrey said. "What's the glass ball on top for?"

Sarah paused, glad to catch her breath after the climb up the mountain. They had taken one of the easier trails, but even so, the route had been four miles of steady rise. She took a bottle of water out of her red paisley bag, opened it, and drank.

"That's the beacon," she replied. "It's lit at night during the summer and winter. Not in the spring and fall when the birds are migrating, because it confuses them." She wagged a finger at Audrey. "I thought the war memorial was the subject of your class project on unsung heroes. Are you trying to get me to do your homework for you?"

Audrey laughed, her freckled nose crinkling. "Grandma, I was just checking to see how much you know."

"Uh-huh." Sarah laughed too. Every minute she had with her granddaughters was a treasure; since they moved to Maple Hill during the summer, she had looked forward to special moments like this with them. There had been too few when they lived across the country in California. "But remember that I won't be the one standing up to give your presentation."

"We know, Grandma," Amy said. She grabbed her cap as a gust of wind tried to pull it off.

"It won't be that bad," Audrey said. "We only have to do a three-minute speech."

"Not that bad for you. My knees are shaking just thinking about it. You'll get up there and ace it."

"It's easy. You've just got to have a few tricks."

"Don't tell me you imagine the audience in their underwear," Sarah said.

The girls stared at her. "Ewww. No way."

Sarah laughed and walked along the dirt path toward the war memorial. The girls followed, still talking about the upcoming presentations that they would be delivering on Open House Night at Hawthorne Middle School next month.

"Who will be your unsung heroes, Amy?" Sarah asked.

"Hikers."

Sarah smiled. Trust Amy to find some athletic connection for her project. "OK, tell me. How can hikers be unsung heroes?"

"Not all of them. Just the ones who make sure they don't leave any litter along the trails. The ones who make sure they carry everything with them to where it can be disposed or recycled." Amy's eyes twinkled with her grin. "People complain about hikers who leave a mess, but never talk about the good ones who don't."

"Like us," Audrey added.

Amy laughed. "I could interview you for my project."

"Both of you are looking for the easy way out." Sarah draped her arms around the twins' shoulders.

About two dozen people were on the grounds of the memorial. Some sat on the base or on the stone wall by the edge of the mountain, enjoying the spectacular views of the valley and the mountains beyond; a few stood with their arms stretched out as if they expected the wind to lift them and let them soar over the valley; and more were bent like trees, waiting for the wind out of the west to die down again. Children raced across the small grassy area and toward Bascom Lodge, a two-story stone building built low to withstand the strong winds and snow. The mountain was closed to visitors in the winter, but Sarah had seen pictures of its trees enveloped in ice.

Fortunately, this late September afternoon was blustery but beautiful. With the trees just beginning to change from their summer

10

green to brilliant oranges, subdued yellows, and fiery reds, it was like standing in a perfect photograph.

"Why don't you girls get your cameras out?" Sarah remembered to ask. The twins slipped off their backpacks. Amy pulled out a still camera and Audrey, a video camera.

"There's the Rosenthals!" Amy called out, leading the way around the war memorial toward the summit road.

"Let's wait here," Sarah said. "Once they've parked, they'll find us."

"You're so lucky to be working with Emma and Cole," Audrey said as she fiddled with the video camera.

"Who are your partners?" Sarah asked.

"Tracy Witherspoon." She didn't look up.

"And who else?"

"Just Tracy. My team is the only one with two because we've got twenty-three kids in class. Seven teams of three and one team of two, and I got stuck with only one partner. I wouldn't mind, except that it's Tracy."

Sarah frowned. Audrey was having a difficult time adjusting to the move from California and it showed in her bitter tone. But Sarah said nothing — she knew the twins' parents were doing their best to help the girls. She didn't want to interfere, though she would mention the conversation

11

to her son, Jason, when they returned home.

"Hi!" Amy yelled, her voice breaking Sarah free of dreary thoughts. Amy ran to meet a girl and a boy her age, who were walking from the summit parking lot, both in the same jeans and shirts as the twins. Behind them came a woman who must have been the boy's mother, because she had the same dark brown curly hair. She waved.

Audrey continued to watch the vehicles coming in a steady parade up the road to the parking lot. The summit was always busy on weekends once the leaves started turning.

"I'm sure Tracy will be along soon," Sarah said.

Audrey didn't say anything as Amy returned with her friends.

"Cole, Emma," Amy pointed to her classmates. "This is my Grandma Hart. She's really cool because she solves mysteries."

Sarah didn't want anyone to get the wrong impression. After greeting the children and the woman, whose name was Diane, she said, "It was only one mystery, Amy, and I don't think Sherlock Holmes has anything to worry about."

"But it was cool anyhow." Without stopping to take a breath, Amy asked, "Can we get to work now?"

With a smile, Sarah nodded. "Just stay where I can see you. If you need to go somewhere else, check with me first."

"Wait!" cried Audrey. "Where's Tracy?"

Cole shrugged.

Emma said, "She called and told me to go ahead without her. I guess her folks are bringing her up." She pulled out her cell phone. "Do you want me to call her if I can get a signal here?"

"I don't think you'll have a problem." Sarah pointed to the cell tower that rivaled the war memorial.

Emma dialed the number and handed it to Audrey.

They stood around while Audrey waited for Tracy to pick up. Finally Audrey spoke. "This is Audrey. I'm on top of Mount Greylock. Where are you?" She stabbed the button to end the call and kicked at the ground. "I'll just start without her, I guess."

"That's a good idea," said Sarah, stroking Audrey's hair. She could feel her granddaughter's tension; even though Audrey was acting somewhat nonchalant, she was upset. But was it just because her project partner was late? Audrey was clearly not thrilled about being paired with Tracy Witherspoon, so there might be more to the situation than the kids were letting on.

"Hey," Sarah said, "there are several hikers coming along the Appalachian Trail right now. Why don't you give Amy the video camera so her team can start their interviews? You can get some photos of the war memorial while you wait for Tracy."

"Go on, kids," Cole's mother said. "Get your footage and interviews and whatever else you need. We've got to leave in an hour."

The four ran past the tower, pausing to pet two pugs walking with their owner.

Diane turned to Sarah. "Do you want to get a cup of coffee? They brew a pretty good cup in the lodge."

"Go ahead. I'd like to keep a close eye on Audrey while she's on her own. I also want to do some sketches."

"You're an artist?"

Sarah shook her head. "Only by the greatest stretch of the imagination. I'm doing some very rough sketches to help me remember the colors and shapes for a wall quilt I'm making."

"Good luck holding onto the paper," Diane replied as another gust of wind blew over the mountaintop. She hunched her shoulders and hurried toward the lodge. To the west, the sky was clear; they should have some time before the summit vanished into mist again.

Sarah walked down to the half wall about thirty feet away from the memorial. She sat on the dry stone wall, finding a spot where the slope allowed her to put her feet on the ground and where she had a clear view of both the valley and the trail. There, Amy's team was now interviewing two hikers only a few years older than the kids, and Audrey was getting photos of the war memorial from every possible angle.

Sarah drew out the sketch pad and her colored pencils and set them next to her. She could have borrowed the camera to take a panoramic shot of the hills, but drawing the scene herself, selecting the colors, and feeling the contours of the land as the picture grew on the page would help her remember the nuances.

She was planning on making the wall quilt from scraps left over from other projects. She wanted to hang it above the mantel in the living room, where she could enjoy it when she sat in the rocker her late husband, Gerry, had made for her. An heirloom painting of Mount Greylock had been displayed there since she was a young bride. When her son bought the house that once had been her parents', she had been happy to return the painting to where it once had hung.

She bent to her work, but an hour later, she had only the beginnings of a sketch. She'd spent more time watching the twins and their friends than drawing. Yet it was enough — each time she checked to make sure they remained safe and in sight, she took in the wondrous panorama of the mountaintop and shifting clouds, and after guiding her pencils along those same splendid lines, she had the basic image she needed.

Audrey and Amy ran to her after the other children left to explore the war memorial. Amy bounded up eager as a pup, and Audrey trailed behind. Tracy had never shown up, but Audrey shrugged off Sarah's attempts at consolation.

"Can we go up into the monument with Emma and Cole?" Amy asked. "They're going up before they leave. We can get some good pictures of the Appalachian Trail from there."

Sarah gave her consent and started packing her sketch pad and pencils in her bag. Amy handed her the digital camera and ran along the wall to look at the view stretched out below. Sarah put it in her bag and asked the twins about the information they had gathered for their reports. Both girls talked at the same time, eager to share, and Sarah did her best to pick out each girl's words.

They entered the war memorial and the girls pelted up the stairs, calling for their grandmother to follow. At the top, about four stories above the ground, windows cut into the granite offered an amazing 360-degree view of the mountain's summit. The twins, giggling, joined the other kids and took turns taking movies out the windows any time other tourists stepped aside and gave them a clear shot. The window closest to Sarah offered her an eagle-eyed view of the valley. From here, she could see the ponds in the valley. She'd add them to her wall quilt.

Soon, though, another cloud crept by, obscuring everything in cottony white.

"Grandma!" called Audrey. "Come look! It's so weird!"

Sarah took a single step, but her cell phone jangled in her bag. She edged aside to allow people to go down the stairs, and she groped in her bag for the phone. From across the room, she heard Audrey's laugh and saw Amy holding the camera up against one of the windows. The view was being consumed, bit by bit, by the clouds.

Her fingers found the phone. She pulled it out and flipped it open. "Hello?"

"Oh, Sarah, thank goodness you had your

phone on. I didn't know what I'd do if I couldn't contact you." It was Maggie, her daughter-in-law and the twins' mother. "Jason drove over to Pittsfield on an errand, and I'm not getting any answer from him." Sarah knew how bad the reception could be in the mountains.

"Maggie, what's wrong?"

"I think someone broke into the store."

"What?" A hundred questions bounced through her head, but that was the only one that escaped her lips. Maggie's antique store in Maple Hill had been open only a few weeks.

"When I got here, the back door was open."

"Broken open?"

"No, just open. But that means it's been open all night."

Sarah took a breath. "Are you OK?"

"I'm fine."

"And the store?"

"I don't know. I haven't gone in yet." Her words spilled out in a rush. "I didn't want to go inside alone." Maggie paused. Then, her voice dropping to a whisper, she said, "Just stay on the line until I make sure everything's fine. OK?"

"OK," Sarah said, even though it wasn't. A chill crept down her spine. If an intruder was still in the store . . . Silently, she prayed, *Dear Father, protect Maggie. Help me to say the right things to strengthen her and comfort her.*

"I'm going inside now."

"Keep talking." The noise around Sarah withered to a distant hum. She watched the kids, but didn't hear what they were talking about as they pointed out the windows and giggled. It was as if she stood between two realities — the one with her grandchildren having fun and the other with Maggie as she walked into the store. "Maggie, keep talking."

"I've got the door open. Nothing out of place in the storage room. A few papers are scattered around."

"The wind could have done that."

"I know. I'm going to open the door to the store."

"If there's someone in there, run outside and call 911."

"I will. I promise." She hesitated, and then whispered, "Thanks for being here, Sarah."

"I'll always be here for you."

"I know. Here I go."

Sarah held her breath and heard Gerry's voice echo in her mind. How many times had he reminded her that there was nothing that she could make better by fretting about it? Better to face it head on, he'd said.

Only silence came from the phone. She shifted it, hoping she hadn't lost the connection, but the call hadn't dropped. She wanted to call Maggie's name. Remind her to keep talking. Tell her to describe what she saw. But she didn't dare to speak. If there was an intruder in the store, a single word coming through the phone might betray Maggie.

Could Sarah's heartbeat be heard in the store? It thumped in her chest like rain on a metal roof.

Maggie gasped. "Sarah, don't bring the girls here. Please take them straight home."

"Maggie, is everything all right?"

"I've got to call the police."

CHAPTER TWO

Magpie's Antiques was the perfect name for Maggie's store on the village green, because everywhere Sarah looked, there was something shiny. A gold-framed mirror, a silver tea service set on a gleaming mahogany table, ornate art-deco jewelry in a glass case. Even the bell over the door that jangled as Sarah came in glistened. She usually enjoyed coming to the store to admire the pretty pieces.

Not today. Even if she hadn't gotten Maggie's call, Sarah would have known something was wrong as soon as she stepped inside the store. The young police officer who had gone to school with her son, Jason, recognized her and let her into the store once she promised not to touch anything. Two other officers were squatting by the back door.

She was relieved to see the store looked untouched. The cases weren't broken, and the china wasn't shattered.

Maggie rushed toward Sarah, her shoulders stiff beneath her light blue blouse, and her beautiful auburn hair seemed to have lost its ruddy glow.

"Where are the girls?" Maggie asked.

"I left them at my house with Rita." Rita French was one of her boarders and Sarah's cousin. She would keep a close eye on the girls. "I told them that you or Jason would pick them up. Is he here yet?"

"Not yet, but he's on his way."

Sarah gave her daughter-in-law a hug, feeling damp tears on her shoulder.

"I'm sorry, Sarah." Maggie stepped away and wiped her cheeks with the back of her hand. "It's been a tough day." Her face got even more ashen.

"Are you really OK?"

"Almost. I know it's just a store and it only contains things, but I feel as if my life's been invaded. What would have happened if the thief had come while I was here?"

"But that didn't happen." She squeezed Maggie's hand. "Thank God for that."

"I have. With every breath."

Sarah smiled. Sarah had always admired Maggie's quiet, unwavering faith. It gave her strength to face challenges — and having her store robbed would demand every ounce of that resilience.

"What have the police said?" Sarah asked.

"Not much. They've asked me a lot of questions and spent the rest of the time checking the store."

"Have they found anything?"

"A folded-up piece of paper. They think it'd been set in the door to keep it from locking securely."

"Did it say anything?"

"It was one of my invoice pages that I keep on the counter."

"So anyone who came into the store could have had access to it?"

"Yes."

"What was taken? It looks like everything is here."

Maggie sighed and pointed toward a Welsh china cupboard. "The only thing missing is the oak wall clock I had hanging there."

"That beat-up old clock?" She couldn't help but notice it the last time she'd been in the store. Everything else in the store was lovely, but the battered clock looked as if it belonged in the garbage. Its wooden case was chipped, the glass over the dial was cracked, and the numbers from 5 to 11 were missing. In addition, the pendulum had fallen to the bottom.

"It *is* an antique. It's over 150 years old."

At Maggie's retort, Sarah weighed her answer carefully. She'd never seen her daughter-in-law so prickly.

"So it is very valuable?" Sarah asked.

"The clock could be nice if someone put the time and money into getting it going again. As it is now . . ." She shrugged. "I've got a lot of pricey antiques here. Why take the clock? It doesn't make any sense."

"Maybe the thief doesn't know what's valuable and what isn't."

"Then why rob an antiques store?"

Before Sarah could reply, a deep voice echoed from the back of the store. "Dust for fingerprints. Maybe we'll be luckier here than we were at the Poplawskis'."

Sarah exchanged a glance with Maggie. Another robbery in Maple Hill? She was astonished. The last robbery Sarah could remember had been more than six years ago — when Gerry was still alive — and even then it had turned out to be kids playing a prank.

Chief Webber walked toward them. He wore a radio on the shoulder of the department's simple blue shirt. He wore black trousers beneath a black windbreaker, but she could easily envision him in camouflage. He'd spent almost ten years in the U.S.

24

Army as a military policeman before joining the Maple Hill Police Department and rising to the position of chief. His hair was salted with gray, the only sign that he was past forty. He was as lean as a police-academy cadet, and his brown eyes seldom missed anything.

"Hello, Mrs. Hart," he said. "Maggie told us that you'd be coming." He looked at Maggie. "I'd like to see those sales slips now."

Maggie nodded. "Let me get them." She went around the counter, took a box from beneath it, and opened it. She took out a handful of sales slips and sorted them. "The ones in the smaller stack are the slips for antiques I've sold, the larger for items I've bought."

He picked up one from the shorter pile and scanned it. "Do you have your customers' names on all of them?"

"Yes. That's my way of keeping track of what they've bought in case I get something similar in."

"And when you buy something yourself?"

"I keep track of those names too."

"Excellent. May I take these with me?"

"Certainly." She put the slips in the box and then handed it to him.

"Can you think of anyone else who's been

in during the past week, but didn't buy or sell anything?"

Maggie blanched. "You mean like someone casing the store?"

He gave her a bolstering smile. "Or just checking things out. Don't worry about getting someone in trouble. Most people are happy to answer a few questions if they can help catch a thief."

"Let's see." She considered for a moment, and then said, "Arnold Kirschner comes in about once a week to look around. So does Peg Girard. She asks about different items I have for sale, but she's never bought anything. Karen Bancroft comes in to chat sometimes, but I can't remember if she did last week. There are others, but I don't know their names."

He wrote down the names she'd given him. "This will get us started."

As soon as he thanked them, Maggie asked, "Was there another robbery last night?"

Chief Webber hesitated. "It may not have been last night. They didn't know anything was missing from their barn until this morning."

"Did they lose antiques too?"

"Sorry Mrs. Hart I really shouldn't say at this point." He gave them a kind but profes-

26

sional smile.

A voice crackled on the radio clipped to his shoulder, "211 reported at 307 County."

"Isn't that out by the Kirschners'?" Sarah said. Chief Webber didn't answer, but Sarah was sure it was. But what was a 211? Dottie and Arnold Kirschner were members of the Bridge Street Church. What was going on in Maple Hill?

Sarah didn't have any answers when she went to her house to pick up the twins. Jason had arrived at the store as the police were finishing up, so Sarah volunteered to take Audrey and Amy home. The girls pelted her with questions, but she halted them simply by suggesting they stop to pick up some pizza. The conversation then turned to a debate of sausage versus pepperoni.

By the time they reached the twins' house, Sarah's silver Pontiac Grand Prix was filled with the aromas of tangy sauce and cheese. Each girl carried a box up the porch steps.

Sarah opened the front door and realized how accustomed she was to the commotion of a busy family in the house. The concert of hammering and sawing and ripping up carpet and tearing down wallpaper and plaster had been silenced. Not a light shone anywhere, and shadows had crawled out of places where Sarah couldn't remember ever seeing them before. She put out her arm to halt the girls from racing into the house. When they looked at her, puzzled, she lowered her arm.

"Don't pepper your mother with a bunch of questions, OK?" she asked.

The twins exchanged anxious glances, and then nodded.

Sarah motioned for the girls to follow. As they reached the foot of the stairs, Maggie stepped out of the door that led to the cellar. Both girls launched themselves at her.

She hugged them close. "I'm fine. Don't worry. The thief is long gone."

"But —" began Amy.

"It's time to let the police do their jobs. All we can do is pray that they catch the thief before he can rob someone else." She released the twins. "So tell me. How did it go up on Mount Greylock?" she asked with feigned brightness.

"Mom, wait till you see the pictures we shot!" Amy said. "They're so cool."

"I can't wait to see them, but I'm going to have to. The power's out again. Your dad is down in the cellar trying to figure out what's wrong this time."

"Ah, Mom!" groaned Audrey. "Why can't

28

we live in the twenty-first century like the rest of the world?"

"We're working on it." Maggie ruffled her daughter's hair.

"By the time this house is fixed up enough for the twenty-first century, it'll be the twenty-second!" Audrey said, holding out her pizza box. "We can't even nuke this."

Maggie took both boxes and set them on the dining-room table. "He shouldn't be long."

"Why can't we live in a new house like we did in California?" Audrey stormed up the stairs.

When Amy followed her sister, Maggie sighed.

"It's OK," she said before Sarah could sympathize. "I'm getting used to the combination of their being twelve and being upset about the move. I think Amy would have settled in by now if Audrey didn't use everything as an excuse to let us know how we've ruined her life forever."

"And they're not even teenagers yet."

A faint smile curved Maggie's lips as the squeaking floors upstairs announced that the girls had gone to their rooms. "Don't remind me. Come on. We might as well sit and chat while we wait for Jason to get the lights on."

"Some quiet would be nice."

"And it'll give me a chance to apologize for biting your head off at the store."

"No apology is necessary."

"Well, you're going to get one anyhow." Maggie went into the parlor and sat in a chair beside the fireplace. "You know, I would have expected this in Los Angeles, but not here." Sarah sat on the pale-blue camelback sofa. The room, with its bay window edged with lace curtains and sunny yellow walls, was brighter than the foyer. "I was excited to think about living in a place where people don't have to lock their doors. I guess it was a silly fantasy."

"There's nothing silly about it," Sarah hurried to reassure her.

The lights flickered and then died again. From the cellar came clumping and a clatter of tools, followed by Jason calling up the stairs, "I'm OK. I'll have the lights on in a minute."

"Don't let Jason's cheerful tone fool you." Maggie's shoulders rose with her deep breath, and then slowly lowered as she expelled it. "He's upset too."

"That's no surprise."

"And thanks for not asking any more questions. I'm not sure how many more I could take now. Before the cops left, Chief

Webber said he'd let me know as soon as they find anything to identify who broke in."

Sarah's smile became genuine. "He's a good man. If there's a clue waiting to be found, he'll be the one to find it."

"Unless you beat him to it, Grandma," Amy said as she came into the parlor. After giving her mother another hug, she dropped down next to Sarah.

"How long have you been eavesdropping?" Maggie asked.

"Long enough," replied Amy. "Can I help you find the thief, Grandma?"

"No," Sarah said, "but thank you for offering."

"Why not?"

"Because I'm going to leave this investigation to the police. I plan to spend the next couple of weeks working on my wall quilt." Was she saying that to convince them or herself? Maybe both. It was tempting to imagine herself playing a small part in the thief's capture.

It was tempting *and* silly.

"Oh, c'mon," Amy said. "What did the police tell you, Mom? They've got to have some clues."

Maggie leaned back in her chair. "Chief Webber asked if I'd seen a man in a dark green cloth coat hanging around near my store. Someone reported seeing someone who fit that description."

"Then again," Sarah said, "the man could have nothing to do with the robberies."

"True." Maggie sighed and turned to Amy. "Where's the camera? With the power out, the only way I can watch your video is on it."

"But the sound is lousy on it. I want you to see it on the TV."

"All right. I'll wait, but tell me. Did you talk to any really interesting people?"

Amy jumped in to answer. She shared a riddle her project partner, Cole, had told and giggled so hard she could barely give the silly answer.

Sarah listened, knowing Amy was doing all she could to lift her mother's spirits. When Amy impersonated the pugs she'd seen by the memorial, Maggie laughed.

The noise coaxed Audrey down from her bedroom. She came in and sat next to Amy, and Maggie asked if she'd had a good time.

"Tracy never even showed up," Audrey said. "Did she call here to say she wasn't coming?"

"There weren't any voice mail messages before I left. Maybe she texted you or sent an e-mail."

Audrey toed off her shoes and folded her

legs beneath her. "I checked. Nothing. She just blew me off, and when we give the presentations, she'll take credit for the work I did. It's not fair."

"Maybe she intended to let you know, but didn't have time," Amy said.

Audrey jumped to her feet. "She could have called me when she called Emma." She walked back out of the room toward the kitchen.

Maggie sighed. "Amy, what's going on between your sister and her friend."

"Friend?" Amy shook her head. "Tracy isn't her friend."

"She's not?" Maggie asked.

"Their lockers are right next to each other. Mine is just a couple away, but I've never heard them talk to each other except when Audrey said hi to Tracy a couple of times."

Audrey came back into the room and glared at her twin. "Thanks for telling everyone my business."

"Audrey," Maggie said.

"Tracy Witherspoon snubs me. All the time. Even in class, she refuses to talk to me or pass papers to me. It's like I'm invisible." She dropped heavily to the sofa. "I can't believe I'm stuck with her as a partner. She's skipping out on the work, and I'm go-

33

ing to fail because of her. It's *so* not fair."

"Why don't you talk to your teacher tomorrow?" Sarah asked as she put her arm around Audrey. "Explain what has happened, and I'm sure she'll help you figure out a way to share the project fairly."

Audrey nodded, but she clearly did not want to be appeased. Sarah remembered how, at twelve, any event could quickly become a crisis of epic proportions.

Suddenly every light in the room blinked and stayed on. While Maggie got up to turn off the lamps on the marble-topped side tables, the cellar door opened and Jason emerged, wiping cobwebs from his hair and shoulders.

He walked over to Sarah, kissed her on the cheek and asked how she was doing.

"Fine," she replied. "Did you get up close and personal with every spider in the cellar?"

"It feels like it." He held up two fuses. "Here are the culprits. That's the fifth and sixth ones we've blown in the past two weeks. I guess I can't put off getting an electrician in any longer. I'll give the handyman a call and see if he can come over tomorrow. Do you have his number somewhere, Maggie?"

"Sure," Maggie said, standing.

34

"Ah, you're discovering the charm of old buildings." Sarah smiled and was glad when Maggie did too.

"Charm isn't the word I'd use. I keep getting zapped whenever I turn the lights on or off." She patted Amy's arm. "Why don't you get your video ready to show us?"

Jason sneezed once, a second time, and then a third time.

"God bless you," Sarah said. "I think I'm becoming allergic to my cellar. If spider webs and dust became valuable, we'd be millionaires."

While the girls hooked the video camera to the TV and Jason went to call the handyman, Sarah shifted to one end of the sofa. When he returned, they started the video.

"Amy and Cole and Emma's video is first," Audrey said. "Then you'll see what I did. Last is what we shot up in the war memorial."

"A triple feature!" Jason said and sneezed again.

"Bless you," the twins said together before Audrey asked, "All set?" She pressed play on the camcorder.

Sarah was pleased to see how polite the twins and their friends were when they approached people to ask for an interview. The questions were insightful, but never made anyone uncomfortable. In fact, all the people interviewed seemed to enjoy it. One of the hikers even unpacked his backpack to show his method for carrying his supplies and his trash to help assure that the Appalachian Trail remained pristine.

The bright sunlight dimmed when the scene shifted to the circular room at the base of the memorial. The camera panned around the walls with the windows set deep into recesses at the four compass points. It slid up to the gilded, domed ceiling before Audrey focused on a father and two children. The questions and the responses became serious, especially after the father identified himself as a member of the National Guard. Audrey had done a good job of showing how servicemen and women were unsung heroes.

Abruptly the scene changed again, and they were looking down over the mountainside to the valley.

"That's the end of our interviews. The rest is what we took while we were goofing off," Amy said with a proud smile that broadened when Sarah applauded.

"Great job!" Jason exclaimed. "Good questions and good use of the camera. Both of you."

As Maggie added her praise, the video

continued to play. Sarah was relieved to hear Maggie's laughter along with the others.

"How about heating up that pizza?" asked Maggie, standing.

The twins raced toward the kitchen, and Maggie and Jason followed right behind.

Sarah picked up the camera while the sounds of the kids' distorted voices played through the TV. In the video, they called to her. She stiffened. That was the moment Maggie had phoned her.

She turned the camera over to find the button to stop the video. She raised her eyes to the TV screen, so she could be certain the video stopped, but her finger froze over the button. There was something on the screen. She stared at a form partially visible in the cloud rolling over the mountain.

It was a man. He was off the trail and among the stunted trees clinging to the summit. What was he doing there? The bushes were thick, and it had to be tough walking. Then she saw him look in every direction. He crouched down farther.

He clearly didn't want to be seen.

Sarah peered closer at the television set, trying to will the clouds aside so she could get a clear view of the man. The mist erased colors as if the girls had shot in black and white. She couldn't tell anything about him other than his shape.

He turned his head to the side, and she saw he was wearing a baseball cap. It was a dark color. Red Sox or Yankees, she assumed. Everyone around here was a fan of one team or the other.

But what if he wasn't from around Maple Hill? She couldn't imagine one reason why one of her neighbors would be lurking in the underbrush at the top of Mount Greylock.

He tugged the baseball cap down over his forehead and checked his coat collar. It was turned up, so even if the cloud hadn't been there, his face would have been invisible.

Then he moved again. He reached down, and his back arched. He was struggling with something she couldn't see because the bushes were too thick. Was he trying to pull something somewhere? No, he didn't move. He must be yanking at something.

What was there to yank on out in the bushes? None of this made sense.

The cloud shifted, and, for just a second, the world regained its color. Like a frightened animal who didn't want to be seen in the sunlight, the man rushed away down the mountain toward one of the toughest trails. She gasped when she saw it.

His coat was made of dark green cloth.

Could it be the same man who'd been seen near the robberies? If so, *what* had he been doing up on the mountain?

She looked toward the kitchen and heard the laughter of her family. Could that man be the one who had stolen the clock from Maggie's store? If there was any chance it was the same person, she needed to find out.

CHAPTER THREE

Sarah woke up the next morning, thinking about the man in the video. There could be any number of people who had dark green cloth coats just as there could be any number of reasons why the man had been in the underbrush.

But she knew that one plus one usually did add up to two, and she was too curious not to check. More important, if she could find some clue to help the police, Maggie might stop flinching at every sound as she had during supper last night. Mount Greylock wasn't too far away. She'd just take a quick look.

Sarah took extra time while she made breakfast to ask for God's guidance. The quiet in the cozy kitchen and the warm glow of the sunrise on the cranberry walls and cream cabinets helped open her heart and her mind. She was a little worried about going up to the summit on her own, but knew, as she had told Maggie yesterday, she would never be truly alone.

She was just about to pour herself a second cup of coffee when the phone rang. Picking it up, she said, "Good morning."

"Good morning, Sarah!" It was her best friend, Martha Maplethorpe, warm and exuberant. "I saw Dottie Kirschner at Liam's this morning. She and Arnold were in there geting muffins for breakfast like they are most days since he retired. She told me about the robberies. She's really upset. How's Maggie?"

"Doing as well as can be expected." She sighed. "All the years they lived in Los Angeles, they never had a break-in. Now they've come to Maple Hill, and Maggie's store is robbed."

"You don't think they'll move away again, do you?"

"I don't think they'd be able to sell their house."

Martha chuckled, before saying, "At least the plumbing works."

"Are you having problems with your pipes again?"

"*Still!* I don't know what's wrong with Bob. He used to be the most dependable handyman in town, but he hasn't shown up for more than a week. He left the kitchen sink in pieces, and the bathroom sink won't stop dripping. I'll go crazy if he doesn't fix it soon."

"Maybe he'll come today."

"No, Ernie called, and Bob's wife said he's gone to Springfield for parts for *their* sink."

Sarah was tempted to laugh, but she knew Martha was too frustrated to see the irony. "Jason and Maggie have a handyman they use. Why don't you have Ernie call him? Is Ernie doing OK?"

"He is. His doctor gave him a new drug to help with the tremors, and it seems to be helping."

"Praise the Lord."

"And pray the medicine continues to work without a lot of side effects." Martha's voice faltered.

Sarah knew she had to distract her friend. "Would you like to come to Mount Greylock with me?"

Martha seemed interested, "Didn't you just go up there yesterday with the twins?"

"Yes, and I wanted to go back." Sarah said.

"Pick me up," Martha said before she had finished, "and I'll go with you."

"I'll be there in five minutes."

"And bring the name of that handyman of Jason's."

■ ■ ■ ■

While Sarah drove her silver car up the steep road, slowing for the hairpin turns, she answered Martha's questions, starting with the name of the handyman: Dave Diamond.

"Diamond?" Martha said. "You know, I think I heard someone say he's not very friendly."

Sarah smiled. "Martha, you don't need him to be friendly. You need him to fix your sinks."

"True. True."

She also shared what Maggie had told her about the man in a dark green cloth coat being seen near the earlier robberies.

In the passenger seat, Martha kept her crochet hook and fingers flying. She was making another one of the child-sized afghans she donated to Project Linus, a charity that donated the blankets to hospitals where they were given to sick children. This one was a wild orange, a shade sure to light up a hospital room. She enjoyed creating the afghans almost as much as she delighted in the notes she received from children who were thrilled with her colorful projects.

"Green cloth coat?" asked Martha. "There

could be any number around Maple Hill. Farmers have been wearing that kind of coat for years."

"I know it's a long shot. But if I can do something to help Maggie, I'm going to do it."

"And I'll try to help you."

Martha began to devise outrageous theories of why a man in a dark green coat would start a "crime wave" in Maple Hill. Sarah appreciated her friend's attempt to make her laugh, but none of the scenarios Martha imagined seemed very likely.

The summit was deserted. Only two cars were parked in the lot. The weekend hikers and tourists had returned to jobs and school. The sunshine was bright, but a chilly wind must have chased the drivers of the other cars into the lodge. Sarah was tempted to join them.

"Which way do we go?" asked Martha. She wore a bright red cardigan and carried a large purse of the same color. Only a couple of inches taller than Sarah, she was the picture of a nice, round grandmother with the perfect lap for grandchildren.

"To the war memorial and then left toward the Appalachian Trail." Sarah buttoned up her navy coat. She started to turn up the collar, but then paused as she thought of how the man had done the same.

Maybe he hadn't been trying to hide. Maybe he'd just been cold.

Doubts about investigating the summit enveloped her again. But how could she do nothing when her friends and her family were so distressed? The very least she could do was look around.

As they climbed the steps to the path to the memorial, Martha scanned the area. "Did you see anything other than the dark green coat?"

"I'm not even one hundred percent sure that the coat was dark green. We replayed the tape several times, and with the mist obscuring pretty much everything, we couldn't tell."

"Not much to go on, is there?"

"Which is why we're here."

Again Martha looked around. "Which way now?"

"Audrey was pretty sure they'd been standing in the window directly opposite the lodge when they noticed something moving in the bushes. That makes sense because I was near the top of the stairs when Maggie called, and the girls were partway around the viewing area."

"Then let's go." Martha pointed toward a sign. "Thunderbolt Shelter and Appalachian

Trail N."

Sarah set off along the pebble path, which was wide enough for two people to walk abreast. It curved into the trees quickly, leaving the open area around the war memorial behind.

Overhead, a hawk rode the thermals. Even while trying to solve this puzzle, Sarah took a moment to savor the glories of God's world. The wind whispering through the trees offered a gentle soundtrack for the bird's dance among the clouds. Bright leaves on the ground hinted at the magnificent palette that would spread across the hills as autumn unfolded.

Every few feet, Sarah glanced back at the memorial to gauge their distance and angle. They needed to go toward where the mountain dropped off sharply. There were no crags along this part of the mountain, but they would have to be careful.

"Do you see anyone?" Martha whispered, glancing around as if she expected an ambush.

"No."

"But we wouldn't see anyone if they were in the bushes, right?"

"Just keep your eyes open."

When Sarah led the way off the path, she held her bag close. Every branch and briar wanted to rip it off her arm. Each twig breaking beneath her feet sounded like a gunshot. Ridges of raw stone burst out of the ground. Centuries of wind and rain had gouged narrow lines into the rock. Sarah watched each step, not wanting to slip.

"Be careful, Martha," she warned.

"I'm trying to. Next time we chase a thief, let's have it be on a sidewalk, OK?"

Sarah eased more deeply into the underbrush. "Or we'll bring machetes."

Again and again, she looked at the top of the memorial. She went a bit to her left and farther down the mountain. She eased aside another bush, holding it until Martha grabbed it. She didn't want any branch whipping back at her friend. And she held her breath, hoping that no one was waiting to jump out from behind a bush. She knew she was being silly. They should be perfectly safe. But she couldn't keep from thinking how deserted the mountaintop was and how no one would be able to see them from the lodge.

Her toe hit something hard. "Ouch!" she yelped. She looked down to see what she'd run into, and gasped.

A weathered wooden door was built into the mountain. Its frame had rotted on two sides. The door itself was made from a single plank and held in place with rusted hinges. A glance over her shoulder told her that they had to be close to where the furtive man had crouched.

"What is that?" Martha asked as she pushed away some of the overhanging branches to allow her to see the door better.

"On the video, the man was struggling with something I couldn't see." Sarah squatted down to get a closer look at the door. "I suppose it could have been this."

She'd been so focused on the man that she hadn't paid enough attention to exactly where he'd been standing.

"What else could it be?" Sarah glanced around. "He must have been trying to get this door open."

"Did he?"

Sarah smiled up at her friend, and then stood. "I don't know. The video ended before I could see."

"Then let's get this door open to find out," Martha said.

Feeling like Alice about to fall into Wonderland, Sarah bent. She set down her bag so nothing would fall out of it. She grasped the latch. Planting her feet against the ground, she gave a mighty tug — and almost fell backward as the door swung open with a creak. If Martha hadn't steadied her, she would have ended up on the ground.

"Wow!" whispered Martha. "Will you look at that!"

Sarah did as she leaned the door against a bush. Wooden steps went down into some sort of cellar. Odors of damp and decay and long-forgotten dust rose up them. At the bottom of the steps, debris gathered.

"It looks like a root cellar," Sarah said, wondering if the wooden stairs were as rickety as they appeared. If they were, she doubted they'd hold any weight. "Or maybe it's something left over from when they built the war memorial in the thirties. It could have been some sort of storage bunker to keep building supplies from getting wet."

"Maybe there's something down there that will tell us." Digging into her purse, Martha held out a small flashlight hooked to her key ring. "Here. Use this."

"I sure hope these hold." Sarah took the flashlight, and then put her foot on the top step carefully.

The wood squeaked, but didn't wobble. It was sturdier than it appeared. She leaned her hand on the stone wall edging the stairwell and eased down, testing each step before she put her full weight on it.

The cellar wasn't large, no more than ten

feet in either direction. Sarah could stand up straight, but Martha's hair brushed cobwebs on the dirt ceiling. Sunshine came down the stairs to light a small square patch in the center. Something skittered away into the shadows. Martha gave a shriek and grabbed Sarah's arm.

Sarah choked out, "What is it?"

"Something moved over there." Her hand tightened on Sarah's arm. "And right here!"

Aiming the flashlight down, Sarah saw bugs rushing to hide under the stairs. Her skin rose in goose bumps as she tried to sidestep the scurrying creatures. Puddles gathered in the low spots, and a drip came from the shadows to the right.

"I can't get away from that dripping sound," Martha said as she inched past Sarah to peer around the stairwell corner. The small flashlight bored a finger of light into the dark, which was reluctant to give up its secrets. "Nothing over here. How about on your side?"

Sarah moved the light slowly to her left. Her eyes widened when she saw something glisten. Was it another puddle? For a second, she shivered at the thought of what could be puddled in such a ghastly place. *Stop it!* she told herself. Vincent Price wasn't about to step out of the shadows.

The glint wasn't a puddle, because it was about a foot or two off the floor.

"There's something over here, Martha."

"What?"

Motioning with the flashlight, Sarah walked toward whatever reflected the light. Three large black trash bags were propped in the corner.

"Trash?" Martha's disappointment burst out.

"Maybe. Maybe not. Hold this." She handed the light to Martha and pointed at the plastic tie around the closest bag. "Keep it aimed right here."

"Don't tell me you're going to open it." Martha's nose wrinkled. "Why do you want to go poking around in some hiker's litter?"

"It doesn't smell like garbage."

"How can you tell? It smells like something died down here."

"Don't say that." A shiver ran down her spine.

"Watch out for broken glass and sharp edges."

"I will."

Sarah reached for the plastic tie holding the bag closed. A single pull revealed she'd need a pair of heavy-duty scissors to break it. Instead, she gripped one section of the bag itself and tugged. She held her breath in case Martha was right and the bags held garbage. She stepped back as the plastic tore.

A hardcover book fell out. She scooped it up before it could tumble into a puddle. When Martha shifted the light to focus on the partially torn maroon cover, remnants of gilt blinked at them.

Sarah opened the book *Leaves of Grass* by Walt Whitman. Small letters below the book's title spelled out BROOKLYN, NEW YORK 1860.

"Is it a first edition?" asked Martha.

"I don't know, but it could be because I think the book came out before the Civil War." Sarah cradled the book carefully. "It's got to be very valuable."

"Then what's it doing here?"

"That's a good question." She handed the book to Martha and then squatted down to tear the bag farther.

She took out three objects covered in white plastic. She drew back one corner. The plastic was lined with gauze to protect the base of a cranberry glass lamp, a cranberry globe, and a clear chimney. She put the lamp together. She guessed it had to be as old as the book. She wasn't an expert like Maggie, but she could see stains where oil still clung to the bowl in the base.

"That's beautiful," Martha said. "I don't understand why anyone would toss out these nice things."

"Me either." She reached into the bag again and, this time, pulled out a piece of cardboard. A discarded box for disposable bed pads. Had the gauze around the lamp come from this box? She turned it over and saw *VNA* stamped on the side. "Look at this. Why would there be something from the Visiting Nurse Association up here?"

Martha took the box. "I don't have a clue." She smiled. "But *this* might be a clue."

"Maybe. Do you know who Maple Hill's visiting nurse is?"

"No, but I'll know tomorrow afternoon."

Sarah looked at her friend, puzzled. "Why tomorrow afternoon?"

"Ernie's doctor arranged for the VNA to stop in. His doctor wants his vital signs checked regularly while Ernie gets used to his new meds, and the visiting nurse will save us from having to go to the doctor's office."

Martha put the box next to the lamp. "Is there anything else in the bag?"

"One more thing, I think." Sarah lifted out the last item.

It was a clock. An oak wall clock with chips on every edge, most of the numbers missing on the dial, and the pendulum loose in the bottom.

Sarah heard Martha talking, but the words didn't filter into her mind. All she could do was stare at the clock, which looked exactly like the one taken from Maggie's store.

Exactly like it.

But that made no sense. Why would a thief steal antiques and leave them in such a damp and dirty place? The book's pages were already crinkling, and the wooden clock would soon warp completely out of shape. The lamp could have broken if she hadn't been careful taking it out.

Setting the clock on top of the other bags, Sarah stood and brushed dirt off her shaking hands. "We need to call Chief Webber and get him up here right away."

Martha's eyes grew wide at the mention of the chief of police.

"I'm sure this is the clock stolen from the store," Sarah went on. "And I wouldn't be surprised if the lamp and the book are also stolen."

"But why bring them up here?"

"I don't know, but the thief obviously knew about this cellar."

"And he would know that nobody would look for them here." Martha warmed to her idea. "Would *you* look for stolen antiques on top of Mount Greylock?"

"It's a perfect place to stash them."

Martha set the book next to the clock. "I wonder what's in the other bags." She reached for the next bag.

Sarah halted her. "I think we should leave them alone. Our fingerprints are all over the ripped bag and these antiques, but maybe the police can find the thief's on what we haven't touched." She opened her purse and dug inside. She pulled out Amy's camera and took several pictures of the clock. She'd show them to Maggie.

Sarah then took out her phone and flipped it open. It wasn't getting a very good signal. Too much earth between her and the tower, she guessed. "I'll have to go up to call them."

"I'll go with you." Martha gave a nervous laugh. "I'm not staying down here alone with that drip-drip-drip." Something moved near the bags. "And whatever else is here."

CHAPTER FOUR

The next fifteen minutes were among the longest in Sarah's life. She and Martha had gone into the lodge to get two cups of hot tea. Though tempted to sit in the sun porch, they went back outside where they had a good view of the road.

"Do you think the police will come up with lights on and sirens blaring?" asked Martha with a grin.

"That would alert everyone within earshot."

"Oh! Do you think the robber is nearby?" All color flushed from her face.

Sarah shrugged. "If he is, he'd be crazy to stay around now that we've discovered his hiding place."

"Unless he wants to silence us."

"Martha, you know no one can silence you when you've got something you need to say."

Her friend laughed. "Let's discuss something else. I hear Amy went out for the field hockey team."

"Yes." Sarah smiled. "I can't wait to see her play."

"And Audrey?"

"Audrey isn't interested in sports. She'll join the drama club."

"It sounds as if the girls are adjusting to their new school. I know my girls are enjoying getting to know them." Martha had three granddaughters around the same age as the twins, and they'd spent some time together over the summer.

"Audrey seems to be having a rough time. She's mad at her partner for a presentation they're supposed to do together. The girl didn't show up yesterday, and Audrey has convinced herself that the girl hates her and is trying to ruin her life."

"Teenage angst." Martha sighed. "No, it's preteen angst, isn't it?"

"This move has been tough on both girls. I wish I could help more." She hated feeling so uncertain about how to reach out to her granddaughters.

Until Jason's family moved to Maple Hill, she had seen the twins for only a week or two at a time. Then, everyone had been on their best behavior, focused on making great memories. It wasn't as if she could just push a button and make the girls feel comfortable talking to her about something important. Such trust took time to build. She knew that. Even so, she wished there were a shortcut.

"You'll find a way to help them." Martha patted Sarah's knee. "You're learning that being a full-time grandmother has its pros and cons. But one of the pros is that you can reach out to your grandchildren in a different way than you did with your own kids. You aren't setting the rules and enforcing them. That lets you be the good guy."

Sarah smiled. "I'll keep that in mind."

"Give them chances to feel comfortable confiding in you, and they will. Watch and see."

Sarah didn't answer because a Maple Hill police car drove into the parking lot. With Martha in tow, she walked toward the memorial. Chief Webber strode up the steps and along the path.

"Thanks for coming quickly," Sarah said after greeting him.

"I probably should ask what you two ladies were doing wandering around in the bushes." He smiled.

"Come with us, and I'll tell you along the way."

It didn't take Sarah long to go through

the story again, and they reached the door in the ground as she finished.

"You know," Chief Webber said as he pulled a flashlight off his belt, "you shouldn't have gone down there before you called me. He glanced at Sarah, "but now that you have, show me what you've found."

"We didn't know what was down there," Martha said in their defense. "We couldn't even be certain that the man Sarah saw on the tape was the thief."

"I'd like to see that tape, Mrs. Hart."

"I'll ask Maggie to make you a copy."

Chief Webber tested the first step down to make sure it would hold him too. "I'm glad you didn't paw through all the bags before you called me."

"I didn't want to paw through any." Martha gave a genteel shudder. "I was afraid the bags were full of garbage. But you've got to admit, Chief Webber, if we'd just shut the door and left, the thief could have returned to get his loot."

"OK. I'll give you that." He went down into the cellar, ducking his head to keep from hitting the door frame.

Sarah followed. She paused at the bottom of the stairs as Chief Webber, crouching almost double, walked across the cellar to check what they'd found. When Martha scurried down the steps, she stopped beside Sarah. They both watched in silence.

Chief Webber whistled a single low note. "It looks like you ladies stumbled on the mother lode here."

He pulled a pair of latex gloves from his pocket and stabbed his fingers into them. Only then did he pick up the lamp to examine it. He said nothing as he put it on the ground and reached for the book. When he opened it to the title page, his brows rose. He set it on the bag. He glanced at Sarah, startled, when he saw the clock.

"No wonder you called me without looking further," he said. "You recognized this clock, didn't you?"

Sarah nodded. "It's the one taken from Maggie's store."

"This isn't everything that's been reported missing." He stepped back and surveyed the bags. "Did you find anything else — chairs maybe?" He sprayed light on the other side of the steps.

"No, just these bags."

"But what about the book and the lamp?" asked Martha. "Were they stolen too?"

"Possibly."

"Possibly?" said Martha. "*We* found these things. Don't we have a right to know if they were stolen?"

He fixed them both with one stern frown. "Actually, you don't, even if I could say unequivocally that these were stolen. I need to check the descriptions of the items taken as well as have the robbery victims give me a positive ID. Proper procedures have to be followed."

Martha sniffed. "That's not how they do it on TV."

Chief Webber smiled coolly before he turned to examine the unopened bags.

"Can you see anything to tell you who's the thief?" Martha continued.

"If only it were that easy." He faced them again. "It would make police work much simpler if criminals would autograph their work."

Sarah laughed. "You don't know how many times I've said the same thing when someone has asked me to date an antique quilt."

He looked at the bags in the corner. "These are standard trash bags that you can buy in any grocery store. These plastic binder ties are usually available only in hardware or home improvement stores, so anyone can buy them."

"What about the box with 'VNA' on the side?"

"It could have come from anyone who's

been seen by the Visiting Nurse Association. It could have been in someone's trash, and the thief picked it up. It's a clue, but not *the* clue. We don't often find *the* clue."

"So there's nothing?" Martha's disappointment filled every word.

"I didn't say that. There are plenty of possible clues waiting for us to find. Fingerprints, something left behind that the thief didn't realize he'd dropped. The thief made one mistake in letting the Hart girls tape him. I don't think we can count on him making another. But if the thief is a kid or a bunch of kids getting their kicks, leaving something that points to them by mistake is more likely."

"But would kids bring everything up here? Wouldn't it be more likely they'd leave it somewhere more convenient?"

"Perhaps."

"Maybe," Martha said pensively, "it's someone who hikes up here and knows about this place. Or maybe it's someone who works on Mount Greylock. Or helped build the monument."

"All interesting theories, and we'll investigate them and any others that come along. Right now, it's too early to make any assumptions. Every possibility has to be considered and investigated." He bent toward the bags again.

Martha continued to ask questions, and he answered each one politely, but without offering any further information.

Knowing they were now just in the way, Sarah turned to go back to the stairs. She hoped Martha would notice and follow, leaving Chief Webber to his work.

She took one step, but then halted. Something had glittered, flashing sunlight into her eyes. But what? Where? She turned her head slowly. There! There it was again. A flash of gold. At the edge of the light coming down the steps.

She moved closer, and her foot sank into softened earth. There must have been a puddle earlier, but the water had seeped away. She edged around the spot and bent to touch something made of wood. It was small and square. Putting out a cautious finger, she touched the wooden square.

"What's that?" asked Martha as she knelt beside her.

"I'm not sure."

"Let me see." Martha dug at the soft dirt and loosened it enough to pull out the small item. She tilted it toward the stairs and blinked. "You figure it out. It blinded me."

Sarah took the wooden square, holding it so it didn't catch the sun like a mirror. It was a picture. A portrait. A man sat, and a woman stood behind him with her hand on his left shoulder. Both of them appeared to be in their early twenties, and she wondered if the picture had been taken to commemorate their wedding. It must have been taken more than 150 years before, because the man wore what looked like a Civil War uniform. The woman's wide skirt was draped with rows of ruffles and lace. Her sleeves were slashed, revealing a simple white blouse that closed at her throat with more lace. It could have come out of *Gone With the Wind.*

Standing, she held the tintype out to Martha. She pulled out her camera again and glanced toward her friend.

Martha nodded and propped the frame on her hands.

Sarah switched off her flash. She took a couple of photos of the tintype's front, and then had Martha turn it around so she could get more of the back. She had seen Maggie examine antiques from every angle.

The second image of the back blurred when Martha moved. Something scurried across the floor. "Sorry," she said. "There are too many bugs in here."

Martha readjusted the tintype so it was straight, and Sarah snapped another picture.

"Ladies?" Chief Webber pulled off his latex gloves. "What's that?"

"A tintype," Martha replied as Sarah slipped her camera back into her bag. "We just found it."

"Found it where?"

Martha related how Sarah had found the frame half-stuck in the ground, but her words slowed when the chief scowled.

"Please, Mrs. Hart, Mrs. Maplethorpe. Don't touch anything else."

"It was just lying there," Martha said. She looked to Sarah for confirmation.

Sarah didn't answer as she stared at the gilded frame that Chief Webber now held. It hadn't been in one of the bags, but it had to be valuable. So why had it been left in the middle of the floor where it could be stepped on and broken?

Martha's eyes widened. "So do you think it's stolen too?"

"That's possible, but I don't recall any photographs —"

"Tintypes," said Martha.

"I don't recall seeing any *tintypes* on any report of stolen goods."

"Maybe," Sarah said quietly, "the thief dropped it. Maybe it's the something that got left behind accidentally."

He set the framed picture on an untorn

bag. "I want to thank you ladies for your help, but I'm going to have to ask you to leave. I need to bring in experts to get whatever information they can from the bags and this site."

"Leave?" Martha asked. "I'm sure Sarah will be glad to help you."

Chief Webber smiled when he saw Martha was serious. "I am grateful for your quick eye, Mrs. Hart, and that you took the time to come up here to follow a hunch. But this is a serious crime, and you need to let us handle it."

"He's right, Martha." Sarah put her arm around her friend. "We've had our fun playing detective."

"Thank you." Chief Webber motioned for them to go up the steps.

Sarah didn't expect him to leave the cellar too, but he did. When they were out, he shut the door and pulled out his cell. Again he thanked them, and Sarah guessed he wanted them on their way before he made calls to whomever would help him investigate.

"Is it all right if I let Maggie know we found her clock?" Sarah asked as she reached to push aside the nearest tree branches.

"Tell her to keep the news to herself until we contact all the victims officially." He gave them both another steady gaze. "Which means you don't mention this to anyone else."

"Not even to Ernie?" Martha looked aghast at the thought of withholding the information from her husband.

"You can tell Ernie, but none of you must make a peep to anyone else. Until I have to, I don't want to let the thief know we've found his hiding place. If he doesn't know, we might catch him creeping up here to take the items away."

"Oh, that puts a whole different light on it," Martha said. "We're still helping."

"Exactly, but promise me that you won't go investigating on your own again."

Sarah looked at Martha, whose eyes sparked with outrage. Martha understood that this wasn't a game.

"I promise," Sarah said as she gave Martha a gentle jab with her elbow.

"I promise too." Martha's words were grudging.

"Good." He thanked them again.

"C'mon, Martha," Sarah said. "I want to talk to Maggie before the girls get home from school."

As she pushed aside the branch and ducked to start toward the path, Chief Webber called their names. Sarah turned to look at him.

"One more thing, ladies." His expression was now grim, and his next words sent a chill down her spine. "Don't forget that we have a criminal in Maple Hill. Keep your doors and windows locked. At all times."

CHAPTER FIVE

When Sarah walked into Maggie's after dropping Martha off at her house, the store appeared to be empty, until a clatter of dishes came from Sarah's left. She stepped around a child's wagon horse to see Maggie on her knees next to a box of dinner plates nestled in newspaper. Unwrapped plates were stacked beside her.

Garish tea roses in brilliant shades of red and pink were painted in the center of the plates, and the edges were gilded.

"To what do I owe the pleasure of your visit?" asked Maggie with a grin. "I thought you'd be spending the day cutting out pieces for your wall quilt."

"I've hardly even had a chance to think about it."

"Do you like these?" Maggie asked as she set another plate atop the others.

"They are . . ." Sarah searched for a word that wouldn't hurt Maggie's feelings and

69

still not be a lie. In truth, Sarah thought the huge roses painted on the plates were a bit garish.

"Go ahead. You can say it. They're hideous. I agree, but you'd be surprised how many collectors out there are on the lookout for this pattern. It's rare, and you know why? Because people had good taste a hundred years ago and thought these plates were ugly too." She stood, wiping her hands on her jeans. "Maybe I shouldn't put them on display. That clock was about the worst-looking thing in the store, and someone stole it. Who knows what will happen next?"

"The police are going to keep a close eye on the store."

"They can't be here all the time. I wish I could afford an assistant." She sighed. "With a new store and a new law practice and a new house that needs so much work, neither of us has the time we want to spend with the girls."

"I have faith in you."

"I wish I did."

"And Jason will want to help."

"I don't want his help." She shook her head. "I mean, we agreed this is *my* store. We need to work this out on our own."

"I didn't mean to butt in."

Maggie nodded, but Sarah wasn't sure she

was convinced. She had to be more careful about what she said and how she said it while they got used to living so close to each other.

"I need to talk to you," Sarah said when Maggie remained silent. "Somewhere where no one else might hear."

"We can talk back in my office." Maggie led the way toward the rear of the store. "I'll have to leave the door open in case a customer comes in. Not likely at this time of day on a Monday, but . . ."

"I understand." Sarah sat on a cane-bottomed chair by Maggie's rolltop desk. She waited until Maggie was sitting too, before saying, "I wanted to talk to you before Amy and Audrey got here."

"Audrey called at lunchtime, as a matter of fact. She's upset because her teacher wouldn't let her switch partners for her project, and her partner is still acting like Audrey doesn't exist. I knew it would be tough moving to a new school, but I thought Amy would have the harder time. Audrey's always outgoing."

"What are you going to do?" Sarah asked.

"Be sympathetic with her frustration, and pray a lot."

Sarah clasped her daughter-in-law's hands between hers. "I'll add my prayers and my

71

sympathy."

"Thanks." Maggie's smile returned. "But you didn't come here for that."

"No, I came here to tell you that your stolen clock has been found."

"It has?" Her face brightened. "How do you know?"

Sarah pulled out the camera and turned it on to show Maggie the pictures she'd taken. Her daughter-in-law clapped when Sarah told how she and Martha had, quite literally, unearthed the thief's cache.

"You're amazing!" Maggie exclaimed as the photos flashed across the screen.

Relieved that the tension between them had faded — at least for now — Sarah said, "Maggie, one more thing. It's important that you don't tell anyone other than Jason, of course, what I've told you. Chief Webber doesn't want anyone else to know about the discovery until he speaks to all the victims, and he doesn't want to give the robber a heads-up."

"I understand." Sitting again, she rested her elbows on the desk. "I'll keep this under my hat. What happens now, do you suppose?"

"I'm sure Chief Webber will give you a call once the stolen items are brought down from Mount Greylock. He'll want you to identify the clock."

"That makes sense. Does he have any idea who might have done it?"

"Chief Webber said it's too early to assume anything. He's going to check every clue and every lead."

She clicked through the images until she reached a good one of the young man and woman in the gold frame. "But in the meantime, look at this and tell me what you think."

Maggie took the camera out of Sarah's hands and looked at it. "What is this?"

"A framed picture we found near the stolen items. We think it's a tintype. Can you tell me anything else about it? You know much more about antiques than I do."

"Hmmm . . . it doesn't look like a tintype." Maggie squinted at the screen. "I think it's probably a daguerreotype."

"What's the difference?"

Maggie explained that daguerreotypes were the earliest photographic images, dating from the 1830s. Holding the camera so Sarah could see the picture too, she pointed out how the image had been produced on a polished silver plate. It was mounted behind glass, and tintypes often weren't. Daguerreotype images were much clearer than the later tintypes, and they almost always were placed in small frames to protect their edges.

"I told Martha that you'd know." Sarah hoped Maggie noticed how proud she was of her daughter-in-law.

"Without being able to examine it in person, I'm not sure what else I can tell you." She clicked to the next pictures. With a puzzled frown, she held the camera close to her face. "What is this writing on the back of the picture?"

"Writing?"

Maggie handed Sarah the camera. "Can you make it out?"

Sarah tried, but the writing was too faint and small in the photo. "I'll print it out at home. I'll let you know what it says."

"I can't tell you much else about it. Sorry."

"Don't be. I'm glad you know about early photography." She switched off the camera. "Maggie, where did you get the clock that was stolen?"

"Neil Lawton sold it to me."

Sarah put the camera in her bag. "Neil? That's interesting."

"Why? He's sold me several nice pieces."

"He doesn't seem like an antiques collector. His house looks like something from the future. Brushed metal and white leather and tile floors. I'm amazed that he'd have

74

anything you'd be interested in selling."

"Maybe he's been keeping a stash of antiques in a secret room." She laughed.

"I doubt that."

Sarah spent a few more minutes chatting with Maggie, and then headed to her own house. As she got out of her car, she thought about what she had found. How had those antiques and the daguerreotype ended up in the cellar? She might be a grandmother, but her curiosity was still that of a three-year old. It wanted to be satisfied immediately.

But Chief Webber was right. She needed to let him and his fellow officers investigate the robberies. Already she and Martha — with the best of intentions — had interfered and could have hurt the investigation.

Instead of thinking about the robberies, she would focus on her wall quilt and preparing her supper. Last week, she had picked up the ingredients for chicken soup, and tonight seemed the perfect time for a quick and simple meal. While it was cooking, she could begin deciding which fabric scraps she would use for the hanging.

There was a pretty red calico that would be perfect for the barns in the valley and also for the scarlet maples. An orange and yellow gingham check would re-create the oaks. She could make tree trunks with dark brown flannel and use white wool for clouds. And deep green dotted swiss would bring the evergreens to life. Because it was a wall hanging, she could mix and match the fabrics. Around the edges, she planned to use an oak leaf and acorn pattern. It'd be the perfect finishing touch for her pictorial quilt. She was eager to get started on what she hoped would be a fun project.

Even so, she couldn't stop thinking about the daguerreotype.

Sarah climbed the steps to the porch, smiling at the squeak on the second one. Her husband had intended to fix that step, but he hadn't gotten to it before he died. And there was no way she would have it repaired now; each time it creaked, she remembered Gerry working on the house, his hair filled with sawdust. He'd been so proud when he'd turned spindles to replace the broken ones on the porch. They'd laughed together while painting each one. They ended up with as much paint on themselves as on the spindles. For days, no matter how thoroughly they scrubbed, they kept discovering paint spots on elbows and knees. Those memories were sweet.

As she stepped onto the porch, her steps faltered. Something wasn't right. But what?

The Adirondack chairs hadn't been moved. She stared at her front door. The screen door was closed, but the inner door was ajar.

Just like the back door had been at Maggie's store.

Then she heard them. Voices in her house — male voices! Her boarder was female. Who was in her house?

She edged toward the steps as she jabbed her hand into her bag. Her fingers found the camera. Her sunglasses. Her wallet. Where was her cell phone?

She found it, pulled it out, and flipped it open. It was off. She pressed the key to turn it on when the screen door opened.

"Hi, Mom! Are you all right? You look like you just saw a ghost."

Sarah lowered the phone and stared at her son. "Only thought I heard one." She let her breath sift out in a sigh as she closed her cell phone and put it back in her bag.

Jason suddenly wore the guilty expression she'd seen when he was a kid and got caught doing some mischief, an expression his daughters had inherited. He was dressed in casual clothes, and she remembered he'd planned to meet with the handyman this afternoon.

"Sorry. I figured when you saw the open door, you'd know someone was inside."

"I did! I thought I was being robbed."

"Now I'm really sorry. I should have thought about that. When we came over and you weren't home, we didn't think you'd mind us going in."

"I don't. It's just —" She waved her own words aside. "Sorry. Just a bit jumpy. Who else is here?"

Jason motioned to someone still inside. "Hey, Dave! Come out and meet my mother."

A tall man came out onto the porch. He looked to be a few years younger than Jason. He had deep-set brown eyes, an angular face, and, on his light brown hair, he wore a New England Patriots cap. It was as dusty as his jeans and gray sweatshirt. His boots were scuffed, and the broken laces had been tied together.

Jason smiled. "Now you can see you've got two law-abiding citizens skulking around your house, Mom." He glanced at the man, who looked as uneasy as Jason had a moment before. "This is Dave Diamond. He's going to be working on the wiring at the house. Dave, this is my mother, Sarah Hart."

"Nice to meet you," she said, trying to persuade her heart to stop beating like a crazed drummer.

"And you, Mrs. Hart." His voice was a pleasant tenor and filled with apology. "I'm sorry if we scared you. We got talking about some projects over at Jason's house, and he wanted to show me the work your late husband did on the walnut paneling around your living room hearth."

"No need for an apology." She squared her shoulders and said, "Jason tells me you're new to Maple Hill."

"My wife and I moved here last November. I'd just gotten out of the army, and we wanted a nice town like this to raise our family in."

"How many children do you have?"

His smile set his whole face alight. "Not quite one. My wife and I are expecting our first very soon."

"Congratulations! You must be excited."

"Closer to nervous." He glanced at Jason. "And I'll only have one to practice on."

"Are you all settled in?" she asked.

"For the most part. We're starting to get to know a few people."

"We go to Bridge Street Church. If you'd like to come some Sunday, you'll find friendly people." She smiled broadly. "And I know plenty of folks there are looking for a good handyman."

Jason broke in, "Don't spread the word

too quickly, Mom. We've got a bunch of projects for him over at our house."

They laughed, and Sarah enjoyed the sound. Since Jason and his family had come to Maple Hill, there had been more joy in her home, which had been too quiet after her husband's death. It was such a blessing.

"Thanks for the invitation, Mrs. Hart," Dave said. "I'll talk to Liz, but we won't be able to make it this coming Sunday. I'm working on a fund-raiser for a charity called Stand Down in Springfield this weekend."

"Stand Down?"

"It's a program that assists homeless veterans, making sure they get medical care and counseling. There are too many vets who have fallen between the cracks or are too proud or sick to get help. Stand Down seeks them out and offers them assistance." He paused, and a flush rose up his cheeks. "It's really a great organization."

"It sounds like something good to feel strongly about," Sarah said as she opened the screen door.

"Thank you."

By the time she stood in her front hall, her heart had regained its usual steady pace. She hung her bag on a peg by the door.

"Can I get you something?" she asked. "It

will take only a moment to make some coffee."

"Nothing for me," Jason said as Dave shook his head. "If you don't mind, Dave wanted to check in the cellar and see how the fireplace is supported in the foundation. Ours need repairs, and we figured we wouldn't try to reinvent the wheel. Dave is the expert, but I thought I'd see how much I could get in his way by trying to help."

"There's more than enough to keep both of us busy," Dave said with a shy warmth that made Sarah like him right away.

She wavered between happiness and grief as she imagined how Gerry would have spent hours talking with Jason and Dave about fixing up the old family home. She knew how proud he would have been of Jason striving to make a beautiful and safe home for his family. If he had been here, he would have worked alongside the two younger men.

"Of course. Check whatever you want," she said.

"While we're here, we could fix that squeaky front step for you, Mom."

"You've got enough to do over at your house, and the squeak will be a good security alarm now."

"That's actually not a bad idea," Jason said.

"It was just a joke."

"Still, it's not a bad idea."

Sarah looked at Dave. "Don't worry, Dave," she said. "Maple Hill isn't usually like this; it's usually pretty quiet."

"Just plain boring is what I hear around my house," Jason said.

Dave seemed to relax. Sarah understood how unsettling the robberies must be for him — a newcomer to Maple Hill with a wife and a baby to worry about.

When the two men hurried down into the cellar, Sarah went to the kitchen and started taking out the ingredients for chicken soup. The sounds of Jason's and Dave's voices came up the basement steps and past the partially opened door. She had cut about half the vegetables by the time footsteps came up the stairs, and the two men pushed the door wider to step into the kitchen.

Dave held up a piece of paper and a pencil. "May I use your counter?"

"Better use the table."

He looked down at his clothes that were covered with dust and cobwebs. "Good idea. We were poking around in the corners." He began to sketch on a piece of scrap paper. "If we copy what your mother has down there, Jason, we should be fine."

"How soon can you get started?"

"The electrical should be done first."

Jason grinned. "I had Dave look at our old knob and tube wiring and the three fuse boxes, and he nearly had a heart attack. I guess we should have looked a bit more closely when the Realtor said it'd been modernized. Sure, except for the wiring, the plumbing, and the foundation. So when do you think you can get to shoring up the fireplace?"

"Jason," Sarah said with a smile, "give the man a chance to finish one project before you ask him about another."

"I just want a safe home for Maggie and the twins." His tone reminded Sarah of Maggie's earlier.

She hadn't intended to scold her son. Rather she had thought he'd see her words as teasing. She was speaking too quickly and without thinking. That was unlike her, and a sign that *she* was more disturbed by the robberies than she'd admitted to herself.

Into the silence, Dave said, "All set." He folded the page and put it in his shirt pocket. "We'll get out of your hair now, Mrs. Hart."

"Sarah, please."

He gave a quick, shy glance in her direction. "Thanks for letting us look around, Sarah."

The two men walked into the hall and then out the front door. It shut behind them, leaving the house in silence.

Sarah chopped the rest of the vegetables. Jason's visit had reminded her again of one important thing: she must be careful of frayed emotions, both hers and her family's. Only now was she realizing that the thief had stolen something other than antiques; he'd stolen their peace of mind.

CHAPTER SIX

With the soup prepared and cooking, Sarah stood by her desk in one corner of her sewing room and looked out the back window at the garden. She held Amy's camera, and if any of her neighbors happened to see her standing there, they would probably guess she intended to take a photo of the burning bush that was donning its scarlet coat — or maybe one of the maple leaves that already had orange at their tips.

But she was thinking about the pictures she'd taken on Mount Greylock. She couldn't stop wondering if the daguerreotype was connected to the robberies. The answer was probably simple. Most were, but for the time being she was stumped.

I'm making God's job with me a little easier by letting him do the worrying.

The words Gerry had often said to her popped into her thoughts. When they had first married, he had thought that her weighing every problem carefully before coming to a decision was worrying. He had learned it was just her way, but they had continued to tease each other about it — one of those special private jokes that couples share. She really missed that.

But the advice was still good. Instead of worrying, she needed to do something productive. Why not try to identify the couple? Doing that would not interfere with the police, and if she chanced to find out something useful, she'd let Chief Webber know in a heartbeat.

Her curiosity refused to be quiet. Why would anyone take valuable antiques and hide them on Mount Greylock? And why those items when, as Maggie said, there were far more valuable antiques for sale in her store?

But she'd promised Chief Webber that she'd stay out of the investigation, she reminded herself. She didn't make promises lightly. Therefore, she'd focus on finding out more about the young man and woman in the daguerreotype.

Linking the camera to the printer, Sarah pushed the proper buttons, and then went into the kitchen to check on supper. The aroma of chicken and parsley and vegetables filled the air. She stirred the broth, added noodles, and turned down the heat to let the soup simmer. Soon it would be ready. Taking some rolls out of the bread drawer, she set them on the counter next to the cookie jar.

The pictures from Amy's camera had printed out when Sarah returned to her desk. She unplugged the camera and switched off the printer. She took the photos from the tray. They'd come out clearer than she'd dared to hope, even though one of Martha's fingers was visible in the lower right-hand corner. But the writing she wanted to decipher was in the center. She couldn't read what it said. She needed her strong reading glasses that she'd left in the dining room. She'd had them on in there recently when she had spread out a quilt restoration project so the owner could approve her work.

Checking the soup again, she went into the dining room at the front of the house. Like the other rooms, it was much smaller than the grand rooms in her son's house. A pair of windows gave her a view of the front porch with its hanging flower baskets and the street beyond the front yard flower beds. Family pictures filled the cream walls between the chair rail and the wisteria-wallpaper border.

In the middle of the room, the long dining table gleamed and the brass chandelier overhead still had most of its hanging prisms and cast a warm light onto the maple floors. A pair of tall bookcases flanked the open pocket doors.

She set the photos next to the sketch she'd done up on the mountain. She asked the couple in the picture, "What do you know?" She laughed. If anyone heard her talking to people from 150 years ago, they'd think she'd lost her mind.

She picked up her reading glasses and a photo of the back of the daguerreotype. Squinting, she read the faded words in the middle: *Adam and Barbara.*

Sarah studied Adam's and Barbara's still poses. First, she looked at Adam. She could make out the insignia on his uniform. Above the stripes on his arm was a diamond-shaped emblem. Barbara wore a cameo brooch partially obscured by Adam's head.

Two more clues.

She had no idea how they might help, but she would try to find out after supper. She had to decide what she would type into the Internet search box to find out what she needed. Even with the right words or phrases, it could take a while to get answers.

Nothing helped her focus better than

quilting, so Sarah returned to her sewing room. She opened her fabric closet and took out her scraps basket and the other supplies she'd need to get started. Carrying them to the dining room, she tipped out the pieces left over from other projects. She spread them across the table, separating the fabrics she'd already decided she would use. She selected some thick lace to edge the clouds. Should she add buttons to give a sense of depth? Possibly. If she found the right color and size, she could use them to simulate wind-ruffled water on the ponds. When she restored antique quilts, she had to be certain that she followed the original quilter's pattern as closely as possible. Sometimes it was fun to create something new, with no rules.

She glanced at the photo, wondering what color Barbara's dress had been. Adam's uniform would have been Union Army blue. Wool, most likely. But what had her dress been made of? A simple fabric or had she posed in something made of richer, more luxurious material?

Focus, she told herself.

She needed a design for her wall quilt. Reaching behind her, she took down one of the pincushions from the mantel. She picked up the tracing paper she'd brought in. Usually she used cardboard or even sandpaper to make a template for a quilt pattern, but on the wall hanging, each piece would be unique.

She joined the pieces of tracing paper with straight pins until she had the exact size she wanted. Lightly, with a dull pencil, she drew the pattern. She simplified the view to make it less cluttered. She added fewer buildings and focused on the ponds and the curves of the mountains.

Even though neither the war memorial nor the hiding place was visible, she couldn't stop thinking about them. Should she include the memorial in her quilt? Avoiding it was useless when every time she looked at the wall hanging, she'd be reminded of these past two days.

Sarah began anew, this time including the war memorial off to one side. That allowed her to have her view of the valley as well.

By the time she was finished, her stomach was grumbling. Her boarder hadn't come home yet, but the enticing aroma of the soup called her to the kitchen. She was ladling out a bowl for herself when she heard footsteps in the front hall.

Even though she knew it had to be Rita, Sarah jumped. She yelped when hot soup splashed her hand. Putting down the bowl, she went to the sink and ran cold water over her hand.

"Sarah?" Rita French's short hair bounced as she rushed into the kitchen. She must have been bird-watching because she had both binoculars and a camera hanging around her neck. "Are you OK?"

"Fine." She turned off the faucet and gingerly dabbed a towel on her burned hand. "I can assure you that the soup is hot."

"Ouch!" Rita drew her binoculars over her head and set them on the table.

"Would you like some soup? I made enough for an army."

"Sounds great. I could use something hot after spending the afternoon chasing the song of a great crested flycatcher through soggy woods. I wanted to see one before they migrate south."

"Did you ever see it?"

She lifted off her camera and smiled. "I got a great picture . . . I hope." Putting the camera on the counter, she added, "You sit, honey. I'll bring your bowl to the table."

"Then I'll get the butter and silverware. As well as napkins in case I decide to take another bath in soup."

"It smells delicious."

Sarah smiled when Rita announced a few

minutes later that the soup tasted just as good as it smelled. Her boarder was one of the most accommodating Sarah had ever had. She was always fun to be around, she kept her room neat, and, despite her love of birds, she didn't want a pet.

Uncertain how to begin what she had to say, Sarah decided the easiest way was to jump in with both feet. "Rita, I'm going to need you to make sure you've got your house key with you all the time. I spoke with the police chief today, and he wants everyone to keep their doors locked until the burglar is caught."

"That's a good idea." She raised her roll to take a bite, and then lowered it untasted. "It's a shame that one bad guy can ruin a whole town's sense of security."

"I agree."

When Rita turned the conversation to other subjects, Sarah was happy to go along. Her day had been consumed by the mystery of who was stealing antiques and why. She needed to get some balance back. Rita gave her the chance when she asked what quilt Sarah was working on.

"Oh, I wish I were creative like that," Rita said after Sarah explained.

"It isn't difficult to learn the basics. If you want, I'd be glad to give you some lessons."

"Maybe later, after the birds have gone south. For now, I want to get photos of as many as possible." Getting up, she put her dishes in the dishwasher. "I can't wait to see how my great crested flycatcher photo came out. Thanks for supper."

Sarah leaned back and, locking her fingers together, stretched her arms high above her head. Her left shoulder gave a satisfying pop while the muscles loosened. Her head ached, and her brain felt dull. How long had she been peering at the computer screen? She was astonished to see that more than three hours had passed.

And what did she have to show for her time?

Nothing.

She had visited genealogy sites and Civil War sites and historical sites. She had quickly been overwhelmed with histories of Massachusetts military units during the Civil War as well as the stories of individual soldiers. She had read through the history of the state reservation on Mount Greylock. She had learned the insignia Adam wore belonged to a Union first sergeant, but she'd failed to turn up one clue to Adam's and Barbara's identities. Without a surname, she had found too many roadblocks along the way. She found Web sites for cemeteries and historical books and a pop-star sensation and the two presidents named Adams, but nothing that helped her.

She needed more specific information to help her search, but she wasn't going to find it tonight. She was too exhausted. With a yawn, she turned off the computer. Tomorrow she could start anew when her head wasn't pounding like an avalanche was tumbling inside it.

From the bookshelf beside the computer, Sarah took down a well-thumbed Bible. "Dear Lord," she prayed with her hands cupping the Bible, "thank you for leading Martha and me toward the truth. I know you will guide Chief Webber too, and I ask for strength and comfort for the thief's victims. Reach out to this man and let him know of your love. Let him know that we don't despise him and are willing to help him as much as we can. Please help him find his way to your righteousness and forgiveness."

The words were from her heart, but difficult to say. She raised her head and looked around the small room, wishing she could find more forgiveness for whomever had frightened her daughter-in-law and set everyone in the town on edge.

Bending her head again, she prayed as well for guidance in her search for the identities of the people in the picture. Maybe one of the robbery victims would know who they were. If so, her search would come to a quick end. It didn't matter who found the answer. Only that the answer was discovered, especially if it could lead the police to an arrest.

Sarah pushed back her chair and stood. She closed her Bible and set it on the shelf before stretching her tired muscles again. For a moment, she considered going into the dining room to work, but a wide yawn halted her. She needed some sleep. Taking her empty water glass into the kitchen, she saw the back porch light was on. Had Rita gone back out without Sarah noticing? Rita's red convertible wasn't in the driveway.

A shiver rippled down Sarah's spine as she grasped how easy it would be for the thief to creep in and out of her house without her noticing. She stretched to close the window above the sink. She twisted the sash lock. That thin pane of glass seemed like a flimsy barrier between her and a thief.

Stop it! she scolded herself. As she turned from the window, she sneezed. That sent the ache throbbing harder through her head. She needed to get to bed and sleep the headache away.

But first. . . . She walked around the house, making sure every window was locked. In the morning, the first floor would be stuffy, but she had promised Jason to be careful. She even closed and locked the small window in the half bath. No one bigger than a kindergartner would be able to crawl through it. At least the windows upstairs could stay open to let in the night breezes.

She turned the lock on the front door and sighed. One of the aspects of Maple Hill that she had always loved was that everyone could trust their neighbors. The town had grown quite a bit in recent years with houses built all the way out to Patriot Park and up and down both banks of the river. Still, that small town feeling had remained.

The distant sound of a clock ticking upstairs broke into the silence. She thought of Maggie's stolen clock. What a shock to find it today! She wondered what had been in the other bags. The stolen antiques had one thing in common — the thief had wanted each enough to steal it. But why? A simple question, but she guessed the answer wasn't going to be easy to find.

CHAPTER SEVEN

Sarah looked up when the phone rang. This morning she had woken to sunshine, and was in good spirits. She'd decided to pin together the small pieces of tracing paper and fabric for her wall quilt. She had been deeply engrossed in her work until the phone's jangle intruded.

It was Maggie.

"I was going to call you later," Sarah said. "I figured out what it said on the back of the daguerreotype."

"Anything interesting?"

"Two names. Adam and Barbara. I haven't found out much more than that."

"If I know you, you will and soon!" Maggie paused, and then asked, "Sarah, are you busy?"

"I could take a break." She put down her scissors. "Why?"

"The police department called. They want me to come in and identify the clock. Just as you said they would." She took a deep breath. "Jason's busy at his office, so I was wondering if you'd come with me."

"I'd be glad to." Sarah smiled. She was glad Maggie felt she could call her.

"Great. I'll be by in about ten minutes."

Sarah fixed her hair and her makeup to hide the lingering signs of her late night on the computer. Collecting her paisley bag, she put the photos inside. She wasn't sure what she'd see at the police station, but she wanted to be prepared.

As she opened the door to go out on the porch to wait, she hurried back to the kitchen and took her key off its hook. Why was it easy to start a bad habit and tough to begin a good one? She laughed again as she walked out onto the porch. She locked the door behind her, testing the knob to make sure. Now she could be honest if Chief Webber asked her if she was being careful.

Sarah led Maggie into the Maple Hill Police Department. They'd talked on the way over about the daguerreotype, but neither of them spoke now as the heavy door with its oval etched-glass window closed behind them. Papers on an overcrowded bulletin board flapped as they passed, wanted posters mixed with town announcements. State-of-the-art security cameras hung from the ceiling, but the marble floor had lost its sheen after sixty years. In front of them, a tall counter cut the long room in half. The round emblem of Maple Hill hung on the front — the town symbol was a single maple tree in front of a mountain, encircled by the words "Town of Maple Hill."

A young officer wearing a name tag that said HOPKINS came forward to greet them. Once he confirmed that they'd been asked to come in to view the recovered items, he had them follow him to a door at the back. Another police officer at the counter was helping two high-school age boys fill out forms, and a man was emptying the trash cans in front of the tall windows. They all halted when Sarah and Maggie walked past with Officer Hopkins.

"Are they all looking at us?" whispered Maggie.

Sarah glanced around. "I think so, but I don't think we look like anyone whose pictures are hanging in the post office."

Maggie gave a nervous giggle. Sarah squeezed her hand and offered a smile.

Officer Hopkins continued around desks topped with the latest computers. He paused to open the closed door at the back. He didn't follow as Sarah and Maggie walked into a smaller room where Chief Webber was talking to Dottie and Arnold Kirschner, also victims of the burglaries. Sarah wondered if the Poplawskis had already come or if they were late.

Sarah looked at the tables in the room and recognized some of the items on them. The others must have been in the unopened bags. Maggie's clock was set to one side. The cranberry lamp had been put together and sat next to a piece of jewelry, a cast-iron kettle, and what looked like a boot scraper. More antiques had been placed on the other table. The book was encircled by a white silk fan, a small handmade doll, and a silver-edged mirror. She wondered where the daguerreotype and the box with the VNA stamp were.

"Mrs. Hart, thank you for coming on such short notice," Chief Webber said, shaking Maggie's hand. "This shouldn't take long." He smiled at Sarah. "I haven't heard any rumors about the stolen goods being found. I appreciate your and Martha's cooperation on this matter. An hour ago, we put out an official press release about finding the items on Mount Greylock."

"Oh, my!"

He quickly assured her that neither her name nor Martha's had been included in the information sent to the local media. "It simply stated that two hikers whose names are being withheld stumbled on the door."

"That's true, quite literally." Sarah was relieved she wouldn't have to field calls from inquisitive reporters.

While the chief of police spoke with Maggie and reviewed a long form that she would need to fill out and sign, Sarah walked over to where the Kirschners were staring at the table. Dottie was a slight woman with almost pure white hair who had raised three children. None of them lived in Maple Hill any longer. Her husband had no hair at all and thick, dark-rimmed glasses. He stood well over six feet tall. He had worked for the Department of Conservation and Recreation, keeping the local parks in good repair. In the summer, he had worked cutting down trees and clearing brush. His work had taken him from the top of Mount Greylock to the Mohawk Trail State Forest in the Cold River Valley. Both appeared overwhelmed at finding themselves at the police station.

"Sarah! It's so good to see you," Dottie said after Sarah greeted them. "How are you?"

"I'm fine. How are *you?*"

"I'm honestly not sure." Dottie spoke

101

calmly, but she flexed her fingers open and closed, betraying her anxiety. "I mean, I'm glad the antiques have been found, but I haven't had a decent night's sleep since Arnold discovered they were missing."

"Now you know your things are safe."

"Things are just things." The woman shook her head. "I worry the robber will come back and get into the house this time."

Sarah understood why Dottie was upset. Last night, Sarah had found herself waking at any sound, even the familiar creaks of the house settling at day's end.

"At least there haven't been any other robberies."

"Thank heavens." Dottie glanced at her hands and unclenched her fists. "Maybe he's found out the police are on his trail, and he's left Maple Hill."

"We can only hope. Dottie, which of these things are yours?"

"These." She pointed to the lamp, the kettle, and the pin.

"So you didn't lose a small framed picture too?"

"Not that I know of. Arnold?"

Her husband squinted through his glasses, and then shook his head. "Nope. That's everything."

"Are you sure?" Sarah asked. "I know

102

you've got a lot of stuff packed away in your barn."

"And he knows every single item," Dottie said with a grin. "That's how pack rats are. If even one thing goes missing, he knows." She bent toward Sarah and whispered, "Otherwise, I'd have gotten rid of Arnold's junk years ago."

"My hearing still works," Arnold grumbled. "Be honest, Dottie. Most of the stuff in the barn is from your family."

"Yes, but that's because you keep scrounging through antique stores and flea markets and heaven knows where else to find more stuff to bring home. And there's no room for anything else in the house."

He frowned. "The items I find *belong* in our house."

Dottie raised her hands in surrender. "I know. I know." She turned to Sarah. "Once this man gets an idea in his head, he can't let it go."

"He's excited about it."

"He's *obsessed!* Neil Lawton came over a few weeks ago with some paperwork for us to sign. Arnold made him look at everything he'd bought in the past couple of months. Poor Neil. He was clearly bored to tears." She shook her head. "I don't know what to do with Arnold. He's been on this redecorating kick since he retired. He used to put some of this energy into his job, but now it's all focused on the house."

Sarah wanted to get back to her question. "You're sure a small picture — a daguerreotype — wasn't taken from your house?"

"Absolutely," Arnold said quickly, and then walked away.

Sarah bent forward to examine the cameo. A woman's profile with long, curling hair was a yellowed white against a pink background. Was this cameo like the one worn by Barbara in the picture? Sarah had been able to see only a portion of it.

"Have you had the cameo long?" she asked.

"Arnold?" prompted Dottie. "How long has that ugly pin been in the barn?"

He frowned as he paced back to them. "What was that doing out in the barn? I thought it was in the dining room."

"There's your answer, Sarah," Dottie said. "If it was supposed to be in the dining room, it's something Arnold picked up in the past three years." She faced her husband. "If it was in the barn, *you* put it there."

Arnold ran his hand across his bald head as if he still had hair to rake. "I must have taken it out with some other things. I need to be more careful. But you must have moved this lamp out into the barn. I knew you didn't like it as soon as I brought it home."

Sarah paid no attention to their bickering as she tried to memorize the filigree around the edge of the cameo, so she could compare it to the one in the daguerreotype. She knew she was grasping at straws, but didn't want to overlook anything that could help her learn more about Adam and Barbara.

"Sarah, you seem very interested in that pin," Dottie said.

She smiled. "I've recently gotten interested in cameos."

"Is Maggie teaching you about antiques?" Dottie asked. "I'd love to know if there's anything in the barn that *isn't* junk. Most of it is rusted or worn out."

"If it's junk," Arnold said, "then why did someone go to the trouble of stealing it?"

Dottie's eyes widened. "I never thought of it that way. We should have Maggie come over. If there are other valuable antiques out there, she'll know. Right, Sarah?"

She didn't answer because Chief Webber had come around the table.

"All right," he said as he picked up a clipboard with a sheaf of papers on it. "Mr. and Mrs. Kirschner, could you please point out the item or items you believe are yours?"

"We don't *believe*," Arnold said. "We know."

"We need to do this the official way," Chief Webber said. "Now would you please point out the item or items you believe were stolen from your barn?"

They did.

Chief Webber thanked them and checked boxes on the topmost page before asking, "Mrs. Hart, will you please point out the item or items that you believe were stolen from your store?"

"I *believe* —" Maggie began and everyone smiled. "That's the clock stolen from my store. I recognize the damage done to the case."

"Thank you, Mrs. Hart."

"Can I take it with me?"

He looked up from the form he'd been filling in and shook his head. "I'm sorry, folks, but we need to keep these items here for the time being. Evidence."

"Oh, I should have known that. Well, at least I don't have customers banging down the door to buy it."

Arnold cleared his throat. "Actually, before you came in, I was looking at the clock. Once this is all settled, I'd like to talk to you about purchasing it."

"What do you need another old clock for?" asked his wife. "We've got three or four perfectly good ones in the barn."

Maggie, with the skill of a diplomat, said, "It may be some time before I have the clock available for sale, so you'll have plenty of time to discuss it."

Sarah gave her daughter-in-law a smile.

Maggie smiled back, and then glanced at the accumulated antiques on the table. Her eyes grew wide. "Is that a first edition of *Leaves of Grass*?"

Chief Webber shrugged. "I'm hoping the owners know."

"If it's a true first, you need to make sure it's secured somewhere safe. Walt Whitman's early editions are very collectible, and it could be worth a lot of money."

"Really?" asked Arnold. "And the Poplawskis had it in their barn?"

"Lots of people have no idea of the value of the antiques they've got stored away." She shifted her gaze to Chief Webber, not seeing the gleam in Arnold's eyes.

Sarah did, though, and she hoped Arnold wasn't counting on finding anything that rare in their barn.

"But why would anyone take a potentially priceless book along with my old clock? It doesn't make sense."

"Not to us," Sarah said, "but it must have to the thief."

"You're right." Chief Webber regarded them. "It may be a sign that the thief isn't thinking clearly or has a very specific plan. That could make him even more dangerous. I hope you're keeping your doors locked."

Everyone nodded.

"Now one final request today," he said. "We need to get a set of fingerprints from each of you."

"Fingerprints?" gasped Dottie, looking down at her recent manicure. "Is that necessary?"

"You've all handled at least some of the stolen items. We need to reject your prints while we search for the thief's. If you'll go out to the desk, Hopkins will take your prints."

As Chief Webber thanked them again for coming, Arnold walked out of the room with Maggie, already asking her questions. Sarah heard Dottie say, "Precious family heirlooms." What a change from her usual "Arnold's junk!" All it had taken was someone besides Arnold thinking the antiques were valuable.

Sarah stopped by the door. "Chief Webber, what about the gauze pads and the box with the VNA stamp on it?"

"They're important evidence. I can't say anything else."

"I understand, but can I ask you a couple more questions?"

"If you don't mind me telling you that I can't talk about an ongoing investigation."

"Did you find the missing chairs?"

"Not yet. Your daughter-in-law told me that they're quite valuable. What's your other question?"

"What about the daguerreotype? The Kirschners said it wasn't theirs."

"They told me the same thing when I asked if they'd discovered any other items missing. They said nothing about the picture, and I wasn't going to ask them any leading questions."

"I'm sorry if I spoke out of turn."

He glanced at the clock. "Once the Poplawskis identify their items, we can talk more openly about what we found."

"So the daguerreotype must belong to the Poplawskis."

"Why are you so interested?"

"I'm curious about the identity of the people in the picture. I thought I might try to figure out who they are."

He smiled. "Well, if you find out anything, let me know."

"I will."

By the time Sarah was finished being fingerprinted, Maggie and the Kirschners had left to clean up. She went into the ladies' room to wash the ink off her hands. Nobody else was there. She rubbed and rubbed, but shadows remained on the tips.

She didn't see Maggie or the Kirschners in the main room either. They must have left already. She walked around the counter and headed toward the door. It opened, and a blonde wearing brightly printed scrubs came in. She looked uncomfortable and unhappy to be there.

"Chief Webber will be with you in a minute, Mrs. Girard," Officer Hopkins said from behind the counter.

"Peg Girard?" asked Sarah.

The woman faced her. "Yes. Do I know you?"

"I don't think so. I'm Sarah Hart."

"Hart? Any relation to Maggie Hart at the antiques store?"

Sarah nodded. "My daughter-in-law."

"Tell her that I'm not happy that this is the second time I've been dragged in for questioning simply because I visited her store." Her whole face grew taut. "You can be sure I won't again."

"Mrs. Girard, the police have to investigate

every possible lead."

"What possible lead could there be with me?"

Sarah was saved from answering when Officer Hopkins walked over and said, "Chief Webber will see you now, Mrs. Girard. His next appointment is late, so he can fit you in."

Sarah rushed out the door and down the steps. Seeing Maggie waiting by her red Chevy Tahoe, she hurried over.

"Whew!" Maggie used her remote to unlock the doors and grimaced at her ink-stained fingers. "I don't want to go through that again. Not ever."

Sarah nodded. "Did Peg speak to you too?"

"No. Why?"

"I just saw her inside."

"Chief Webber is being very thorough."

"That's what I told her."

Maggie frowned. "I'll have to apologize the next time I see her."

"I know it had to be hard for you too. Today must have brought back all the bad feelings from Sunday."

"Oh, no, not that!" Maggie smiled wearily. "While we were being fingerprinted, I got the third degree from Mr. Kirschner. I should never have mentioned that the book might sell for big bucks. He thinks they're going to be millionaires once he goes through their house and barn. I kept telling them that I couldn't give them a value on an item I haven't seen, but when I said that about one thing, he asked me about something else."

"Uh-oh. It looks as if we've started the Maple Hill gold rush. Only with antiques."

"The problem is that things can be old and not worth a penny. It depends on what other people want to collect." She walked around to the driver's side. "I finally agreed that we could set up a time for me to come over, but he needs to get everything arranged before I can examine it."

Sarah opened the passenger door. "Then don't worry. Arnold will need *years* to sort out the mess."

"That's good to hear." Maggie smiled as she set her purse behind the driver's seat. "I hope Chief Webber will tell the Poplawskis what I said about that book. Even if it's not a first edition, it's still too valuable to be left in a barn." She laughed without humor. "I know several collectors who would give their eyeteeth for a first edition of that book."

"You could try contacting the Poplawskis to let them know."

"I'll do that. I want to talk to them about the missing chairs too."

"Chief Webber said you think they're valuable."

"It's possible. I know a lot more about antique furniture than first editions. Apparently they were a pair of hand-carved mid-nineteenth-century chairs, which with their original finish, could be worth some money."

"You're going to have everyone in Maple Hill checking what they've got hidden away in their barns and attics."

She laughed. "Oh, I almost forgot. I promised the girls I would ask you if you wanted to make Tuesday cookies this afternoon."

"Sounds yummy." Sarah got into the car and pulled the door closed.

Maggie slid behind the steering wheel. "When the girls were young, we made cookies after school all the time. This is the first chance we've had since school started to make any."

"What a wonderful idea!" She snapped on her seatbelt.

"It was, but I'm not sure how long we'll be able to keep it up." She twisted the key to start the engine before pulling on her seatbelt too. "The twins are so busy with

113

those school projects and getting settled in their new classes. But we're definitely making cookies this afternoon. Why don't you come over around four? The girls will be home around then on the late bus."

"I'd love to. Thanks for including me."

"You don't know how happy they are to be able to share our traditions with you."

That thought made Sarah smile. It was the best thing she'd heard all day.

CHAPTER EIGHT

As soon as Maggie dropped her off, Sarah finished pinning together the pieces for her quilt. Pleased with her progress, she decided to make some tea. She craved a spiced chai tea with a mountain of whipped cream, but would settle for Earl Grey while she tried to sort out everything that had happened since Sunday. The doorbell rang as she put the kettle on the stove. She opened the door. "Martha!"

Martha was wearing a sweater almost as brilliant an orange as the afghan she'd been crocheting on the way up Mount Greylock. She had her yarn bag, which went almost everywhere with her. "Sarah, I just spoke with the Poplawskis on the town green. I didn't talk to them long because Mrs. Poplawski is on crutches after the foot surgery she had a few weeks ago. Imagine that! Surgery and now being robbed. They were on their way to the police station, but

I came straight here. I couldn't wait to tell you what they said."

"Hi, Martha," Sarah said with a grin. "How are you today?"

Her friend smiled back as she came in. "OK, hi. Sorry. I'm a bit excited."

"So I see." She closed the door and motioned toward the kitchen. "Come on in. I just put the tea kettle on."

"No time for tea now. I need to get home to make sure Ernie takes his medicine."

"I can't imagine Ernie not being conscientious about his meds."

"He is, but he'll start reading and the time slips away." Martha leaned forward, her eyes twinkling. "I asked the Poplawskis about the daguerreotype. They didn't know what I was talking about. So you see? It isn't theirs."

"Oh." Sarah frowned. "It doesn't belong to the Kirschners either. Now what does that mean?"

"It could have already been there when the thief stashed the stolen goods in the cellar."

"Maybe," Sarah said. "Or else the thief dropped it after stealing it. But nobody has reported it stolen."

"Unless . . ." The excitement returned to Martha's voice. "Unless there's another robbery out there that hasn't been reported. Maybe the victims don't know they've been robbed."

"Wow!" Sarah hadn't thought about that. "It's possible, I guess. It's also possible that the daguerreotype belongs to the thief, and it was dropped by mistake. I think we need to find out more about that cellar. What it was used for and how long it's been there."

Martha smiled. "I've been thinking about that too. That's why I went to the library. I wanted to read up on Mount Greylock's history." She pulled a sheaf of papers out of her yarn bag. "Here's what I found. Lots of nothing."

"What do you mean?" Taking the papers, Sarah scanned the first page. It was about Mount Greylock's early history. Martha must have printed it from the Mount Greylock Reservation Web site page.

"None of them mention a cellar on the peak. I looked on every possible site and link I could find. Nothing."

"We'll probably need to talk to an expert. Maybe one of the park rangers up there."

"Oh, that's an interesting idea. Can you go now? Let me stop and check on Ernie, and then we'll go up."

Sarah took only enough time to turn off the stove, grab her coat and purse, and lock the door. It was time for some answers.

Clouds were closing around the peak when Martha parked in the almost empty lot. Getting out, she grabbed her umbrella. "Looks like we're going to need this."

Sarah glanced at the forbidding sky. "Let's hurry."

The open area around the war memorial was even more deserted than the previous day. The wind shoved them toward the Bascom Lodge. Lamps had been lit, but shadows still clung to the dark plank walls and rafters. Nobody was inside except a bored young woman behind the refreshment counter. She wasn't sure where any of the park rangers were, but suggested they try the memorial tower.

Heading out into the wind, Sarah looped her arm through Martha's. "This way, if one of us gets blown off the mountain, both of us will."

"Thanks." Martha chuckled.

Rain spat at them. Sarah peered into the tower. The rotunda was empty, and the door to the upper area closed. "I don't see anyone here."

"Over there!" Martha pointed toward the trail they'd taken yesterday. A man was hunched over against the wind.

They bent their heads and walked into the steady wind. The ranger must have noticed them too, because he came forward to stand by the trail sign. The only bright spot on his dark greenish-brown uniform was his gold badge. He raised his arm to block their way.

"I'm sorry, ladies. No one is allowed down this trail today."

"Because the police are still investigating?" asked Martha.

Sarah looked past the park ranger and saw yellow warning tape flapping in the wind.

His eyes narrowed. "I'm sorry. I can't answer that question."

"But we're the ones who found the cellar."

"I'm sorry, ladies. My orders are that no one is allowed down this trail today."

Sarah pulled up her collar as the wind blew harder. "We understand, but we've got a few questions about the history of the peak. Could you answer them?"

"I could probably do that." He hunched into his coat as wind-driven rain pelted them. "One minute." He pulled out a radio, called for someone to take his position, and then motioned toward the lodge. "Let's go."

A few minutes later, Sarah and Martha sat on leather chairs in front of the large fireplace. Ranger Belden — according to his name tag — faced them. Sarah explained how they'd stumbled on the cellar. She didn't say anything about the man in the green coat.

"We're curious why a cellar would have been dug on the top of Mount Greylock. Was there a house up here at one time?"

Ranger Belden shook his head. "As far as we know, there never was anyone living up here permanently. It's too brutal in the winter. There have been farms along the base of the mountain since the late eighteenth century. Some of the fields extended quite a way up the mountain as forests were cleared. There were logging camps on the mountain's sides during the nineteenth century, and the state set up the reservation."

"So there weren't any buildings up here before then?"

"Students from Williams College down in the valley built an observatory up here in the 1830s. That was pretty much it until this lodge and the memorial tower were built during the Depression."

"We thought we'd discovered someone's long-lost root cellar, but I guess not." Sarah relaxed in her chair. "What do you think it is?"

"We'll study it further when the police are

120

done, but our best guess is that it was dug by the Civilian Conservation Corps in the 1930s. The CCC built our hiking and ski trails and most of our buildings. They had to store their equipment near where they were working because the roads were so bad." He grinned. "You must have seen signs for the CCC Dynamite hiking trail. Do you know why it's called that?"

Sarah shook her head.

"Because we found a large metal box along it. The CCC stored their dynamite in it when they blasted away rock ledges to make the trails. We've found several other boxes and a few storage cellars. We left the boxes intact, but filled in the cellars. We don't want campers using them as shelters, especially if a bear has already moved in."

"Wow," Sarah's eyes widened. "I had no idea." Her mind was whirling. "Thanks so much for explaining all that, Ranger Belden." Sarah stood.

As he shook their hands, he said, "Glad to help. A word of advice, though, ladies. From now on, stay on the marked trails."

They both agreed and went out into the rain. Martha didn't open her umbrella; the wind would have immediately turned it inside out. They half-ran to the car.

Closing the door and shutting out the roar

of the wind, Martha put her hands on the steering wheel. "Well, that was interesting, but not exactly helpful."

"No, it does help. Now we know that the daguerreotype couldn't have been left behind when someone moved away from here." Sarah smiled. "One possibility crossed off, so now we can focus on the others."

"So what do we do now? I've still got some time before the visiting nurse comes to see Ernie."

Sarah glanced at her watch. "If we can stop somewhere to grab some lunch on the run, I can spend a couple of hours at the library before I go over to Maggie and Jason's house. I promised to make cookies with Maggie and the girls this afternoon."

Martha smiled and started the car. "You can't be late for that! Let's get going."

The Maple Hill Library was an imposing building near the village green. Made from local stone, the two-story building had a Palladian window above the main entrance. The other windows were tall and marched in perfect precision across the front of the building.

When Sarah walked in that afternoon, librarian Spencer Hewitt was not at the circulation desk. That wasn't unusual. He liked to help patrons find what they were looking for. She noticed him talking to a woman by a bookcase about halfway down the long room. The young woman was hanging on his every word. Sarah wasn't sure if it was because what Spencer was telling her fascinated her, or if the librarian himself held her attention.

Miss Carpenter had been Maple Hill's librarian for as long as Sarah could recall, but when Spencer took the job, there had been a buzz among the younger women in Maple Hill. Many suddenly discovered an interest in books and the long-ignored book club, because Spencer looked more like a leading man than a librarian. He was tall enough to reach most of the shelves and had the slim build of an athlete. His dark hair framed bright blue eyes and a smile that lit up the library.

Sarah waited by the circulation desk for Spencer to return. He did when he finished answering the woman's question. He seemed completely unaware of the woman watching him walk away.

"Hi, Sarah," he said as he faced her across the counter. "What can I do for you today?"

"I'm trying to identify some people in an old photograph. I was wondering if there's anything here to help me."

"What do you know about them?"

"The man's wearing a Civil War uniform, and their names are Adam and Barbara."

"No last name?"

"That's what I'm hoping to find. I've done some research on the Internet about Massachusetts units, hoping to find something."

"He could have enlisted in one in Vermont or New York instead. We're close enough to either state for a man to ride to Bennington or Albany to enlist."

She nodded. "I never considered that, but it really doesn't matter. Without a last name, I haven't gotten anywhere."

"There are some great books of town history in the special collection. I have one that might help. It was written late in the nineteenth century. It's the best history of Maple Hill." He walked around the desk and opened a drawer. Taking out a key, he said, "I can't let you take it out of the library, but you can go through the book here. I'll be right back. Wait here."

Sarah did, and Spencer came back within minutes with a brown book. He placed it on a reading table. She thanked him and sat.

"Let me know when you're finished," he said. "I'll put it away, and see if any of the others might be useful."

She thanked him again and gingerly opened the book titled simply *The Maple Hill Book*. The paper was thicker than the paper in modern books. She turned the pages with care. One page had the names of the people who had served on the historical committee that had compiled the book. The next listed the illustrations. The five pictures were of important buildings in town. She turned to the chapter on the Civil War and began reading.

Hope turned to disappointment as she read. The authors gave a history of how regiments were raised in Berkshire County. They included the names of the high-ranking officers as well as men who had risen to positions of authority and respect in Maple Hill. But there was no listing, as she'd hoped, of all the men who had served.

Closing the book, Sarah got up. She took the book to the circulation desk and gave it to Spencer. "Thanks."

"If I'm reading your expression right, you didn't find what you were looking for."

"Not yet."

He smiled. "I have some other books that may be useful. Want me to see what I can dig up?"

An hour later, Sarah had skimmed through a pile of books on the town's history, but she hadn't found anything useful. She stacked the books up and brought them back to Spencer. "Sorry you didn't find what you needed," he said.

"That's OK. I'm not going to give up."

"If there's anything else I can do to help you research the photo, let me know."

"I will, but I think I'll see what Irene might have at the historical society."

"That's a good idea. Good luck, Sarah."

"Thanks. I'll take all I can get."

CHAPTER NINE

Sarah arrived at Jason's house to make cookies a short time before the girls were due home from school. The rain had slowed to a gentle sprinkle by the time she parked behind a green truck with DAVE DIAMOND, HANDYMAN on the doors. It had a cab on the back with a missing rear window, and a bright blue tarp covered the truck's contents, which jutted at strange angles.

As Maggie welcomed her with a kiss on the cheek, banging sounds and loud music came from upstairs.

"Dave is hard at work," Maggie said as she hung Sarah's tan raincoat on the coat tree in the front hall. "He started right after lunch today. So did that music. Let's go into the kitchen. It's a bit quieter there."

By the time they reached the kitchen, the music had dimmed to a distant rumble, like the remnants of a thunderstorm. The old house's thick horsehair-plaster walls offered excellent sound insulation.

Because the kitchen was decorated in country style with a few of Maggie's favorite antiques, the old cabinets didn't look out of place. A new granite countertop and appliances had been installed before Jason and his family moved in. The walls had been painted a glorious persimmon that seemed to shift tones with the sunlight. Wide pine boards spread out from the oak cupboards and took on a golden glow beneath the round kitchen table. A door just past the table opened to a back staircase. The kitchen was a room meant to be lived in.

"Something smells good," Sarah said.

"I've got chili in the Crock-Pot." Maggie lifted the lid to let more zesty aromas swirl through the kitchen. "You'll stay and have some with us, won't you?"

"You know I love your cooking." Sarah smiled. "You were asking me a week or so ago what you should bring to the next church potluck. Bring that, and you won't have to worry about taking home any leftovers."

Maggie colored at the praise, but Sarah wasn't exaggerating. Her daughter-in-law was a wonderful cook, using Latin and Asian influences in common dishes to make them delicious.

As they talked, Sarah took the mug of tea that Maggie offered her. The scents of cinnamon and apple steamed around her as she took a sip.

"Oh, perfect," she said. "It makes me think how much I'm looking forward to taking all of you out to Graham's Orchard this fall."

"I'm looking forward to it too." Maggie sipped from her mug. "I've never been apple picking."

"There's nothing like an apple fresh off the tree." She noticed Maggie was staring down into her cup. "What's wrong?"

Maggie looked up, pasted on a smile, and said, "Don't mind me. It's just been one of those days."

"Anything I can do to help?"

She shook her head. "Not unless you can pull an assistant for me out of a hat. I had to spend the past two hours at the store, even though it's supposed to be closed. I got a request to open it. They said for just a few minutes, and they were there for more than an hour. I need someone to cover for me on my days off, and it'd be nice to have someone to chat with when there aren't any customers." She hesitated, and then added, "I knew it'd be tough on the girls leaving their friends behind. I didn't stop to think that I'd be doing the same."

"Hasn't Jason introduced you to his friends?"

"Of course, but they're *his* friends from high school. And you've been kind enough to introduce me to your friends at church. Don't take this the wrong way. I'd like to make some friends of my own."

Sarah put her cup on the counter. "How could I take that the wrong way? Is there anything else I can do to help?"

"I'll let you know if there is, but right now making friends has to be on hold while I get the store under control."

"I can ask around if anyone is looking for a part-time job."

"Not yet." A flush rose up Maggie's cheeks. "I have to check my cash flow."

Sarah hadn't intended to embarrass her, and she sought for a cheerful reply to make Maggie feel better. Before she could speak, a sudden silence swept through the house, followed by someone coming down the back stairs.

Dave opened the door slowly to make sure it wouldn't bump anyone. Earplugs and a dust mask hung around his neck, and he pulled off a pair of very worn work gloves. "Was my music too loud?"

"A bit." Maggie opened the spice drawer.

"But we're fine here in the kitchen."

"I must have bumped the volume up by mistake." He tapped the earplugs hanging on a string. "I wear hearing protection when I drill. I didn't realize how loud it was until I took these off. Let me know if it happens again, OK?"

Maggie set several spice jars on the counter. "I'll do that."

"How was your fund-raiser?" Sarah asked, taking out the cookie sheets.

Dave's smile got so wide she wondered if his face could hold it. "The weekend went really well. We'll be able to help a bunch of homeless vets on our next weekend. We collected a lot of supplies to distribute. Thanks for asking."

"Is that what you've got stacked in your truck?" asked Maggie.

"Yep. I volunteered to take them to a homeless-vets' shelter."

The front door opened and closed, echoing through the house.

Maggie put her cup on the counter. "That's the girls. Let me go and get them washed up. Then we can begin baking."

"I'd better get back to work too," Dave said. "I don't want to leave those wires hanging."

"Dave, can I ask you something?" Sarah

picked up the two tea cups and put them by the sink.

"Sure. Anything."

"You were in the army, and you work a lot with veterans. Do you know anything about soldiers in the Civil War?"

"Civil War?" He swallowed so roughly that she could hear it over the voices from the front hall. He put his hand to his throat. "Sorry. Plaster dust."

Sarah opened the refrigerator and took out a bottle of water. "Here. This should help."

"Thanks." He opened it and took a deep drink that drained most of the bottle. He screwed the top on. Setting the bottle on the counter, he said, "I've recently gotten interested in the Civil War, and I've been reading a lot about it. Why?"

"I found a daguerreotype that I'm trying to get more information on. The man in it is wearing a Civil War uniform."

"All I ever find are cobwebs and mouse droppings in these old houses."

"I didn't find it in my —"

He began to cough again. Grabbing the bottle, he finished off the water. "Sorry. That tickle is persistent."

"It's OK."

He glanced toward the hallway as Maggie

132

and the twins approached. "Do you have the picture with you? I'd need to see it to be able to tell you anything."

"No, but I'll try to remember to bring it the next time I come over here."

"That would be great. I hope I can help."

As Dave went upstairs, closing the door behind him, Sarah began to gather the rest of the bowls and measuring spoons they'd need to make cookies. She was looking for the mixer when Audrey stormed into the kitchen.

"Hi, Audrey," Sarah said, smiling at her granddaughter. Her smile faded when Audrey stamped past her and threw her backpack down beside the table.

Before she could ask what was wrong, Amy and Maggie came into the kitchen. Both of them looked upset. Maggie went to put her arms around Audrey, but Audrey wasn't in the mood to be comforted.

She evaded her mother and said, "Tracy Witherspoon is *so* obnoxious."

"Audrey!" said Maggie. "Just because you and Tracy don't see eye-to-eye, there's no need to insult her."

"I wasn't insulting her. It's the truth." She jabbed an elbow at her sister. "Tell her."

Amy mumbled something, and then slipped off her own backpack. Going to the sink, she washed her hands.

Scowling at her twin, Audrey said, "Amy won't say anything because she hopes maybe Tracy will let her be one of her friends. She wants to sit at the popular table in the cafeteria."

"No," Amy replied as she opened the cookbook. "That's not it. I don't care about being friends with Tracy. All I want is to make sure we both get good grades on our projects."

"Do you like Tracy, Amy?" asked Sarah as she began to measure flour.

"She's OK."

Maggie joined them at the counter. "Audrey, you've got to stop letting Tracy get under your skin."

"Don't tell me to turn the other cheek, Mom!" Audrey said. "She'd just snub that one too."

Maggie began talking about the cookies they'd make. Sarah and Amy quickly joined in the conversation, but Audrey remained a dreary shadow lurking in the kitchen. She participated in mixing up dough and putting them in the oven. She spoke when someone asked her a direct question. Otherwise, she said nothing. When the last tray of cookies was baking, she excused herself and went upstairs.

"I'm sorry, Sarah," Maggie said as soon as Amy — with cookies for her and Audrey — had gone upstairs too, to start her homework. "Not quite the fun family moment I'd promised."

"It's OK. Even though it's not easy right now, you should be glad that she shares her true feelings with you."

Maggie laughed. "Sometimes I think I'd like her to share a little less."

A few minutes later, Jason took a deep sniff as he came into the kitchen. "Tuesday cookies and chili? Yum!" Giving Maggie a kiss, he picked up a cookie. He winked as he asked, "How's the sleuthing going, Mom?"

"It's not. Every idea I have takes me nowhere." Sarah told him about the trip she'd taken with Martha earlier. "I know there's something I'm missing. Something that's probably right in front of me." She poured him a glass of milk to drink with the cookies. "How was your day?"

"Lots of paperwork for the Commonwealth of Massachusetts. Remind me again why I decided to become an attorney instead of flipping burgers." At the high-pitched whir of a power drill, he glanced at the ceiling. "How's the work going here?"

"Dave is taking out that extra fuse box in

the guest room," Maggie said.

"He's still working in the guest room?" Jason frowned. "I thought he was going to be finished with that a couple of days ago."

Maggie nodded her thanks when Sarah poured her a glass of milk too. "He must have run into some complications. Don't worry. He'll get to the fireplace before it falls into the cellar."

"Let's hope so."

"Now we know where Audrey gets her attitude from," Maggie said.

He gave her and Sarah an apologetic smile. "Where are the girls?"

"Upstairs. Amy is doing her homework, and Audrey is sulking."

"More Stacy trouble?"

"*Tracy*, and yes." She pushed herself away from the counter. "Audrey doesn't need us sticking our noses in. She needs to learn how to solve her own problems. But I'm going to keep an eye on both Audrey and Tracy at the auditions for the fall play tomorrow and maybe discover a way for them to bridge their differences."

Another thud reverberated through the house.

"I hope that's Dave and not the girls." Jason took a generous bite of his cookie and smiled.

"You're lucky you found him, Jason," Sarah replied. She began moving the cookies into the snowman cookie jar.

"I hope so. His work is great, but slower than I expected."

As if on cue, Dave opened the stairwell door again. Plaster dust whitened his clothes and his face. "One circuit traced in the attic fuse box."

"Attic? I thought you were working in the guest room," Jason said.

"I finished that one up and figured I'd start on the attic one before I headed home. About twenty more circuits to go, assuming we don't find another fuse box or two hiding somewhere."

"It's a wonder this house hasn't burned down by now." Jason shook his head.

"Nick of time, I'd say." He handed Jason a section of old wire where the insulating cover was torn away. "I cut the wire at the end, but you can see how someone else stripped it and just left it like that. If there had been current running through it, we wouldn't be having this conversation here." He gestured toward the foyer. "I want to check under the stairs out there. A wire I was tracing went in that direction."

"Go ahead." Jason set the wire on the table and grinned. "Just poke around wher-

137

ever you need to. I'm glad you can figure out what to do. I couldn't make head or tail of that tangled mess."

"I'd like to say I've seen worse, but I haven't."

The twins thundered down the stairs and into the kitchen with their empty plate. They gave Jason a quick hug, both asking at the same time if he liked the cookies.

"They're the best." he told them.

"Do you want some cookies before you go back to work?" Maggie held out a plate to Dave.

He took two oatmeal raisin cookies and a chocolate chip. "If these taste half as good as they smell, they'll be heavenly." He bit into one of the oatmeal raisin cookies and closed his eyes. "Mmm . . . delicious."

Sarah bent and whispered to the girls as Jason asked Dave another question about the wiring. As the men went out to the front hall, Amy and Audrey got busy. They carried a foil-covered paper plate toward the stairs and held it out to Dave.

"What's this?" he asked.

"For the baby," Audrey replied with a grin. "Cookies for the baby."

"I'll make sure Liz eats a couple of extra cookies for the baby."

Sarah could see he was really touched by

the kindness Jason's family was showing him. She remembered Martha's comment about Dave not being very friendly, and now she wondered if anyone had given him a chance.

As Dave got to work, the girls went into the parlor. Jason and Maggie followed, talking about their day.

"It's been stressful," Maggie said with a sigh. "I got another call from the police with more questions about the clock."

From the corner of her eye, Sarah saw Dave flinch. His usual smile faded as his jaw tightened. It was the same expression she'd seen on his face at her house when Jason spoke about the robbery. She couldn't help wondering if it was because he worried about his wife being home by herself or if there was another reason.

When Sarah returned to her own home that evening after enjoying supper with her son's family, she found her front door unlocked. She was going to need to remind Rita to keep it locked when she came home in the evenings. Simply because there hadn't been more robberies didn't mean they were safe.

No one was on the first floor, but the dishwasher was running. Rita was very considerate. Checking the refrigerator, she saw that the leftover chicken soup, which she had marked as "help yourself," was gone. Good. She was glad Rita felt at home in the house.

Sarah was about to go upstairs to get ready for bed. She halted, with one foot on the lowest step, when she remembered that she'd promised to bring Dave photos of the daguerreotype next time she went over to Jason's house. She should print up extra copies so he could look them over at his leisure. Not that a man who worked as long and as hard as he did and had a baby on the way probably had much spare time.

She went into her office and turned on the computer. Waiting for it to boot up, she sat down to read her evening verses. She opened the Bible to Psalms and lost herself in the inspiring words. As she had often, she wished she could go back in time to hear their original music. She and Gerry had enjoyed reading them aloud. His deep baritone had been perfect for the beautiful words.

Pausing only to send another set of the pictures to the printer, she returned to her reading. She bowed her head over her Bible and said her nightly praises of gratitude for family and friends. She added a prayer for Audrey and Maggie to weather their difficult transition to their new lives, and she finished with her now-familiar prayer for security to return to Maple Hill and for the thief to change his ways.

She closed the Bible, putting it on the shelf. Switching off the computer, she reached for the photos. One fell to the floor. She set the others on the desk and bent over to pick it up.

The photo was of the back of the daguerreotype. She put it on top of the others, and then picked it up again. It wasn't the same as the other pictures. Martha's hand had shifted when she readjusted the frame. Without Martha's finger covering the bottom of the frame, Sarah saw lettering she hadn't noticed before.

She'd been concentrating on the writing in the center of the old photo, but, this was in the lower left corner by the frame's edge. She tried to make out the teeny letters. It was impossible even with her reading glasses.

She took the photo to her sewing machine and held it under the magnifying glass that she wore when she did close work. It hung on a string, balancing against her chest. She gasped as the words came into focus:

Foxton's Studio

Maple Hill, Massachusetts
1861

That's when she realized she knew exactly where to look. The daguerreotype had been taken in Maple Hill.

Chapter Ten

The Maple Hill war memorial was a simple bronze plaque bolted to a large rock at one end of the town's green. On Memorial Day, July 4th, and Veterans Day, small flags were placed beside it, and American Legion members fired blanks over it while a member of the high school band played taps. She and Gerry and the children had made it a tradition to attend every year. However, the rest of the year, few people paid much attention to either the rock or the memorial.

On the plaque, which was about a foot square, were the names of Maple Hill residents, both men and women, who had died serving their country. It was the town's way of honoring them.

When Sarah stopped in front of the rock the next morning, which was surprisingly warm for late September, she couldn't remember the last time she'd paused to read the names. Too long ago, she knew. Even if she got nowhere in identifying the people in the picture, she was grateful for the excuse to come here to acknowledge the fallen.

A few leaves that had dropped early crunched as she knelt. She tried to read the small, raised letters on the plaque, but then gave up and opened her bag to take out her reading glasses. Settling them on her nose, she leaned forward again. She ran her fingers over the bronze letters. She scanned through the names once, then a second time just to be certain.

No Adam was listed there.

She sat on her heels. Maybe Adam had been the man's middle name or a nickname. Or the man in the daguerreotype might not have been from Maple Hill, even though the studio had been.

Don't play "what if," she reminded herself. *Focus on clues you have.*

She had two first names and the name of the studio. That wasn't much, but it was more than she'd had the day before.

The answer she sought wasn't here. Pushing herself to her feet, Sarah brushed leaves off her khaki pants. Time for Plan B: a visit to the Maple Hill Historical Society.

Before she walked away, she rested her hand on top of the sun-warmed rock. "Thank you for what you did and all you

144

sacrificed," she whispered.

She crossed the village green, which was edged on the two longer sides by stores. The big box stores had moved out beyond downtown Maple Hill, leaving the three-story storefronts to be filled with art galleries, stores, and delightful places to eat. Most of the buildings had striped awnings hanging over their doors and large windows. Each awning was a different color, giving the street a festive appearance. Atop the false fronts of the tallest buildings were the names of businesses that once had been there. Maple trees, some already changing to golds and reds, shaded the sidewalks.

Traffic flowed around the green, or at least it was supposed to. Right now, it was inching along. The putt-putt of a tractor at the far end of the green revealed why. Harry Graham was perched on his tractor and moving at about ten miles per hour. He ignored the line of traffic behind his large flatbed trailer that was stacked high with the bales of hay he delivered each week to stables around town. There weren't many working farms near Maple Hill, but the Grahams hung on, growing vegetables as well as hay. On a steep hillside, they'd planted an orchard that soon would open for pick-it-yourself apples. Just the previous year, they'd rebuilt the old cider mill, and Sarah had been fascinated by the great press squashing juice out of hundreds of apples at once.

She couldn't wait to share that with Audrey and Amy.

When a driver stopped to let her cross, Sarah hurried to the sidewalk. She paused to look in the window at Wild Goose Chase. She didn't have time — or a reason, though she often went in just to look — to stop in the fabric store, but she waved to Vanessa Sawyer, the proprietor. Vanessa waved back, bouncing from one customer to signing for a delivery and then back to the customer. Sarah knew Vanessa was efficient even when she was frazzled — she could always tell Sarah where to find what she needed in the shop.

Sarah continued along the street toward the historical society building, which wasn't far from the library and the police department. Whoever had set up Maple Hill years ago had done a great job of keeping town services close together.

Not too many people were out on the streets on a Wednesday morning. She nodded and said, "Hi!" to the few she passed. When she saw Neil Lawton getting out of his black Mercedes, which he'd parked in front of the Spotted Dog Bookstore and Café, she called a good morning to him.

He was a few years older than she was. He had graduated from Maple Hill High — or Maple Hill Central as it'd been then — the year she was a freshman. She remembered that because Martha had had a big crush on him that year and talked of little else. Neil had been a very handsome young man and was now a distinguished man. Silver glistened at his temples, and though his strong jaw had softened a bit with the passing years and glasses now perched on his patrician nose, he still had the movie-star good looks that had made Martha's heart beat fast.

Where had he gotten the clock and other items he'd sold to Maggie? Antiques were what his mother liked, not him. In fact, Mrs. Lawton had a magnificent house full of antiques that she displayed proudly every December for the Old Town Holiday Home Tour.

A horrible suspicion crept into her mind. Mrs. Lawton had been put on the Bridge Street Church prayer circle a couple of weeks before because she had to have a bypass. Was Neil taking antiques from his mother's house while she was recovering? Sarah wished she could rid herself of that thought, but it was too late. He had sold Maggie antiques, including the clock, which could not have come from his ultramodern house.

Neil stepped onto the sidewalk and waited until she came nearer before he said, "Good morning to you too, Sarah. How's Maggie doing?" He didn't give her a chance to answer. "Terrible thing, her being robbed like that not long after she opened her store."

As soon as he took a breath, she replied, "She's fine. Thanks for asking. How's your mother?"

"She's doing as well as can be expected. They've moved her to the cardiac-rehab unit at Bradford Manor Nursing Home."

"That's where my father lives. The staff is very kind."

"I'm glad to hear that." He took a deep breath and released it slowly. "I'm grateful she can have her rehab here in town."

Sarah nodded. "I'm sure your clients don't want an accountant who's unavailable for hours at a time."

"Yes." He folded his arms over his chest. "Keep the clients happy. If your daughter-in-law hasn't learned that yet with her new business, she will."

"She has." She thought of how hard Maggie worked. "Tell me. How are *you?*"

"Me?"

"Did you know the clock you sold to Maggie was the only thing stolen from Magpie's Antiques?"

"I'd heard rumors that the thief took just one thing from her store, but I didn't know it was that hideous old clock until the cops showed up." Neil kicked at the sidewalk. "I never thought when I sold that clock to Maggie that I'd have the police appearing on my doorstep to ask me questions. They were curious about the clock, and they seemed to think there is a connection between me, the Kirschners, and the Poplawskis."

"Other than that you all live in Maple Hill?"

"I've done their taxes for the past few years." He looked out at the village green as he added, "I was worried more about my clients getting audited than the police asking questions about their relationship with me."

Sarah nodded. "Maggie is unsettled by the questions too, but we'll be relieved when the thief is caught."

"If he is." His mouth turned down, and he looked past her as if impatient to be on his way. "I wish the cops would stop bothering us and spend more time investigating. Other than when I do their taxes, the only time I've seen either Poplawski is when they've brought their car in for service at the same time I have. Tell me, how does knowing that help the police find a thief?"

Sarah needed to take another tack to keep him talking. Neil was so disgusted at how he'd been treated by the police — though she couldn't imagine Chief Webber and the other officers being anything but polite — that speaking of the police department would add to his irritation.

"I'm sorry you've been dragged into this," she said. She was rewarded by the return of his smile.

"It seems like too many of us have been. You and your family. The Kirschners. The Poplawskis." He stepped aside to let a woman walk past.

"What a shame all of the Poplawskis' antiques haven't been recovered."

"Well, I can understand why the thief would have dumped that clock in a hole and kept other pieces."

Sarah laughed. "You really don't like that clock, do you?"

"I was glad to be rid of it. I never have understood why fixing some broken old thing takes away its value. The clock doesn't work, and I wasn't interested in fixing it."

"Did you own the clock long before you sold it to Maggie?"

His brows lowered. "Sarah, I didn't expect *you* to be asking the same questions the police did."

"You've got to admit that the clock doesn't look like something you'd own."

"It isn't. When I went to an auction fundraiser for the high school newspaper last month, I bought a box of miscellaneous junk in order to get a silver tray. It's mid-century modern, so it's perfect for my dining room. I spent more than I wanted because there were other people bidding too." He made a face. "The Kirschners were there — there's a connection the police missed. Anyway, I thought about throwing out the clock, but then I decided to see if I could get something for it. I sold it to Maggie for almost as much as I paid for the whole box." He gave her a grin. "Once I found out Maggie would pay good money," Neil continued, "I brought over some other items from the house a few days later."

"Your house?"

He frowned. "Sarah, why are you giving me the third degree? That's not like you."

"There are many rumors flying around. I'm making a real effort to make sure I get *my* facts straight."

That seemed to work. "The whole box I won at the auction was full of junk, as far as I was concerned, except for the tray. If Maggie can resell it to someone with more money than taste, good for her."

"Thanks, Neil, for putting up with my questions. Tell your mother that she's on our prayer list at church."

He thanked her, bid her a good day, and walked in the opposite direction from where she was headed. She wasn't sure if he or she was more relieved at that. Suspecting a person she'd known her whole life of committing a crime made her uncomfortable. Yet she couldn't disregard the fact that he'd had business dealings with all the robbery victims.

The Maple Hill Historical Society was in a white clapboard building with a simple sign hanging from one of the porch columns. Its age was announced by a hitching post out front and the sign over the door:

Maple Hill
Incorporated 1786

The wide plank door squeaked as Sarah opened it and walked in. A large fireplace stood at the far end of the main room. Cooking pans and utensils were arranged around it, and stacked wood waited for the weather to turn cold. The pine floors were uneven but smoothed by decades of foot-steps.

Bookshelves popped out in every possible direction. They battled with filing cabinets of various sizes for floor space. A few over-stuffed chairs that had been stylish before Sarah was born were arranged by the tall windows. Four long display cases held dozens of small objects, each carefully labeled with its name, its use, and who had donated it to the historical society. Floor lamps next to them were off, leaving the room in shadows.

To her right, a counter edged through an arched doorway and around a corner. A sign on the wall asked visitors to ring the bell on the counter for help.

Sarah walked into the other room and tapped the bell.

A door opened at the back, and a cheerful voice called, "I'll be with you in a sec. Don't leave!"

"I won't, so don't hurry."

"Sarah, is that you?" Irene Stuart came out of her office, an average woman in every respect except her intelligence. She'd been an archivist at the John F. Kennedy Presidential Library in Boston, but had come to Maple Hill when her husband was transferred about ten years ago, and so the library's loss was Maple Hill's gain. "I thought you were the UPS guy. It's early for him, but —"

"Are you waiting for something important?"

Irene smiled, and her face lit up with excitement. "Yes!"

"The historical society —"

"It's not for the historical society. It's for Chris and me. Our fifteenth wedding anniversary is coming up, and I decided to surprise him with a trip to participate in a real archeological dig near Williamsburg, Virginia."

"What a fabulous idea!"

"Yes. Digging in the dirt and getting excited over broken pottery. It's perfect. And so romantic when at the end of the day, we're creaking with aching muscles and covered with dirt." She laughed. "Chris is going to love it! We've done some small digs on our own around here, but this is a professional site. Chris may spend his days working on a computer, but in his heart of hearts, he's a swashbuckling historian."

Now it was Sarah's turn to laugh. "I don't

know if I've ever heard anyone use swash-buckling and historian in the same sentence."

"Maybe I'm starting a trend." She put her hands on the counter. "Now what can I do for you?"

"I'm looking for information about two people in a daguerreotype I found on Mount Greylock." Sarah placed the photos on the counter.

Irene picked up one and then the other. She examined them closely before handing them to Sarah. "How can I help?"

"Have you ever heard of the photography studio listed on the back of the daguerreotype?"

She shook her head. "But I don't have much information about businesses. Our focus is family and social life. The Chamber of Commerce has some records, but not before the 1940s."

"Is there anything that can help me find out about Adam and Barbara and Maple Hill around the time of the Civil War?" she asked as she put the photos in her bag.

"I can order census records for you, but the ones I have access to may still be on microfilm. You'll have to go through the files page by page because you won't have a search feature like a computer does."

Sarah frowned at the idea of paging through so much information. "They haven't been made into searchable files yet?"

"Some have. Some haven't. The older the census, the less likely it's been scanned."

"I need the information. I'll take it in whatever form you can get for me. How long will it take to get here?"

"Let's see. Today's Wednesday. It usually takes a couple of days, so it should be here by Friday or next Monday at the latest."

Sarah glanced around at the bookshelves and display cases. "Is there any other source you can suggest to find out more about Foxton's Studio?"

Irene bit her lower lip and pondered the question. Abruptly she snapped her fingers. "There's one place we could look. In the years just before the Civil War, engravers started making city views. The artists would go to a high point where they were able to get a good view of the city, and then they would draw each building and the streets and even throw in railroad lines and trees for good measure. On many of the maps, they labeled the important buildings and the stores."

"And you have one of Maple Hill?"

"I think it was done after the war, but the studio may still have been in existence when the engraving was done." She crooked a finger. "C'mon. It's up near the front."

Irene came around the counter and led the way past the display cases. She stepped between two sections of bookshelves and stopped in front of a framed map. It was about two feet wide and a foot tall.

Sarah pulled out her reading glasses and peered at it. The black frame appeared to be covered with a fine layer of dust, but a closer look revealed that the finish had faded. It must have been as old as the map itself, which was dated 1874.

The map showed the buildings that had existed then. She could pick out her grand-parents' house, where Jason and his family now lived. Her own street had only a few houses.

"Help me take it down," Irene said. "We'll put it on a table and get out the magnifying glass to see what the small print says."

With care, they lifted the heavy map off its hooks and maneuvered it to the closest table. Irene hurried into her office to get a magnifying glass, but Sarah kept studying the map. It was fascinating to see what had been in Maple Hill many years ago — and what hadn't.

"Let's see what this can tell us," Irene said as soon as she returned and set the magnifying glass over the tiny print at the base of the map. "Look! It *is* a listing of important businesses in Maple Hill. Number six is Foxton's Photography Studio."

"Where is it?" Sarah squinted at the map. "There! Is that a number six?"

Irene moved the magnifier. "Wow! You must be eating your carrots. That *is* a six." She put her finger on it. "OK, let's get oriented. There's the mill, and that must be Bridge Street Church. That means the photography studio is . . ."

"Where Liam's is now." Sarah smiled at Irene. "I think it's time for lunch. Would you like to join me?"

"I can't stay for lunch, but I'll walk over there with you. I can't wait to hear what Liam knows about Foxton's."

"Me either."

CHAPTER ELEVEN

Sarah loved everything about the Spotted Dog Bookstore and Café. The awning outside had been painted to resemble a giant dalmatian, white with black spots. On the wooden sign hanging by the door, a portrait of owner Liam Connolly's dog Murphy welcomed everyone with his usual tongue-lolling grin. The café menu next to it was changed daily, and the special-events board always announced when Liam was sponsoring an author or having a program aimed at a specific book club. All summer, the children's reading club had met one week at the library and the next at Liam's. There always had been a larger crowd at the bookstore, because the kids couldn't wait to spend time with Murphy.

When she opened the door and motioned for Irene to go in first, Sarah saw Murphy heading toward them at an easy lope. He must have been over by the pair of sofas set among the tall bookcases that ran along the walls and stretched out like eager fingers. The dog was a white corgi mix with black around his eyes and ears. The single black spot on his back had inspired Liam and his late wife to name their bookstore and café in his honor.

"Howdy, Murphy," Sarah said, bending to pat his head. "Are you keeping track of everything today?"

She was rewarded with a tail waving at Mach 1 before he turned to Irene, wanting her attention too. She complied with a smile.

"Oh, look, Liam has the new Darryl St. James novel!" Irene picked up a thick book that was set, front and center, on a table. "I read the previous book and loved it. Have you ever read him, Sarah?"

"I'm more of an Elizabeth Michaels reader myself — her historical mysteries."

Irene opened up the book to scan the first page. "That's no surprise." Sarah went to the left. The café started where the bookstore's wooden floors met black-and-white checkered tiles. It was busy with the lunchtime crowd; the pleasant weather had lured everyone out to enjoy it as well as the camaraderie of the café. There were ten tables in addition to the half dozen bright red stools at the counter. When Liam first opened, the stools had been the only place to sit, but word had spread quickly about how delicious the soups, quiches, and desserts were along with a never-empty cup of coffee. Within a year of opening the café's doors, he had expanded into the neighboring storefront, adding both eating and bookshelf space.

The Spotted Dog also took its name seriously. Everywhere you looked, there were spotted dogs: stuffed ones hanging from the ceiling; stickers and posters decorating the ends of bookshelves; a ceramic one that sat between the restroom doors as if guarding them; and, of course, the real one. Murphy was too well-trained to come into the café, but patrons always paid him attention and, Sarah suspected, slipped him treats. He was a well-rounded dog, even though Liam made sure he was walked twice a day.

A sign at the edge of the black-and-white floor asked that diners wait there until a table was available. Not being shown immediately to a table suited Sarah. She went to the counter and folded her arms on it.

. When Liam saw her and Irene, he walked toward them, wiping his hands on his apron. Liam had left his native Ireland almost forty years before, but he'd never lost the brogue that delighted his patrons. His hair was more steel gray than red, and laugh lines edged his green eyes.

"Two lovely ladies!" he said with a broad smile. "Just the perfect addition to a perfect day."

"Liam, you sure know how to make us feel welcome," Sarah said.

"All part of a grand plot to persuade you to come to the Spotted Dog more often. Your bright smile lights up the place."

"If my granddaughters were here right now, they'd be rolling their eyes at such blarney."

He lifted his hands up and shrugged. "I'm an Irishman. I can't help having a wee bit of the blarney. It's in my bones."

"Do you have a minute?"

He glanced around the bustling café. "Not a moment to spare." He winked at her. "Not even for an intriguing woman like you."

"Liam!" She hoped she wasn't blushing.

He looked past her at Irene with an expression that would have been perfect on a choirboy's face. "What did I say wrong? If a woman who designs things is a designing woman, then why isn't a woman who looks into intrigues an intriguing one? And what does that make you, Irene? You must be a history-making woman."

Sarah laughed along with the others. Liam

made everyone feel more than welcome in his bookstore and café. But knowing she couldn't keep him much longer from his other customers, she asked, "Can you spare me a minute after lunch?"

"Now *that* is definitely an intriguing question." He nodded. "Give me a half hour to get through the lunch rush." He went to the bakery case and took out two pies.

Irene said, "Let me know what he tells you, Sarah. I can't wait around any longer. I don't want to miss the UPS man." She waved as she left.

"Liam, is my order ready?" another voice called out before Sarah could answer. Looking over her shoulder, she saw Dave behind her, plaster dust still clinging to his hair and boots. She guessed he'd spent the morning at Jason's house. She wondered how long he'd been standing there waiting.

Liam smiled. "Do you need another cup of my amazing coffee? I warned you it was a bad habit. First you come in every morning for a cup. Now you're coming here for lunch."

"I was on my way home for lunch, and I thought I'd stop in and get some more pie." He gave them a shy grin. "No pickles and ice cream for Liz; just coconut cream pie."

"She's not the only one." Liam winked

before going to cut a generous slice and put it in a takeout tray. Closing the top, he asked, "Are you sure you don't want to take two slices?" Liam's face now had become a martyr's weary one. "I'd hate to see you at my door in the middle of the night like Oliver Twist, asking for more."

"No need to worry," Dave said. "If Liz has a craving in the middle of the night, she's kind enough not to wake me." He backed away a step. "See you later."

"Dave?" Sarah called after him.

He turned.

She opened her bag and drew out the manila envelope. "Here's the picture of the man in the Civil War uniform."

"Oh, good!"

"If you can tell me anything about his unit, I'd appreciate it."

He took the envelope. "This is too thin for a daguerreotype."

"It's a photo of the daguerreotype."

Opening it, he drew out the picture. He stared at it, and then quickly slid it back into the envelope. "Where's the original?"

"The police have it."

"The police?"

Sarah motioned him to follow her into the bookstore. Except for Murphy, it was empty. Quietly, she related how she'd found the daguerreotype at the top of Mount Greylock along with the stolen antiques.

"With Maggie's clock?" he asked.

"Yes. I hope if I can find out more about the couple in the daguerreotype, it'll help solve the robberies."

"I'll do my best." He didn't meet her eyes. "Unfortunately some of his insignias are hidden. It may take some time."

Sarah tried not to show her disappointment. She'd hoped he would have a quick answer and the breakthrough clue she needed. "Thanks."

He nodded and went to the door without looking back. His steps seemed heavy and his head was down as if he were deep in thought. She wondered why the sight of the photo had taken the wind out of his sails.

Chapter Twelve

Liam called Sarah's name. "Karen has a table ready for you." His part-time waitress wound her way among the tables toward her. Karen Bancroft was tall and slender, with stylishly short black hair, vivid eyes, and a nose lightly sprinkled with freckles. Her jeans were frayed around the hems, but Sarah wasn't sure if they were a fashion statement or just well worn. On her faded green T-shirt, a stain peeked out above her apron.

"I'm sorry you've had to wait," she began as she adjusted her apron so the stain wasn't visible.

Sarah interrupted her by saying, "Don't worry."

"Thanks. It's good to see you."

"And you too. I haven't seen you for the past week or two."

"I've been busy with the new semester, but I'm glad to be back here more. I could definitely use the money." She pushed her hair away from her forehead. "Crazy weather, huh? Rainy and cold one day, and then hot as summer the next."

"You know what they say about New England weather," Sarah said with a grin.

"Wait five minutes and it'll change. You'd think, being born and raised here, that I'd be used to it. Follow me, please." Karen led her toward a table at the back. As Sarah pulled out one chair, she looked up in surprise.

"Sarah!" Martha jumped to her feet from a nearby table and rushed over to give her a hug as if they hadn't seen each other in years. "Why didn't you tell me you were coming here today?"

"It wasn't planned. I stopped in at the historical society for help on my little project." Sarah held up her hands in an approximation of the size of the framed daguerreotype.

Martha nodded and dropped her voice to a whisper. "Now I understand. We'll talk about it when we aren't in a public place with who knows who's listening." She glanced at Karen. "Ernie and I are having lunch. Won't you join us?"

As her friend started toward her table, Sarah tried not to grin. Martha's zeal was infectious.

"Will that be OK, Karen?" Sarah asked, knowing from working during church dinners how such an innocuous change can create problems for the kitchen.

"Fabulous," the waitress replied with her scintillating smile. "Now I can seat the people who came in after you." She handed Sarah a menu. "I'll be over to get your order as soon as I get them settled. Oh, do you know what you want to drink?"

After she'd ordered, Sarah went to Martha's table. Sarah was glad Martha had invited her, not only because she could spend time with her friends, but also because their table was close to the window. The view of the green, with the traffic circling it like dancers at some fancy ball, was one of Sarah's favorites.

Ernie stood as they approached. He was as thin as Martha was round, and he had the gangly, disconnected appearance of a scarecrow, even though he was dressed in a blue golf shirt and khakis. Not a hint of gray marred his full, black head of hair or his neatly trimmed mustache. He gave Sarah a kiss on the cheek.

Sarah pretended not to notice how his right hand shook today, because she was glad to see him at the café. When Ernie was

168

first diagnosed with Parkinson's, he had been very self-conscious of the tremors he couldn't control on his right side, so it was good to see him out and about.

As she drew out the chair next to Martha, Sarah asked quietly, "Are you upset with Karen?"

"Not now! I'll tell you later."

Astonished, but hearing tension in her friend's words, Sarah said to Ernie, "I'm glad we're going to have a chance to catch up." She sat and reached into her bag to get her glasses. She wanted to look over the menu.

"Yes!" Martha nearly bounced with excitement. "So how has Irene helped with your *little* project?" Her eyes grew as round as plates while Sarah explained. "That's exciting!"

"It will be if Liam can help with more information. I gave Dave a copy of the photographs we took up on Mount Greylock. He's interested in the Civil War, so I'm hoping he can tell me more about the uniform. It could get us the name of Adam's unit. That would be a big step toward identifying him."

"Who's Dave?"

"Jason's handyman. He seems to be doing

a good job over at Maggie and Jason's house."

"Maybe we should hire him," Ernie said.

Sarah looked over the menu at him. "Are you still having trouble with — ?"

Martha's hand clamped over hers as Karen came to take their order and deliver a cup of steaming spiced chai tea topped with whipped cream for Sarah.

Again Sarah was curious why her friend was upset about the waitress. She swallowed her questions. She selected the potato and leek soup, one of her favorites, Sarah waited until Karen had left for the kitchen before she asked, "Martha, are you OK?"

"Too many ears," Martha hissed.

Still unsure what had put a bee in Martha's bonnet, Sarah nodded. "Hasn't Bob gotten your faucets fixed yet?"

"I don't know what's wrong with him," Martha said. "He used to be dependable, but he hasn't come to finish the job. From what I've heard, he's left jobs half done all over town. Ernie gave him a house key, because we thought that would make it easier and let him come and go when he needed to, but even that hasn't helped. I bet I've left two dozen messages —"

"At least," interjected Ernie with a smile.

"I haven't gotten one call back. Not one."

She paused dramatically, and then said, "Then, out of the blue this morning, he calls and says he'll be there tomorrow."

"I guess he figures he needs to finish up some jobs," Ernie said, "if he wants to get paid."

"That's a good thing, isn't it?" asked Sarah before taking a sip of her chai tea.

"*If* he finishes up instead of leaving it even more torn apart." Martha sighed. "Listen to me. Looking for trouble when I should be grateful that God has decided to ease my annoyance and has sent Bob to finish the job."

Sarah put down her cup. "As the old hymn goes, God moves in mysterious ways, his wonders to perform."

"I'll just be grateful if Bob moves the faucet in a regular old way with a wrench," Ernie said.

They laughed. Sarah was thankful to hear Ernie joking.

As they enjoyed lunch, she continued to see Martha eyeing Karen suspiciously. "What's up?"

"Later." Martha watched as Ernie excused himself, stood, and went to speak to a friend who'd just come in.

"He's doing so much better," Sarah said.

"That's what Peg said when she saw him

again this morning. His blood pressure is down, and Peg told me that visiting nurses don't stress people out like doctors do."

"Peg who?"

"Peg Girard."

Sarah sat back in her chair, stunned. Maggie had mentioned Peg's name to Chief Webber as a regular visitor to the store. Sarah also remembered the police chief cautioning Maggie not to jump to conclusions. Sarah knew she shouldn't either, but the chief must have had his suspicions too, since he'd asked Peg to come in a second time to answer questions. Or had he asked her to come back simply because he wanted her insight as a visiting nurse?

"I'm glad she stops by," Martha said. "Have you ever met her?"

"Once."

"I'm surprised it's only been once, because she lives just a couple of houses away from Jason and Maggie."

"I didn't know that."

"She's so nice, isn't she?" Martha didn't give Sarah a chance to answer, which was just as well. "Dottie Kirschner told me Peg was so good with Arnold after his surgery last spring."

"So she was Arnold's visiting nurse too?"

"She covers most of Maple Hill. Did you

172

hear what she did a few weeks ago? She gave more than $100,000 to Berkshire Hospice. When I asked her where a visiting nurse gets that kind of money to give away, she said she didn't want to talk about it. She just wanted to get on with her job."

Sarah remained silent. She couldn't keep from thinking about the VNA box that had been in the bag with the antiques. Peg Girard had nursed at least one of the robbery victims. Was the visiting nurse checking in with Mrs. Poplawski after her surgery too? If so, that was two of the robbery victims, and Peg had been in Maggie's store often. She had, according to Maggie, inquired about many different items. Had the visiting nurse been trying to learn about the value of antiques she'd stolen?

Ernie came back to the table, and the conversation turned to grandchildren. Sarah tried to relax and enjoy Ernie's story about teaching his youngest grandson how to fish. She couldn't stop thinking about the possible suspects.

They were finishing up their meal when Sarah saw Neil Lawton walk past and get into his car. Sarah considered giving him a friendly wave, but he did not glance in her direction as he backed the Mercedes out and drove away.

She thought of how Neil hadn't met her eyes when they talked about his business earlier. Usually he was a jovial salesman, eager to offer his services to anyone who would listen. Was he having trouble balancing work and tending to his mother? Sarah knew from reviewing her own father's bills at the nursing home that not everything was covered by insurance. With the added burden of his mother's medical bills, Neil might have been pushed into doing something desperate.

Like stealing from his neighbors.

She didn't want to believe that, but anyone could have taken the antiques from the unlocked barns. And he *had* been to Maggie's shop and knew what kind of money he could get there. Had he been there the day before the robbery? Even if he hadn't, the folded slip of paper could have been lodged in the door for a couple of days before the thief went into the store.

This was getting complicated. She had a growing collection of suspects. She needed information to eliminate some of them.

The scratch of a chair being pulled out from the table drew Sarah out of her thoughts.

"Mind if I join you?" asked Liam.

She smiled. "It's your café. You should be

able to sit wherever you want."

He set a cup of coffee in front of him. "But not *when* I want. Sorry I had to put you off earlier."

"Not a problem. Martha and Ernie will be interested in hearing this too. Liam, I was over at the historical society this morning, and Irene showed me an old map of Maple Hill. We noticed there was a photography studio named Foxton's where the café is now."

"Was there? Isn't that interesting?" His bright green eyes narrowed. "Why were you looking at the map?"

She told him about the daguerreotype, and he chuckled. "Well, don't that beat everything? A picture no one will claim of people no one knows. A real mystery any way you look at it. I can see why you're interested in solving it."

"Do you know anything about the photography studio?"

"Sorry, Sarah." He rubbed his chin. "I can't help you. If you remember, this building was the farm supply store before I opened the café. Where we're sitting now was a shoe store for as long as anyone can recall."

"You don't know anything about what this building was used for before the farm supply moved in?"

"Jeannie and I tore this place apart when we bought it. We found lots of things left by the farm supply, but no signs of the Foxton Photography Studio." He shook his head. "Strange, huh? The place used to be named for a fox and now it's a dog. Wish I could tell you something, but I'd only be," he added, deepening his Irish accent, "spinnin' ye more blarney."

"So it's another dead end," Martha said.

"Not really," Sarah said. "The photography studio would have been here . . ."

"Until the Depression, I would guess," Ernie said. "People wouldn't have had money for luxuries like photographs then."

"That makes sense," Sarah said. "But that also definitely means there won't be anything in the Chamber of Commerce archives to help." She smiled at her friends. "I can't believe this is a dead end. Hopefully something will turn up to point us in the right direction."

Liam stood and put his hand on her shoulder. "I'm sorry I can't help more."

"Thanks."

When he went to the cash register, where a customer was waiting, Martha motioned to Sarah. They both got up, and Martha drew Sarah aside. In a frantic whisper, she asked, "Did you know that Karen was away from Maple Hill when the robberies took place?"

"Really?"

She glanced in both directions. "She mentioned that she'd been in Boston for several days, and there haven't been any more robberies once everyone saw her here."

"Why would she mention that if she was worried that someone would connect her with the robberies?"

"Maybe she's trying to throw us off her trail."

Sarah picked up her bag and put it over her shoulder. "We aren't on her trail. There's no reason to suspect Karen."

"No? Come with me." Martha took her arm and led her toward the restrooms, which were down a short hallway. She opened a door next to the ladies' room. "I was looking for some toilet paper earlier, and this is what I found. Look."

Sarah gasped. Hanging in the closet with the broom and a mop and pail was a dark green jacket with a simple collar and no decoration.

"But you can't be suggesting Liam is the man in the video," she said, shocked.

Martha reached into a pocket and drew

out a cell phone. Flipping it open, she held it up for Sarah to see the picture of a smiling woman with a dark-haired man who had his arm around her. "It's not Liam's jacket. It's Karen's. Think about it, Sarah. You didn't get a close look at the thief. Karen is as tall as most men. Could the man in the dark green coat actually have been Karen?"

CHAPTER THIRTEEN

Raising the presser foot on her sewing machine, Sarah clipped the threads from a seam on the wall quilt's top. She was using a zigzag stitch to allow her to join the different fabrics with uncreased seams. Even the gray felt for the boulders didn't bulge. She had selected green thread, and the color blended with the cloth forest and mountainsides.

But for once, quilting wasn't settling Sarah's mind. Thoughts sped through like traffic on the Mass Pike — so many questions about the robbery and the daguerreotype, too many worries about Jason, Maggie, and the girls.

Irene had shared her disappointment that Liam didn't know anything about the photography studio. She told Sarah she'd put a rush request on the microfilm order.

Sarah hadn't expected to add Karen to her suspects, but she couldn't ignore that

Karen owned a coat like the one in the video. Also, Maggie had mentioned that Karen stopped into the store frequently to talk. Why? Sarah needed to ask Maggie about those conversations.

And Peg Girard? She'd been to the store too, and Sarah was curious what she'd told Chief Webber about the VNA box.

How long would it take Dave to find out about Adam's unit? At Jason's house, he'd been so enthusiastic about helping, but once he saw the photo, that had changed. He seemed almost reluctant. She was curious about his reaction, but the puzzle was hers to solve. If he could help her, great. If not, she'd keep looking on her own.

Sarah glanced at her computer. Quilting wasn't helping her organize her thoughts. Maybe she should put the wall hanging aside for now and get back on the computer. Instead of searching on Web sites, she could try doing an image search. Maybe she'd find insignias like the ones Adam wore. It was worth a try.

The phone rang just as Sarah stood. When she answered it and heard her daughter-in-law's voice, she smiled. "Maggie, I was just thinking about talking to you. I wanted to ask you about something you said to Chief Webber on Sunday."

"What's that?"

"You mentioned Karen has been stopping by the store to talk. Has she been interested in any antiques?"

"Not really. We've chatted about interior design in general, though she said she's been trying to learn more about antiques and their value."

"That's good to hear." Sarah smiled. Karen remained on her suspect list, but not at the top. "What can I do for you today?"

"Sarah, I hate to do this, but I need to ask you for another favor."

"You can ask whenever you want. If I can help, I will."

"I don't want to take advantage of your kindness, but I don't know what else to do. Audrey has her audition this afternoon, and I can't get away from the store in time to go."

"I'd love to see her on stage. What time is it?"

"Three-thirty in the gym."

"I can do that."

Maggie's smile warmed her voice. "I owe you big time for this, Sarah."

"Let's not keep track of who owes whom."

"Deal. Oh, there's the bell. Got to go. Come to supper tonight. Jason's picking up pizza." Maggie hung up before Sarah could answer.

Sarah whispered a heartfelt prayer that Maggie would regain the balance in her life.

Hawthorne Middle School once had housed kindergarten through high school classes. When the new high school was built ten years ago, fourth and fifth graders had stayed in the building along with junior high students.

Voices were faint in the two-story building. Sarah passed a few rooms where students had gathered to work on a project or for a school activity. The glass windows in each door revealed that most of the rooms were deserted.

She walked toward the back, where the gym also served as an auditorium. A trio of girls ran past her, giggling, and disappeared through the open double doorway into the gym. The noise rose sharply as Sarah followed them in.

A teacher stood on the edge of the stage. He was tall and skinny and wore glasses that kept sliding down his nose as he read instructions for the audition.

Sarah saw Audrey sitting with her back against the wall beneath one of the basketball hoops. She had her knees drawn up, and her arms wrapped around her legs. Her gaze was riveted on the teacher. Sitting on the lowest tier of the bleachers where a few parents had gathered, Sarah listened too.

"You may try out for up to four parts," the teacher said. "Or you may try out for fewer."

"Why not more, Mr. Lightfoot?" called a boy.

"Because we want to get auditions over before the play opens."

The kids laughed. They seemed to like their teacher.

"OK, first," he called, getting their attention again, "we're going to have auditions for Zanny. Any boy who wants to read should come up on stage now."

As the boys lined up, the girls began to talk. Sarah noticed that all the girls had sat on one side and all the boys on the other. How that would change in the next couple of years!

Audrey saw her and came over. "Hi, Grandma! I didn't know you were coming today."

"I'm glad I could."

"Where's Mom?"

That was the question Sarah had dreaded. "She got delayed at the store."

"Oh." Audrey stuck her hands in the back

pockets of her jeans.

"Which parts are you trying out for?" she asked.

"Janie. She's got lots of funny lines, so I really want that part."

"And which others?"

"I don't want any other part." She started to say something else, but paused as five girls, chattering and watching the nervous boys on the stage, passed by. Sarah recognized Lexie Maplethorpe, Martha's granddaughter among them.

All five said, "Hi!"

"This is my grandmother," Audrey said, her voice cool. "Mrs. Hart. Grandma, you know Lexie. And these are Zoe, Mikayla, Esme, Claire and . . ." She glanced at her grandmother, and then back at a girl who wore stylish glasses. "Tracy."

"Nice to see you," said Zoe, her smile sparkling with her braces. She looked at Audrey. "C'mon. Do you want to run through lines with us?"

Audrey shook her head. "No thanks."

The girls walked away.

"Audrey," Sarah said, "you don't have to stay and talk with me. Go and practice with your friends."

"They're not my friends, and why would I want to help make Tracy better? She wants my part! She didn't want it until she heard I intended to try out."

"Why do you say that?"

"I heard that she was going to try out for the lead character's best friend."

"Heard? What if it was just a rumor?"

"Well, she must have *heard* I was trying out for Janie, because then she decided to also. Why are you taking her side?"

Before Audrey could stomp away, Sarah rose and took her gently by the arm. She hoped Audrey wouldn't want to make a scene anywhere but on the stage. Sarah was relieved when her granddaughter walked with her out into the hall.

"Audrey, I'm always on your side. Don't forget that."

"I won't."

"Why were you rude when those girls were nice to you?"

She looked up, her eyes snapping. "Zoe was nice. And Lexie is always nice. But the rest of them were *acting* nice because you're here. When it's just me, they act as if I don't exist."

"But they asked you to join them today," she said. "One step at a time, Audrey. When they ask you again, why don't you try saying yes?"

Audrey mumbled something, and then ran

into the gym when Mr. Lightfoot called for girls interested in the part of Janie to come up on stage.

Sarah went back in and sat. After the five girls who'd asked Audrey to join them climbed up on the stage, two of them went over to stand by her. Zoe and Lexie. Audrey thawed enough to join in their conversation.

"One step at a time," Sarah murmured, hoping that her granddaughter would take the next one before the girls wearied of reaching out to her. Then Audrey would be left only with her anger for company.

Later at home, Sarah clicked on another image on her search screen. The photo of a soldier from a Massachusetts unit appeared in the upper left-hand corner with a Web site below. She paged through the site, but found no close-up view of the man's insignia. The sites she'd visited earlier to learn about Massachusetts soldiers in the Civil War had few photographs. Finding listings of battles fought was easy. Finding out about a specific soldier when she didn't have a surname seemed impossible.

But she'd made some progress. She'd found the names and e-mail addresses of two college professors who were experts on the period. She wrote each an e-mail explaining that she was trying to identify two people in a daguerreotype. She asked if they'd be willing to advise her if she sent them photos. When she clicked SEND, she smiled. Between Dave and these two professors, she was certain to get some helpful information.

A new message popped up. She sighed when she saw it was an automatic "out of office" reply from one of the professors. He would not be back in his office until mid-October. She hoped the other professor would be picking up his e-mail.

Before she got up, Sarah looked for one more bit of information. Finding Peg Girard's phone number and address was simple. She wrote the information down, and then turned off the computer and the lights.

She checked that the front door was locked before she went upstairs and through the sitting room to her bedroom. It was at the back where she had a view of the changing seasons in her garden. She flipped the switch to turn on the bedside lamp. The room, with its dark molding and whimsical wallpaper, emerged from the dusk. A log cabin quilt in shades of blue green covered the brass bed. At its foot, the painted flowers on a blanket chest had faded to a shadow of their original colors.

She changed into her nightgown and sat in the overstuffed chair next to the dresser. It had been an incredible day. She couldn't believe it'd been only that morning that she'd gone to the memorial on the village green. So much had happened, so much to think about. She was making progress, but very slow progress. She couldn't let her impatience to find an answer make her miss something important.

She reached for the Bible she kept there for evening and morning prayers. It had been Gerry's, and she always felt him close when she held it. As she began reading, she smiled when she reached Paul's urging in Hebrews to *let us run with patience the race that is set before us.* She could imagine no better advice.

CHAPTER FOURTEEN

The answering machine was blinking when Sarah came inside from picking some mums in her garden. She put them on the kitchen table in the vase she'd gotten out earlier, and hit the play button.

Martha's voice filled the hallway. "Sarah, don't forget we've got an author as our luncheon speaker at church today. I know how you get caught up with your sleuthing, so I wanted to remind you."

Smiling, Sarah tapped the button to delete the message. She knew Martha was just eager to learn if Sarah had discovered anything new. The reminder about the woman's group meeting at church was just a pretext.

"Hi, Sarah," began the second message. "Irene calling to let you know that the census records you asked for have come in already. We're closed today, but the historical society will be open tomorrow from nine till noon. I know you'll want to look them over as soon as you can. Have a nice day, and I'll talk with you soon."

Excitement welled up in Sarah. Here was her next step in the search to learn more about Adam and Barbara. Until she heard back from Dave and the college professor, she was stymied on trying to match Adam to a specific army unit.

As she deleted that message, she realized that Irene didn't say whether the files were on microfilm or computer files. Not that it mattered. If necessary, she would sift through every entry of the census.

Taking the phone, Sarah went into the sewing room. She sat down by the computer and called the number she'd found last night. It rang until an answering machine picked up.

"You have reached Peg Girard of the Visiting Nurse Association. I can't come to the phone right now, but leave your name, number, and a brief message. If you have called during normal business hours, I will get back to you within three hours."

As soon as she heard the beep, Sarah said, "Hi, Mrs. Girard. This is Sarah Hart. Could you give me a call back?" She spoke her number slowly, and then added, "I really need to talk to you."

Sarah frowned as she hung up. Had she sounded too desperate? She *was* desperate to get some answers.

"An excellent program," Dottie said to Martha as she peeked into the Bridge Street Church's kitchen, where Martha and Sarah were finishing the dishes.

Martha beamed and put more cups and plates in the sink. Her apron was splattered with water and pink icing.

"Now that it's over," Dottie said, "I think I'll go home and try to light a fire under Arnold. He still hasn't begun cleaning out the barn. Maybe I should just light a fire under the barn."

Sarah laughed. "If he won't clean it to let Maggie appraise his treasures, I don't know what will convince him to do it."

"That old fool!" she replied with affection. "He can't bear to part with a single item. 'Just in case' is what he always says. Do you think we'll ever need a rusty washboard?"

"I *hope* not!" Martha said, turning away from the sink.

"Yet he keeps bringing more things home. Two days ago, he came home with a child's rocking horse and a lady's fan. Now what does he need those for? He's been looking at rocking horses for a couple of weeks, taking off to look at them whenever he hears about a new one on the market. And listen to this. He spent a whole afternoon polishing up the rocking horse so you can see the red stars painted on it."

"Did he explain?" Martha asked.

"Just says that they belong in the house. All he ever wants to talk about is that house! I figured when he retired, he'd get a hobby, but not this. About the only thing we ever do together now is go to Liam's for breakfast, and if he keeps buying overpriced antiques, we won't be able to afford to do even that."

"Has he always been interested in the house?" Sarah asked.

"No. He used to walk through in his work boots, bringing dirt from every place where he'd chopped down trees or cut back brush. I got so I could tell where he was working just by looking at the debris in the cuffs of his pants. The pine needles are different from the ones in the valleys. Probably more than you wanted to know." She looked around the kitchen. "Can I do anything else to help?"

"These are the last dishes," Martha said. "Go on home and get out your matches.

Try to light the fire under Arnold, not the barn."

Dottie waved good-bye and left with a laugh.

As soon as the sound of the outer door could be heard, Martha said, "Now that it's just you and me, what else have you found out?"

Sarah dried the dishes Martha had washed. She knew how difficult it had been for Martha to be patient. First, there had been the women's group meeting, where there had been some debate about the holiday bazaar and the need to appoint someone to the education committee. That had been followed by a buffet luncheon. By the time the author had begun to speak, Martha had been aiming glances in Sarah's direction every few seconds. Sarah was amazed her friend had been able to restrain her curiosity during the book signing and then the cleanup of the large Sunday-school room where the program had been held. She wished she could reward Martha's patience.

She shared what little she'd discovered last night on the computer. "I hope the professor gets back to me quickly."

"Want to know what I hope?" Martha's smile spread across her face. "I hope the thief has left Maple Hill."

"Or given up the life of crime." Taking a stack of plates, Sarah put them in the cupboard. "I can't shake the feeling that it's important to find out who Adam and Barbara are, that if we discover that, the whole puzzle of the robberies will be answered." She closed the cabinet door. "I think there may be a few glasses left. I'll check, and then we can finish up. I want to visit Dad this afternoon."

"Then you go ahead too, Sarah. I'll finish up."

Sarah untied the apron she'd put on over her dark green skirt and print blouse. "I'll let you know as soon as I discover something."

"You'd better." Martha shook a finger covered in soap suds at her, and they both laughed.

Sarah slowed her car as she turned out of the church parking lot onto the road leading to Bradford Manor Nursing Home and yawned. Sleep had evaded her last night. Her brain had played through the information she'd learned — and hadn't learned — yesterday. She couldn't ignore the dark green coat Martha had found. And Karen had been candid about needing money. Would Karen resort to robbery to make ends meet? Sarah didn't want to believe that. Maybe if she looked at the video again, she'd see something to prove Martha's suspicions wrong. She should have had Maggie make another copy for her.

She decided to swing by Jason's house on her way to the nursing home. Amy met her at the door and explained that Audrey had taken the tape to school that morning to show their teacher how much work she had done . . . alone. Sarah was glad to hear that Audrey was alerting her teacher about the situation, but disappointed that she wouldn't get to see the tape after all.

"Mrs. Jefferson isn't happy that they're not cooperating," Amy said with a sigh, "and Audrey isn't happy about being stuck working after school with Tracy."

"You don't look very happy either."

"The power is off again, and I always get antsy when it's off." She wrapped her arms around herself. "It feels so weird."

"Is Dave working on the wiring?"

Amy shrugged. "I haven't seen him since I got home from school. Can I come over to your house, Grandma?"

"I'm going out to see your great-grandfather."

"Can I come?"

Sarah didn't hesitate. "Of course."

Amy grabbed her coat, and once Sarah had checked that the house was locked, they walked out to the car. Amy waved to a passing minivan.

"One of your friends?" Sarah asked.

"No. Mrs. Girard. She lives down the street."

Sarah watched as the minivan pulled into a driveway two houses down.

"She's a nurse. She came into our class last week," Amy said. "She taught us to take our pulses and temperatures. It was cool."

As the garage door came down, Sarah was tempted to walk over and ring the front bell. She curbed her impatience. She'd left a message for Mrs. Girard, and she didn't want her to think Sarah was stalking her. Especially if there was a message at home on Sarah's answering machine.

Sarah motioned for Amy to get in the car. Doing the same, she started it and pulled out for the short drive to the nursing home.

The pleasant lawns surrounding Bradford Manor were welcoming in afternoon sunshine. Residents sat on the patio, playing cards or reading or just taking a nap. As Sarah parked her car in the small lot in front of the single-story building, she glanced at her granddaughter. Was the power being off the only reason Amy had for coming along this afternoon?

When Amy got out of the car and closed her door, Sarah got her answer.

"Grandma, can we talk before we go inside?"

"Sure. Let's walk down to the creek behind the manor. It's quiet there." She put her arm around Amy and gave her a squeeze.

Amy stayed beside her as they crossed the neatly trimmed lawn that sloped down to oaks along the creek. Water tumbled over flat rocks. It wasn't deep at this time of year, but the steep bank would keep in the spring's flood of melted snow. Even when Sarah suggested they sit on the bank, Amy sat close by as shadows from the trees dappled across them. One tree had already completely thrown off its summer foliage and burned with fiery gold. A few other trees hid a hint of bright colors among their green leaves. On the hills surrounding them, more trees added to the resplendent palette.

"I need some advice, Grandma," Amy said as she stared at her hands balanced on her knees.

"I'll give you the best I've got."

"I'm tired of Audrey making everyone miserable because we've moved to Maple Hill and she had to leave all her friends behind. I'm making friends here, and I'm not as outgoing as she is. Why can't she? Lexie and Pru and Trina are being so nice to us both. In our old school, she had lots and lots of friends. Her friends were nice to me too, but they weren't mine. I had about three or four really good friends."

"BFFs?"

She laughed. "Grandma, don't say BFFs."

"Hey, Martha's *my* BFF. Bet you didn't know your grandmother was so hip."

"Hip?"

It was Sarah's turn to laugh. "Never mind."

Amy's smile faded into a frown. "I'm really worried about Audrey."

"She hasn't made any friends yet?"

"A few, but not like what she's used to."

Sarah hated to fall back on platitudes, but said, "You two have only been at school a few weeks. Building friendships takes time."

"Not for Audrey. In California, she could walk into a room and everyone would be her friend. She loves being with people and always knows the right things to do and say."

"You're a friendly girl too, Amy."

Amy drew up her legs and locked her hands around them. "You don't have to try to make me feel better, Grandma. Audrey and I always joke that she got the outgoing, and I got the *in*going. She can't handle being alone, and I love spending the afternoon reading."

"You know the saying like two peas in a pod?" Sarah smiled. "Whoever said peas in the same pod are just alike clearly never saw real peas in a real pod. Each one is unique, just as you and Audrey are."

Amy picked up a leaf and twirled it between her fingers. "Audrey blames Tracy for all her problems. If someone passes the ball to Tracy in gym instead of Audrey, Audrey's feelings are hurt."

"What do *you* think?"

Amy tossed the leaf into the creek and watched it swirl around the rocks. "I like Maple Hill. It's nothing like Los Angeles, but I like it OK. I mean, if Dad said we were heading back to California, I'd be thrilled, but I'd miss Maple Hill too. And I'd miss you even more, Grandma."

Sarah gave her a quick hug. "My heart is happy to hear that, because I would miss you more than I can say. Let's think about the Audrey and Tracy problem. Do they have anything in common?"

"They're both in drama club." Lines threaded in Amy's forehead as she frowned. "Audrey tried for the lead in the drama club play, and Tracy did too. I know Audrey wants that role big time."

"So she believes she's vying with Tracy for winning that part and the most friends?"

Again Amy took time to consider that question. She started to answer once, and then a second time, but halted herself. At last, she said, "I don't think Audrey worries about the number of her friends. She's never really had to, but it's bothering her that she hasn't made friends with everyone in the drama club." Her mouth tilted in a wry grin. "Including Tracy. She's so angry that they ignore her. That makes her miserable, and she's making me miserable too. I wish there was something I could do."

"I wonder if you should let Audrey work this out herself. She's facing a challenge she's never faced before, and, if you solve her problem, she won't know how to deal with it next time."

"But I want to help! There's got to be *something* I can do."

Sarah put her hand on her granddaughter's hair and stroked it. "You can always pray for her to find a way to set aside her anger so she is more open to friendship when it's offered to her."

Amy considered that for a moment. She asked quietly, "Will you pray with me?"

"Always."

As they bent their heads together, the song from the water slipping by the stones and the light breeze swirled through their heartfelt words. It was a moment Sarah knew she would remember with joy for the rest of her life, and she added a few extra words of gratitude.

CHAPTER FIFTEEN

"You don't have to go inside if you aren't comfortable," Sarah said as she walked with Amy toward the nursing home. "I know it's not easy to wonder if your great-grandfather will know who you are or not."

"I want to see Grandpa William. He tells cool stories about when he was a kid."

Sarah held the door open so Amy could go in ahead of her. "He loves telling those stories. Your dad and I have heard most of them already, but I always find them fascinating."

"Me too." She slipped her hand into Sarah's as they walked to the desk and signed in as visitors.

Minutes later, they walked down the hall to Sarah's father's door. It opened, and a man in a wheelchair rolled out.

"Good afternoon, Mr. Zambrano," Sarah said as she stepped aside. "You are looking well." Mr. Zambrano had been a resident for years and liked to visit with her father.

His face was as wrinkled as crepe, and his arthritic hands, gripping the wheels, looked more like talons than fingers. Even so, he smiled up at her with a twinkle in his brown eyes.

"My dear, you are looking especially lovely today," he said back, his voice creaking with his ninety-plus years. "Have you two beautiful ladies come to brighten my day?" He leaned toward Amy and added in a stage whisper, "If I were a few years younger, I'd be waltzing you down the hallway now. Wouldn't you like that?"

"I — I —"

Sarah came to Amy's rescue by saying, "Mr. Zambrano, you know the rules. No dancing in the hall."

"Stupid rules," he muttered as he propelled his wheelchair toward a door leading outside.

"That was so weird," Amy said.

"He likes to visit Grandpa. He considers himself quite the Don Juan. By now, he's forgotten us and will be flirting with the female residents and nurses."

"Better them than me."

"You don't want to date older men?"

"Grandma, an older man for me is fourteen."

Sarah laughed as she knocked on the open door to her father's room. Her father raised his head, and she realized he'd been napping in his wheelchair. He seemed to do that more with every passing day.

"What a wonderful surprise," he said.

"We're sorry to disturb you, Dad." She bent and kissed his withered cheek.

"Every day I am here to greet you is a blessing." He looked past her to Amy and asked, "Sarah?"

"No, Grandpa," Amy said with a gentle patience that pleased Sarah. "I'm Amy. Your great-granddaughter."

"Is that right? Well, we sure do think highly of ourselves." He reached out a vein-lined hand and squeezed Amy's.

"How are you doing today?" asked Sarah when she saw Amy was again at a loss for words.

"Good. We had oatmeal for breakfast, and they had extra brown sugar. Not as good as your mother's oatmeal, but I ate every bit."

Sarah sat beside his wheelchair. "Sounds yummy. I remember when you used to paint pictures with maple syrup on Jenna's and Jason's oatmeal. Do you?"

"Yes, I do. Flowers for Jenna and a baseball player for Jason." His eyes grew clearer with every word and his voice a bit stronger.

"Exactly. Did you hear that the Red Sox might make the play-offs this year?"

"No surprise. Could be another World Series for us this year." He started rattling off the batting averages of players past and present as if they'd played on the same team. He was a rabid baseball fan. Talking about Ted Williams and David Ortiz and Curt Schilling always helped to focus his mind.

"Unless the Angels stop them," Amy said with a smile at Sarah.

"Impossible." He wagged a finger at Amy. "Don't tell me we have an Angels fan in the family. I told you, Sarah, not to let that son of yours move to California."

"I know, Dad." Sarah relaxed and smiled. Her father was back in the present. He knew who they were. She was grateful each time he emerged from the past, which seemed to have a stronger grip on him every day.

"Look at all the foolish ideas he's put in his daughter's head."

That's all that was needed for Amy and her great-grandfather to get into a debate about which players were stronger in each position, spouting statistics like sportscasters. Soon they were laughing. Sarah's father even had Amy open up the top drawer in his dresser and take out the home-run baseball he'd caught during a long-ago game.

As the sun began to drop toward the horizon, Sarah gave Amy a meaningful glance. Amy put the baseball away.

Sarah said, "Dad, we need to be going. Can I ask you a question before we go?"

"As long as it's not about those bogus Angels."

"Bogus?" Amy laughed.

"It's a good word. I hear the young orderlies using it." He smiled, his wrinkles rearranging on his face. "I may be an old dog, Amy, but I can still learn a few new tricks." He winked at her. When she winked back before she left the room, he gave a rusty laugh.

"She's a good girl, Sarah. You've done a good job with them."

"Dad, they're Jason's daughters, not mine."

He looked puzzled. "Is that right?" He trailed off and for a moment he was somewhere faraway. "What did you want to ask me?"

"Do you remember a photography studio in Maple Hill?"

"Foxton's?" He sat straighter. "Sure, on the town green, right next to Willis's shoe store."

"Do you know why they closed down?"

"There was a fire. Yes, a fire . . ."

"I'm sorry to hear that." She sighed. Even if she went to the library and read about the fire in the archives of the *Monitor,* she doubted she'd learn anything to help her search. Any clues to Adam and Barbara must have burned up, if they'd even still existed.

"When I was courting your mother," her father went on, "I used to think about having my picture taken. I wanted to give it to her. That way she could think about me even when I wasn't around. I didn't want any of the other young bucks trying to cut in on her and me."

"I'm sure she didn't look at any guy but you."

"You're right about that. I was quite the catch."

Sarah knew his mind was drifting into the past.

"We did have our wedding picture taken there." He smiled at a memory only he could see. "She was the most beautiful bride there ever was."

Sarah remembered the photograph. It had hung in her parents' front hall for as long as Sarah could remember. As a little girl, she'd had a tough time believing the elegant woman in the bridal gown was her practical mother. The only time she'd seen Ruth in a floor-length gown was at Sarah's own wedding. Her mother preferred simple clothes scented with the lavender potpourri she made herself.

"And, Dad, you were the handsomest groom." Standing, Sarah kissed him on the cheek again. "I'll be back in a few days to visit."

He didn't reply, but his features had softened into a smile.

Sarah went out into the hallway where Amy waited. As they began to walk along the busy corridor, Sarah said, "I didn't know you were such a big baseball fan."

"Yeah, soccer's more my speed," Amy said with a bashful grin, "but I know that Grandpa William likes to talk about baseball, so I've been reading up on it."

Sarah nearly burst with pride. "You really made Grandpa William's day. But just be prepared. He's going to want to talk baseball with you every time you visit."

"Not a problem, Grandma. Maybe I'll even get to like the Red Sox."

Sarah drew Amy to one side to let a nurse pushing a resident in a wheelchair go by. The nurse made consoling noises as the resident complained loudly about one of the physical therapists, and smiled at Sarah and Amy as she passed.

Sarah started to follow, paused, and Amy turned to ask what was wrong.

"Will you wait for me by the front desk?" Sarah asked. "I want to look in on someone else while I'm here."

Amy nodded and headed down the corridor leading to the main door.

When the resident mentioned physical therapy, Sarah remembered that Mrs. Lawton had been at the nursing home since her bypass operation. Sarah hoped she would be allowed a short visit to share with Neil's mother how many people were praying for her quick recovery.

There was as much activity in the rehab wing, but it was more hushed. Monitors hung in the hall, allowing each patient's vital signs to be seen from anywhere in the unit. A red-haired woman at the nursing station looked up from her computer as Sarah approached.

"Can I help you?" she asked with a smile. The name on her nurse's aide tag was Grace.

"I'm Sarah Hart, and I'm hoping you can tell me which room Lenore Lawton is in."

"I'm sorry, Mrs. Hart. Mrs. Lawton isn't accepting visitors right now."

"I hope she's well."

The nurse's aide nodded. "She's doing fine, but all visitors must be approved in advance."

"I understand. How do I get on the approved list?"

"You'll need to speak with Mr. Lawton. He approves all of Mrs. Lawton's visitors."

Again Sarah nodded, but as she walked to where Amy waited, she couldn't help wondering why Neil was being so protective. She hoped her worst fears weren't true, but if he hadn't been completely honest with her about the clock, was he trying to protect his mother or himself?

CHAPTER SIXTEEN

Sarah glanced at the clock as she opened up her ironing board. She looked at it again after she'd filled the iron with water and plugged it in. As she picked up the wall hanging from her sewing machine, she took another peek at the clock.

The hands were moving too slowly.

She had woken before six. By six thirty, she was dressed and drinking her first cup of coffee. Breakfast was done by seven. She'd checked her e-mail and found no response from the college professor. By then it was ten minutes after seven. She checked the answering machine again in case she hadn't heard the phone ring; then she listened to make sure there was a dial tone. She'd expected to hear from Peg Girard by now, but there had been no call back. She called and left another message, asking Peg to call her. She gave her cell phone number as well this time. That took up five more minutes.

She couldn't sit and twiddle her thumbs. That would make the time go even slower. To fill the time before the historical society opened at nine, she decided to work on her wall hanging. She had finished the stitching, so the next step was to press the seams.

She mused about how Barbara kept her beautiful gown and her husband's uniform so neat as she tested the iron to make sure it was hot. Maybe those were new clothes they got just for the sitting.

She went to work. The iron hissed every time she set it upright on the ironing board. She opened each seam and held the sides apart. Carefully, she ran the iron along the seam. With the edges smoothed against the fabric, the connected pieces would be easier to quilt. Ironing was her least favorite part of quilting, but she'd tried to skip it once, and the finished piece had resembled someone eating a lemon — puckered and ugly. She hadn't made that mistake again.

And she had to be as patient with the questions and the worries haunting her. One step at a time. Jumping ahead could mean something more disastrous than a ruined quilt. Especially where her family was concerned.

Once she was done with the seams, she'd

pin the quilt top to the batting and the backing she'd already cut to the proper size.

Then she could begin the actual quilting. Because it was a wall hanging, she planned to use the quilting lines to build depth. She would outline certain shapes, bringing them forward and leaving others as background. The colors she had chosen would help create that illusion of depth.

Unplugging the iron when the last seam was done, Sarah turned over the quilt top. She was pleased with it. In a simple Grandma Moses style, the variety of fabrics and textures matched the breathtaking views at the top of Mount Greylock. The top of the war memorial at one side glistened. She'd used satin for its top. The cream border was appliquéd with oak leaves and acorns. When she hung it in the living room, the colors would make the picture pop against the dark wood molding above the fireplace.

She massaged her lower back and looked at the clock: eight thirty. Good! She was about to burst with anticipation.

When Sarah walked into the historical society, she heard, "Hi! Be right with you."

She was startled. The voice was too deep to be Irene's. Maple Hill's high school basketball star, Tim Wexler, came out of the office. He was well past six feet tall and still growing. He had won a spot on the varsity basketball team as a freshman, and now as a junior, Tim was already getting calls from college scouts.

"Oh, hi, Mrs. Hart." He grinned.

"Is school out today?"

He smiled. "I'm doing an internship here as part of my junior-year volunteer project. I got my classes arranged so I can have two hours here two days a week. On those days, I open up for Ms. Stuart. She says she's developing the bad habit of sleeping in late twice a week."

"Why did you pick the historical society?"

He gave the lackadaisical shrug that teenagers use when they are embarrassed to speak about something near and dear. "I like history. I figured I'd give it a try. Besides, when it's quiet and Ms. Stuart doesn't have anything for me to do, I catch up on homework." His smile returned as he bent to pull something out from under the counter. "Ms. Stuart said you'd want these." He gave her a shallow tray holding four small boxes. "The dates are stamped on the top of each box to make it easy for you to find which decade you want to reel through."

"So these haven't been scanned?"

He shook his head. "She said to tell you that she'll keep looking to see if anyone anywhere has them on CD, but for now, this was the best she could find quickly."

"It's a good starting place."

"Let me know if you need anything. Do you know where the microfilm reader is and how to use it?"

"I've used it before."

"Great. Give a shout if you need me." He hooked a thumb toward the office. "I'll get back to my filing. I never knew when I learned my ABCs how much I'd be using them."

Sarah carried the tray into the back room and switched on the lights. Books and boxes were stacked as high as her knees against the walls. The microfilm reader was set on the room's only table. It was a simple-looking machine. A hood that kept the light out on three sides was connected to a flat panel on the bottom that resembled a TV screen.

She selected a box labeled 1870 CENSUS, BERKSHIRE COUNTY, MASSACHUSETTS, REEL 1. The daguerreotype had been taken in 1861, so Adam and Barbara wouldn't have been married in 1860. Opening the box, she carefully threaded the film through the gears at the top of the microfilm reader and onto the take-up reel. She sat and put on her reading glasses. Taking out a notepad and pen, she set them beside her and began to turn the film slowly.

The census was written in a neat hand, and she realized how huge her task was. At each address, the head of the household was listed first along with age, gender, and occupation. Below his or her name were the rest of the occupants of that home, each on a separate line. How many people had lived in Maple Hill in 1870?

She was about to find out.

Two hours later, Sarah had a headache from looking into the light panel, a crick in her neck, and too many names written on the notepad. She was less than halfway through the third reel of four. She'd completed 1870 and gone back to look at 1860. So far, she'd found six Adams and eight Barbaras, but only one married couple. That couldn't be the right match because their ages were wrong. She'd written down each name and its census information.

It was a real needle in a haystack. She was going to need more patience than she thought to run the race set before her.

The information she had found was certainly fascinating. Most of the men had been farmers or artisans, and only a few of the women had worked at jobs other than homemaker and wife. Of those women, all but one had been seamstresses.

Removing the reel from the microfilm reader, Sarah turned the machine off and set the reel into its box. Two and a half down, one and a half more to go. Maybe those would go more quickly because she would already have written down some of the Adams and Barbaras. She stood and carried the tray to the counter.

Tim was waiting there. "How did it go?"

"I got a good start." She noticed he had a backpack slung over one shoulder. "I haven't kept you from getting back to school, have I?"

"Nope. I stay around till noon, and then lock up." He took the tray and put it beneath the counter. "The reels will be here any time you want them, Mrs. Hart, for the next two weeks. If you're going to need them longer than that, let Ms. Stuart know."

"Thanks, Tim." Sarah turned to go, then stopped as something occurred to her. "Have you heard about the robberies around town?"

"Yeah. Some old antiques, right?"

"Yes. But about six years ago, there was a robbery, and it turned out some high school students did it as a prank. Have you heard anything at school that would make you think kids stole the antiques this time?"

"Nah. Actually, my friends' older brothers were a part of that prank. It was a senior-class stunt, and they stole from another student's house. They were all friends."

"Good to know." It wasn't definite proof, but it did seem Tim would have known if students were talking.

He walked with her to the door. "Hope you find what you're looking for on the microfilm."

"I do, too."

CHAPTER SEVENTEEN

Wild Goose Chase was a mad collage of colors and textures and fun. On every flat surface, bolts of cloth vied for customers' attention. Even white and ecru refused to be ignored, catching sunlight through the large windows.

A mural ran around the store just below the high ceiling. It depicted a flock of Canada geese in flight with one gosling trying to keep up.

"Sarah, have your ears been ringing?" called Vanessa from the back corner where she kept comfortable chairs and a tea kettle for customers. Her Southern accent no longer sounded strange to Sarah.

Sarah wove between the tables and the racks that held every possible tool for needlework. She had come into the store to pick out a rod to hang her wall quilt. "Good things, I hope."

"Would I admit to anything else?" With a

throaty laugh, Vanessa stood to look over a low case holding thread and buttons. She pushed back her black curls and smiled. She was dressed in jeans and a casual shirt with a needlework logo. Today's shirt had Sew What . . . ? emblazoned on it.

"How are the kids?"

"At friends' houses." She wiped her hand with an exaggerated motion across her brow. "I've started getting more Christmas pattern deliveries, and the kids are too eager to *help*." She laughed, her dark eyes twinkling. "Are you in a hurry, or can you come and join us? I've got some mango tea brewed."

Curious who *us* included, Sarah noticed a woman sitting with her back to Sarah. The woman half-turned and Sarah saw she was very pregnant. Her large eyes were the perfect blue of an autumn sky, and her light brown hair had a glorious blond streak that couldn't have come from a salon.

"Sarah Hart, this is our resident newcomer at the Wild Goose Chase: Liz Diamond," Vanessa said.

Sarah shook the young woman's hand, after urging her to remain seated. "I've met your husband several times, and I'm glad to finally meet you too."

Liz smiled. "Yes, he's mentioned you and your family. He's grateful for the work Jason has given him. It's his first steady job since we moved here."

"From what I've seen, he does a great job. Once word gets around, he's going to be a very busy guy, especially with so many old houses in Maple Hill." She included Vanessa in her grin. "It seems something falls apart in my house every week or so."

"I know about that." Liz's smile widened. "We live in an old house too. We bought Gavin Krauss's house on Mill Road at the beginning of the year."

"Then you *do* know about fixing up. I've been wondering who'd started rehabbing it."

"Started being the operative word. Dave worked on it while he tried to get other jobs. Now that he has work, our house is a low priority. That's OK. It's fixed up enough for us and the baby."

Sarah sat. "When's the baby coming?"

"Looks as if it could be any minute." Vanessa handed Sarah a cup of fragrant tea and set a plate of cookies on the low table.

"He's supposed to come around Columbus Day," Liz replied, "but my doctor said first babies come when *they* decide."

Vanessa agreed, "They all do, hon. Don't let anyone tell you otherwise. And it's always at the most inconvenient times. Mine both came in the middle of snowstorms." She sat next to Sarah. "I think it's their way of reminding us that they'll be ruling the roost from now on."

Liz stroked one side of her belly. "I'll be glad when he's born. I haven't seen my own feet in so long that I couldn't pick them out of a lineup."

"Oh, don't remind me," Vanessa said. "My youngest is six, but I remember how tough it was to put on my shoes."

"And socks," said Sarah. "Socks were the worst, but it's worth it when you're holding that precious bundle in your arms."

Sarah liked Liz immediately, as she had Dave. There was nothing pretentious about them. Neither complained about the difficulties of coming to a new town to build a business and a life. Instead they were filled with hope and a quiet joy that shone in their eyes.

"Show Sarah what you've made," Vanessa said and turned to Sarah. "The girl has talent with a needle and thread."

Liz flushed. "It's just something I've been working on. I was bored sitting at home because I'm used to working, so I decided to try something new."

"Liz was an executive assistant to some big-time army general," Vanessa added. "I bet she had a direct line to the Joint Chiefs of Staff."

"I spent most of my time making sure the right people were around for scheduled meetings." Liz reached into a sewing bag beside her chair and pulled out white fabric the perfect size for a crib blanket. Turning it over, she held it up. Bright blue bears were embroidered on it. Two of the bears danced. Another played football while a fourth held a baseball bat.

Sarah ran her finger along the even stitches. "This is lovely work."

"I told you she's talented," Vanessa said.

"It's kept me busy since I got pregnant. Before that, Dave and I liked finding and restoring furniture."

"That sounds interesting," said Sarah.

"We like to drive around on weekends and trash days. If we see a chair or a table left out on the curb, we bring it home. Dave fixes what we find, and I paint it to match our mismatched pieces. Over the weekend, we hit the jackpot out on County Street. A couple of pretty chairs and a side table."

"If you ever run out of room for what you fix up," Vanessa said, "you should rent space at a local crafts fair next summer. I'm sure you wouldn't have any trouble selling your finds."

"What a good idea! I've been looking for something to do after the baby is born. It will give us an excuse to keep finding furniture and making it usable again. Not only that, but we'll be able to continue having treasure hunts. People leave all sorts of things in drawers when they toss furniture out."

Sarah hadn't considered that. "What sorts of things have you found?"

"Strange things." She reached for another cookie. "In the first thing we found after we moved here — a dresser — Dave found a trash bag filled with candy bar wrappers. It had been hidden behind a drawer."

"Someone didn't want anyone else to know about a chocolate addiction."

"That's right. Also, broken toys, old clothes, new clothes. If we find anything valuable, we return it to the house where the furniture was left out with the trash."

"What's the most interesting thing you've ever found?" Vanessa asked.

"The most interesting?" She paused, considering. "There have been a lot of curious items, but I guess the most interesting is the page stashed behind a dresser mirror. The same dresser that had the candy bar wrappers."

"What did you find?" Sarah asked. "A

membership form for a diet plan?"

Liz laughed. "Now that would have made sense, but we found the front page of an old newspaper. It was so fragile it almost fell apart in our hands. We had it framed in order to protect it."

"What a find. Were there any interesting articles?"

"All of them were, but most were continued to pages that no longer exist. It was an issue of *The Maple Hill Monitor*. You'll have to come and see it."

"I will," she said.

Vanessa grinned as she moved the cookies and picked up the embroidered fabric. She smoothed it on the table. "Your son is going to love these bears, Liz."

"Especially the football bear." She grimaced and put her hand on her belly. "I think he's ready to try out for the football team. As a punter. He's kicking up a storm today."

"The high school team needs a good punter. My son is Maple Hill's biggest football fan, and he says that all the time."

"I don't think the baby will be eligible to play for a few years."

"How about nursery school? They might want to scout him now."

Sarah laughed and then asked, "Is he your

parents' first grandchild?"

"Yes." Liz's smile dimmed. "My folks weren't happy about us not moving back to Syracuse, but we liked the idea of a smaller town. On top of that, Dave wanted to start his own business. He's had trouble working for other people."

Sarah gawped.

"I know," Liz said with a sigh. "Dave is such a nice guy that nobody believes me when I say that."

"I don't *disbelieve* you," Sarah replied, setting her cup on the counter behind her. "But Jason says Dave is always there when he says he'll be." She thought of Martha's complaints about her plumber. "That's a real plus for a contractor."

Liz's face grew more troubled. "Dave is skilled, and he's considerate, but his bosses believed he didn't have ambition."

"Why would they think that?" asked Vanessa, balancing her cup on her knee.

"Dave never asked for overtime and seldom would work it because he doesn't like to give up his spare time, which he uses to help veterans."

Sarah nodded, understanding what Liz was trying to say. "He told us about his fund-raiser."

"It's always been important to him. His

Eagle Scout project was to help a World War II veteran get the medals he was due. They had a big ceremony to present them. Even the governor came."

"Your baby is going to have a daddy to be proud of."

"That's what I tell him every day." Liz held her cup out for a refill. The women chatled for a while.

Twice, Vanessa had to excuse herself to take care of customers, but Sarah was amazed when she glanced at her watch and saw it was past one. She wanted to get home and see if Peg Girard had called. Later, she needed to call Audrey and find out if the cast for the play had been posted.

Sarah thanked Vanessa for the tea and both she and Liz for the pleasant company. As she stood, she added, "Oh, Liz, will you tell Dave that I'm looking in town census records to see what I can find out about the people in the photo?"

"Photo?"

Sarah explained, and Liz's eyes glistened with amusement.

"No wonder he's interested." Liz got awkwardly to her feet, resting her hand against her lower back. "He's been busy learning about the units from Massachusetts that fought in the Civil War and what happened to the veterans after they came home. I heard him asking questions about it when I picked him up at the end of the fundraiser." Liz hesitated, and then, looking at Vanessa, she added, "I was hoping to make the embroidered bears into a quilt. Do you know someone who can quilt it for me?"

"You're skilled with a needle. Why do you need someone else to quilt it for you?" Vanessa asked.

"I don't know how to quilt."

Sarah put her hand on Liz's arm. "If you'd like, I'd be glad to teach you. Vanessa is right. You have a real gift with a needle. You should pick up the quilting fast. Why don't you write down your phone number? I'll give you a call, and we can set a time for a quilting lesson. If it's easier for you, I can come to your house."

"Much easier." She stroked her belly again, and then raised her eyes to Sarah's. "You're as kind as Dave says. Thanks so much."

"It'll be fun."

"Sarah," Vanessa asked, "will you be seeing Martha soon? I've got a bag of single skeins of yarn for her Project Linus afghans." She hurried to the counter where a brass cash register stood. From beneath it, she pulled out a large shopping bag. She handed the bag to Sarah. "I hope Martha can use these."

"I'm sure she can." She wondered if her smile was as wide as Liz's. "This is very generous of you, Vanessa."

She waved aside the words. "She's doing me a favor by getting these one-of-a-kind skeins off my hands. They're just taking up shelf space."

Sarah didn't believe for a second that that was the real reason. Vanessa had a big heart.

With a wave good-bye, Sarah went out. She took two steps along the street, and then spun and walked back in. With a laugh, she said, "I forgot what I came in here to get in the first place — a dowel for my wall hanging."

Sarah pulled into the convenience-store parking lot and up behind another car at the gas pumps. The car had less than a quarter of a tank of gas, so it was time to fill up again.

Getting out, she undid her gas cap and fished her credit card out of her purse. She pushed the proper buttons, and then picked up the nozzle. The pump whirred as her car filled.

She glanced around. She looked at the

person pumping gas into the car in front of her.

It was Peg Girard. Her blond hair was pulled back in a bun, and she wore light green scrubs.

"Hello!" Sarah called.

Peg turned. Her eyes suddenly widened with fear. "Mrs. Hart?"

"Did you get my messages?"

"Yes," her voice faltered. "But I've been busy with my patients."

"Do you have time to talk now? Just for a few minutes. We could get a cup of coffee and —"

"I don't want to talk about it. What I do with my money is my own business, so stop calling me." She turned off her pump, shoved the nozzle into place, and twisted her gas cap on. Rushing around her car, she got in. The car tires squealed as she sped out.

"What's gotten into Peg?"

Sarah looked over her shoulder to see Fred Daniels. He had been Jason's classmate, and was now a history teacher at the high school. His dark hair fell over both his collar and the black rims of his stylish glasses.

"I'm not sure," she said. She had her suspicions, but she wasn't going to speak of

230

them until she had facts.

"Strange. She's usually very friendly." He shoved the nozzle on the other side of the pump into his rusty old car.

Sarah finished filling her car and drove out onto the road. Peg had been scared. She'd been scared that Sarah was going to ask about the donation to the hospice. What was she hiding?

CHAPTER EIGHTEEN

Instead of going home, Sarah parked near Maggie's. She went into the store and saw Maggie was on the phone. Maggie waved, but kept talking to her caller and writing on a piece of paper.

Sarah looked around the store while she waited for Maggie to finish. There were several new items on display. A doll with beautiful curls was propped in a wicker pram. Leaning against a wall was a large pub sign. The words "Railway Inn" were painted over a picture of a train spewing clouds of steam.

"Hi, Sarah," Maggie said as she came around the counter. "Isn't that sign amazing? It's from England. The guy I bought it from found it on the Internet, but then didn't have room for it when it arrived."

"I'm not surprised." She pointed to a small map of Berkshire County in a distinctive gold frame, edged with maple leaves.

"Did you move that from somewhere else in the store? It looks really familiar."

"Actually, I just unwrapped it and hung it about an hour ago. I was thrilled when Neil offered it to me along with that beat-up clock."

"Strange, because I'm sure I've seen that frame before."

"It's unique, so it'd be hard to forget."

Where had she seen it? She doubted it'd been in Neil's house, because it was too Victorian for his taste. Maybe it had been in his office. Had she — and she hoped she was wrong — seen the map in his mother's house during Maple Hill's annual Old Town Holiday Home Tour? That could mean he was selling his mother's beloved antiques. Mrs. Lawton was so proud of her home, and she had collected beautiful antiques for as long as Sarah could remember. Sarah couldn't imagine Mrs. Lawton willingly parting with a single piece.

No, none of those theories felt right. She *had* seen the map and that amazing frame, but not at Mrs. Lawton's house. Where?

Leaning back against the counter, Maggie said, "If he comes back in, I can ask him." She smiled wryly. "Not that I expect to see him soon. The police investigation has scared off several of my customers. They don't want to get mixed up in it."

"I just tried to talk to Peg Girard." She explained what had happened at the police station and by the gas pumps. "She acted terrified that I might ask her about her donation to the hospice."

"That's not a surprise. Everyone but Peg is talking about it. She should have guessed keeping her mouth closed when Berkshire Hospice revealed she'd given them such a big donation would make people even more curious." Maggie raked her hand through her hair. "And then I gave her name to the police, so they started asking questions too. Poor Peg."

"Don't blame yourself. I showed Chief Webber the VNA stamp on the box up on the mountain, so that's probably why he asked her to come back to talk to him. No wonder she doesn't want anything to do with either of us."

The phone rang again. Maggie picked it up. "Magpie's Antiques. This is Maggie." She paused, and then said, "OK, Mr. Kirschner. I'll add it to the list. Another cranberry bowl with a silver edge. Got it." She set the phone back on the counter. "There's one customer who hasn't been bothered by the investigation. Arnold Kirschner is going to drive me crazy."

Smiling, Sarah asked, "Why?"

"He's given me a whole array of antiques he wants." She counted down the lines she'd written. "Fifteen different items. Look what's at the top."

Sarah did. "Your stolen clock."

Maggie nodded. "He's called every day since he saw it at the police station to remind me that he wants to buy it as soon as I get it back. And it's not just the clock. He bought a cranberry bowl this morning. He wants to be the first to know if I ever get one identical to it. He said there should be two, though how he knows that I've got no idea. On top of that, he's insisting I look at some pieces he no longer wants. He said he bought them by mistake and doesn't want them any longer."

"By mistake? What does he mean?"

"I don't know." She folded her arms on the counter. "I told him that I'll make a few calls and see if anyone has what he's looking for."

"Poor Dottie," Sarah said. Arnold's wants included items as different as a round oak table and a painting of the Maple Hill Green. "At the rate he's buying antiques, everything they used to have in the house will be out in the barn." She handed the page back to Maggie.

"Maybe she plans to send him out there too."

The store's door opened. The twins came in.

"What are you doing here?" Maggie asked. "You were supposed to take the bus home."

"Emma's mother gave us a ride," Amy said. "The principal said it was OK today because . . ." She glanced at Audrey whose eyes were lowered.

"Uh-oh," Maggie murmured.

Sarah remained by the counter while her daughter-in-law went over to the twins. This was a mother moment, not a grandmother moment. Maggie reached out to give each one a hug, but Audrey edged away. Amy looked almost as woeful as her sister.

"How was school?" Maggie asked.

"Horrible," Audrey said. Amy didn't answer.

"Why?"

Sarah admired how Maggie didn't jump in with any questions about why her daughters were troubled — but Sarah knew there could be only one reason for Audrey's long face.

"They posted who got the parts for the play," Audrey said. "I didn't get picked for the lead."

This time, when Maggie held out her

arms, Audrey flung herself against her mother and sobbed. Maggie stroked her back in silence.

Amy came over to lean on Sarah. The girl was shaking almost as much as her twin.

"Are you OK?" Sarah asked quietly, but not quietly enough.

Audrey whirled toward them. "Why are you asking her? I'm the one who's been humiliated in front of the whole school."

"Audrey Hart," said Maggie, "You owe your grandmother and your sister an apology. Can't you see they're both worried about you?"

Audrey wasn't ready to be appeased. "All I got were three lousy lines." Sarah knew better than to suggest it was better than nothing.

"I hope you'll be supportive of whoever got the lead," Maggie said.

"I won't mess up the play, if that's what you're worried about."

"I'm not. I know you'll do what's right." Maggie looked from one girl to the other. "Why don't we go over to Liam's for a piece of pie?"

Audrey shook her head. Even that favorite treat couldn't ease her disappointment. When Amy said she had to go to field hockey practice and Audrey decided to head home, Maggie told them to go out and wait by the car.

As soon as the girls left, Maggie said, "I think I just lost my mother-of-the-year award."

"I usually lost it the first week of January," Sarah said with a smile, hoping Maggie would give her one in return. When Maggie stared out the window, she added, "If you want me to keep an eye on the store while you take the girls, I'll be glad to."

Her daughter-in-law sighed. "I hate to ask you to do that. I vowed that when we moved here neither of us would impose on you."

"You're not asking. I'm offering, and it's not an imposition." She motioned toward the door. "Go!"

"I won't be long." She grabbed her purse and her keys from under the counter. "And if Mr. Kirschner calls, just put whatever he wants on that page."

Except for the wind shaking the eaves and rain pelting the glass, Sarah's house was quiet. The aroma of blueberry pie came from the kitchen, teasing Sarah to set aside her work and get a piece.

She ignored the temptation as she worked on her wall hanging. Even more delicious than the idea of the pie was having a moment to think. Since she'd gone with the twins up to Mount Greylock, she'd had too few quiet moments. Once she finished pinning the layers of the wall quilt together, she could begin the basting that would hold layers in place while she quilted.

"One step at a time," she reminded herself. The windows rattled in answer as a gust screamed past and vanished into a rumble of thunder. She bent to her work, letting her fingers follow the familiar motions while she tried to sort out the unfamiliar facts.

She weighed what information she had. It was scant. Plenty of people had been in Magpie's Antiques last week. Maggie had specifically mentioned Neil and Arnold and Karen and Peg. Chief Webber must know more, but he couldn't tell Sarah, so she'd have to figure out the clues on her own. Again she wondered what Peg had told him. It was clear she wasn't going to tell Sarah anything.

She stretched at a precarious angle, a straight pin in her hand. Pushing herself up straight, she jabbed the pin into her tomato-shaped pincushion. The way her hands shook with tension, she shouldn't be working on her quilt.

How many times did she need to remind herself of Gerry's advice about letting God do the worrying? She smiled. Apparently at least one more.

Walking to the living room, she switched on a lamp. She sat in the chair that Gerry had made for her, a simple mission-style rocker so she could enjoy the fireplace and the view out the front windows. She wished Gerry were here with her tonight to help her sort out the truth. She missed his clear, insightful way of looking at each side of a problem.

Maybe she could copy that skill. What facts did she have?

Some of her neighbors had visited the antiques store. Neil and Peg had complained about being questioned, but Karen had said nothing about it. Though she owned a green coat a lot like the one in the video, plenty of other people could have a green cloth coat too. On the other hand, Neil had sold antiques to Maggie, and he usually had nothing to do with them. Yet he'd told Sarah about the auction and that Arnold had been there too.

Arnold still wanted to buy the clock, but that fit with his obsession to redo his house. Could that be just a new hobby? Or was it something more? He'd always been active. When he worked for the state, he spent every day cutting down trees and clearing brush. Maybe his new hobby was simply a way to keep busy.

So there it was. Four neighbors who were acting oddly. Or were they? Maybe she was seeing trouble where there wasn't any. Peg was the Maple Hill visiting nurse, so she'd be in many different homes each week. Neil could sell whatever he liked to whomever he wished and he could buy from whomever he wished.

Arnold and Dottie! Memory burst forth. The map had been in the Kirschners' front hall. She'd noticed the ornate frame when she attended a church committee meeting at their house a couple of years ago.

"Don't jump to conclusions," she said. A couple of years was a long time, and neither Dottie nor Arnold had said anything about it being missing. Maybe they'd sold it or given it to someone else. It could have been in the box Neil won at the auction.

She checked her watch. It was too late to call the Kirschners now, but she'd call tomorrow and ask Dottie about the framed map.

"It could all be a coincidence," she said.

"What's a coincidence?" asked Rita's cheerful voice from the doorway. "You're going to rock that chair right through the floor."

She smiled at Rita. "I'm glad to see you home safe and sound. How was the driving?"

"Horrible. I got soaked just coming in from the car. I hope you don't mind. I put my wet umbrella in the hall. If I'd left it on the porch, it'd be halfway to Boston by now."

As if to confirm her words, more wind battered the house.

"Just as long as the whole house doesn't blow away," Sarah replied with a laugh. "A couple of months from now, a storm like this will be a blizzard."

Rita shrugged off her black coat. "Don't remind me that winter is right around the corner. We got spoiled with the summer weather this week." Folding her wet coat over her arm, she said, "I wanted to let you know that I'll be away for a few days. I'm heading up north into Vermont tomorrow with a couple of friends."

"You'll have to go far north to see a lot of color this early." Sarah glanced out the window. "Of course, if all the leaves blow off the trees tonight, there won't be any color to see."

"We're hoping to go *before* the leaf-peepers. We want to visit craft shops and antique stores. Will you be all right here by yourself?"

"Don't be silly! I'll be fine. Go and have a good time."

"You're right. I'm being silly, especially now that the thief is probably long gone from Maple Hill."

Sarah was puzzled. First Martha and now Rita acted as if everything were OK. Or was she the one ignoring the truth? Was she so determined to discover a connection between the daguerreotype and the robberies that she couldn't see that it no longer mattered? The Poplawskis' stolen chairs hadn't been returned, but the police were still on the look-out for them.

"I'm glad it's over, and no one was hurt," continued Rita. "Thank God!"

"I have thanked him over and over, grateful that he is watching over us." She reached out and clasped Rita's hand between hers. "But for now, I think I'm going to continue to lock the doors, front and back, every night."

"And my windows are locked." She laughed. "Not that I expect anyone to climb up the tree in the front yard to find a way into my room."

"Then we have done all that is humanly possible. The rest is in God's hands, and that's a good place to be."

Later that night, something roused Sarah from a pleasant dream. Half-asleep, she wasn't sure what it had been. The wind whistling under the eaves? Or was it already morning and her alarm had gone off?

Then the phone rang.

In one motion, she was out of bed and glancing at the clock, which showed it was an hour past midnight. She lifted the receiver from the phone on her night table.

"Hello?" she croaked.

"Sarah?"

Martha's frightened gasp brought Sarah fully awake. "Martha, what is it? Are you OK? Is Ernie OK?"

"Sarah! We've been robbed!"

CHAPTER NINETEEN

Sarah told Martha that she would be over right away. She hung up and dressed in a hurry. As she came out into the hallway, no lights shone from beneath the front bedroom doors — she must have gotten to the phone before Rita woke.

Tiptoeing down the stairs, Sarah got her coat and purse. She took Rita's umbrella and opened it as soon as she was on the porch. The fierce storm was now a chilly drizzle. She shivered as she rushed to her car.

She gripped the wheel with both hands because she was trembling with more than the cold outside. By the time she turned onto Martha's street, she couldn't think of anything but how scared her friend had sounded on the phone.

Two police cars were parked in front of the Maplethorpes' white Cape Cod house. One had bright blue lights flashing, almost blinding her.

As Sarah got out of the car, the young policeman who had escorted her and Maggie into the evidence room came toward her.

"Ma'am, I'm going to have to ask you to stay back," he said in a calm voice.

"Officer Hopkins, isn't it?"

He nodded. "Yes, ma'am, but I'm going to have to ask you to stay back. This is an active crime scene."

"I'm Sarah Hart. Mrs. Maplethorpe called and asked me to come over."

"Please wait while I confirm that."

Sarah buttoned up her coat as Officer Hopkins spoke into the radio he had clipped to his shoulder.

"All right," he said, motioning for her to follow him.

She did, wincing each time the flashing lights burned into her eyes and reflected off the windows on both sides of the street. She doubted any of the Maplethorpes' neighbors were sleeping because every house along the street was lit. People had come out on their porches to watch.

The house's front door was open, and the officer stepped aside to let Sarah in. He didn't say anything as he returned to his post along the walk.

Sarah gasped as she went into the living

room. The picture window had been smashed. The furniture had been tipped over. Books lay like broken birds on the floor. Martha's yarn had been ripped out of her crocheting bag. Balls of every possible color had been tossed aside, and a spider-web of loose threads made the floor an obstacle course.

"Sarah!"

At Martha's pained cry, Sarah turned to see her friend burst out of the kitchen. They embraced, and Sarah asked, "How's Ernie?"

"Angry." Martha looked past her to the living room, and tears rose in her eyes. She shook herself and took a steadying breath. "Sarah, thank you so much for coming! I shouldn't have called you in the middle of the night, but we came home to *this*."

"You know you can call me any time."

"It's horrible." Martha's lower lip quivered, and a single tear ran down her cheek. "I heard Maggie talk about how atrocious it was to have her store robbed, and I *thought* I understood. Now I do, and I wonder if I'll ever feel safe again."

"You will," Sarah reassured her. "Don't forget that our Father is watching over you. He kept you safe."

Martha raised her head. "I'm glad you're here. You've always been steady in a crisis."

Putting her hands on her friend's quivering shoulders, Sarah said, "I know Ernie's angry. I am too. But, tell me, are both you and Ernie OK?"

"Yes, except Ernie cut his finger when he picked up a piece of glass." She started to laugh, but then clamped her lips closed.

Sarah gave her a gentle shake. "It's OK, Martha. Keep telling yourself that. It's OK, and it will be OK."

"This mess . . ."

"Do you know what was taken?" she asked when Martha didn't add anything more.

"Mostly electronics."

Sarah's brows rose. "Electronics?"

"The thief took the TV and Ernie's computer and the video games that the grandkids play when they visit. New things." She forced a smile. "I guess you could say the anti-antiques."

Sarah gave her best friend another hug. "I'm glad you haven't lost your sense of humor."

"It's either laugh or cry. I'd rather laugh." She shuddered. The tears returned to Martha's eyes, but they were grateful ones now. "You are a blessing tonight."

When they went into the kitchen, Ernie was talking with Chief Webber and another officer Sarah didn't know. The aroma of coffee made Sarah crave some.

Chief Webber gave the officer some instructions, and then added, "Mr. Maplethorpe, if you've got some plywood around, we'll get a few of your neighbors to put it over the broken window."

"Out in the garage," Ernie replied, "there are a couple of — couple of — you know. Plywood — you know." His face wrinkled with frustration at not being able to find the exact word he wanted.

"I'll tell them to look," Chief Webber said.

Martha made sure both policemen had cups of hot coffee before they went out the back door. She insisted Ernie have something to eat. Sarah suspected Martha wanted her husband to sit quietly. He agreed to have a sandwich only if his wife and Sarah joined him.

Sitting at the kitchen table was like being on an isolated island in the midst of chaos and destruction. Sarah let Martha and Ernie talk, knowing from their disbelieving tones that they couldn't accept their house had been broken into.

"We spent the day in Worcester," Martha said. "Ernie had his monthly appointment with his neurologist at the University of Massachusetts hospital. We decided to have a nice dinner at one of the restaurants on

Shrewsbury Street."

"Italian," said Ernie as he took another bite of his sandwich.

"That's why we got home late." Martha blanched. "Someone must have known we wouldn't be home until late tonight."

"Or saw your car wasn't parked out front and the lights were off," Sarah said.

"That's exactly what Chief Webber said." Martha took an apple pie out of the refrigerator. She cut three pieces and put them in the microwave. "You'd make a good cop, Sarah."

The microwave beeped. Martha took out the pie, setting one piece next to her husband's sandwich and a second in front of Sarah. She handed them forks, and then sat again. She stared at her piece of pie.

Sarah said, "Assuming it wasn't just someone who saw a chance to break into an empty house, who knew you weren't going to be here today?"

"Our kids," Ernie said through a mouthful of apple pie.

"Unlikely suspects."

"Our grandkids."

"Ernie." Martha shook her head. "Let's be serious."

"I thought I was."

Martha said, "Ernie's doctor here in town

sent him to Worcester."

"Did his staff make the appointment?" asked Sarah.

"Only the first one. We make the follow-up appointments ourselves."

"So his doctor probably won't know he's been there until he gets a report back. Anyone else?"

Martha shook her head. "I can't think of anyone."

"Peg," Ernie said.

Sarah looked from him to Martha and back. "She knew you were going to be gone today?"

"She's my visiting nurse. She's been asking about my appointments." He put down his fork. "You can't believe Peg would have anything to do with this. She's such a nice person."

Again Sarah wasn't sure how to answer. Both Maplethorpes believed Peg was a godsend. Even so, the visiting nurse had been acting suspiciously. And Sarah couldn't forget that box with "VNA" stamped on it. She needed to think about this before she said anything to her friends or to Chief Webber.

"Would you like to stay with me tonight?" Sarah asked.

"Thank you, but no." Martha gave her a

quick hug. "I don't think we'd feel right about leaving the house with a broken window. We'll be fine."

"Then let me stay with you."

Tears glistened in Martha's eyes. "You don't need to."

"I know, but I want to."

"Thank you." She embraced Sarah again. "You are the sweetest friend." She wrapped her arms around herself. "I'm glad you didn't tell me 'I told you so.' "

"Why would I do that?"

"I was certain yesterday that the thief had left Maple Hill. Now he's proved he hasn't."

Sarah frowned. "I'm not sure this robbery is connected to the others. Your antiques weren't touched, and in the previous robberies, the only things taken were antiques." Her heart lightened at her own words. Why hadn't she thought of that instead of focusing on her suspicions that Peg might have robbed the Maplethorpes? When he came to take Maggie's report about the stolen clock, Chief Webber had warned them not to jump to conclusions. Sarah was still having trouble remembering that. She needed facts, not guesses.

"Maybe he's changed his M.O.," said Martha.

"M.O.?"

"*Modus operandi.* The way he operates."

"Martha, maybe *you* should be a cop." Sarah was glad to let her frown become a smile. "You know the vocabulary."

"That's why we're such a good team." With a sigh, Martha became serious again as she looked toward her living room. "And we've got to discover who this thief is and stop him before someone else comes home to find the same thing."

Saturday morning, Sarah was determined to get some facts. She was babysitting the twins that evening, and she didn't want to waste a minute before then. As soon as she finished breakfast, she called the Kirschners. Arnold answered the phone.

"Good morning, Arnold," she said, "this is Sarah Hart. I was wondering if —"

"Dottie's out, and she won't be back until later this afternoon."

"I'll call back then."

"We're heading over to North Adams then. Can it wait until tomorrow after church?"

"Maybe you can help me."

"Can it wait until tomorrow? I'm dripping paint on the floor. We'll see you at church tomorrow." He hung up before Sarah could ask about the framed map.

"Well . . ." She put down the phone. "Time to look in another direction."

Sarah drove into town and found a parking space not far from Neil Lawton's office. When she went in, she saw the office was decorated with modern furniture that looked extremely uncomfortable. When Nancy Armstrong, his secretary, asked Sarah to take a seat and said that Mr. Lawton would be with her soon, Sarah found the odd chairs quite comfortable.

She had finished one travel magazine and was starting on the next by the time Miss Armstrong said that Mr. Lawton would see her now.

"I'm so sorry to keep you waiting," Neil said as Sarah walked into his office. It was even starker than his waiting room, all white and steel except for two vibrant modern paintings hanging on the back wall. One was done in shades of red and the other in blues. A smaller print that appeared to be by the same artist was set on the desk next to his sleek computer.

"No need to apologize. I didn't have an appointment, and I know you've got clients to worry about."

He motioned for her to sit on the small sofa beneath the paintings. "If a client were giving me half the trouble this new computer system is, I'd suggest he find another accountant." He grimaced as he put his hand on the computer monitor. "I was told this fancy new system would change the way I do business. I didn't guess it would be because I can't make it work."

"That's terrible, Neil. Can you return it?"

"Maybe, but I don't want to admit I can't make this high-priced computer program work." He gave her the charming grin that had made Martha's heart quicken in high school. "Male pride."

"I know. Gerry never could admit there might be a woodworking tool he couldn't master, even if he didn't have any skin left on his knuckles."

Neil started to laugh, but then paused as the phone rang. "Excuse me." He picked up the phone and listened. "No, you've got to have receipts for everything you're claiming as business income. What's the problem? You've always been great about keeping good records. Why the change?" He paused to listen again, and then said, "I can't bend on this. You've got large amounts of money coming in without work invoices to match. Get your customers to pay you by check like they used to." Another pause. "All right. If that's the way you want it, come by on Monday. I'll have your files ready for you to take to your new accountant." He hung up the phone. When he turned back to Sarah with another apology, she waved it aside.

"What was I saying about troublesome clients?" Neil asked, taking a seat behind his desk. He smiled. "Be careful what you ask for, I guess."

"I guess."

"What can I do for you today?"

Sarah hesitated. Neil had just lost a client, and now wasn't the time to pester him with questions about the antiques he'd sold Maggie. But she couldn't say that she'd dropped by to chat while walking around the green.

Inspiration came, and she said, "I'd like your permission to visit your mother at the nursing home. The staff told me that you'd asked for all visitors to be approved."

"I did."

"So may I visit her while I'm visiting my father?"

He leaned back in his chair. "Let me explain why I need to discuss this with Mother first. She's been very hesitant to see anyone while recovering from her surgery." He smiled faintly. "My mother is a very vain woman."

"I wouldn't want to do anything to make her ill at ease."

"Thank you. I promise I'll talk with her

when I go there this afternoon, but you must make me a promise, Sarah."

"What is that?"

"You must never speak to her about the antiques I sold to Maggie." His gaze met hers steadily. "I know you've been curious about where I got those pieces."

"The auction —"

"I got some of them at the auction, but the rest are from my mother's house."

She drew in her breath sharply. Was he about to admit that he had stolen from his mother? She needed to give him a chance to explain.

"Even though," he went on, "I wanted Mother to come home and stay with me, she believes it's time for her to move into assisted living. There are some personal hygiene requirements that she doesn't want to ask her son to help with."

"That's understandable, but why make it a big secret?"

"Mother asked me to sell her antiques somewhere where no one would recognize them, but I didn't have time. She'd be annoyed if she thought someone in town recognized her things in Maggie's store, and stress isn't good for her now."

Sarah met his eyes steadily. "Neil, I need

to ask you about a map you sold to Maggie."

"The one with the hideous frame? My mother bought it at a yard sale at the Kirschners' a year or two ago. Dottie's yard sale. Arnold was out of town — he tried to buy it back from my mother, but she always said it looked perfect in her guest bedroom." He smiled. "To be honest, I think Arnold annoyed her so much that she didn't want anything to do with him. It was the first thing she asked me to sell." His smile vanished. "You can't tell anyone this. The only people I've told are you and Chief Webber."

Sarah was relieved to hear why Neil had sold the antiques to Maggie. Truly relieved. She might never have had a crush on Neil, as Martha had, but she had always thought he was a good and honest man.

"I won't tell anyone," Sarah promised, wondering how she could assure Martha that Neil hadn't been selling stolen antiques.

One possible suspect off her list. Now it was time she got back to learning more about the two names she did have: Adam and Barbara.

Getting to his feet when she did, Neil said, "I'll let you know what Mother decides."

"Thank you." She walked with him to the

door. "I appreciate your asking her."

"And I appreciate your wanting to visit her." He opened the door to the outer office.

As Sarah went to the front door, she couldn't help hearing Neil say to his secretary, "Do a reconciliation on the Herron account. Bob's picking up his records tomorrow."

That surprised her. Bob hadn't finished the job at the Maplethorpes' house, and she remembered Martha talking about complaints throughout Maple Hill that Bob had left jobs undone. Odd that he would have lots of money then.

Lots of money without invoices to show he'd been paid for work?

She closed the door and turned to face Neil. "Can I ask your opinion about something before I go?"

"Of course." He looked puzzled, but motioned toward his office. "Come back in."

As she walked into his office, she gathered her thoughts. She had been wrong in her suspicions already, as she'd learned moments ago while talking to Neil. Yet she was bothered by Bob's apparent change from dependable to erratic and from keeping immaculate records to keeping slipshod ones. Bothered and curious. If she shared those misgivings with Neil, he might be able to allay them or tell her she wasn't on the wrong track.

Neil listened quietly while she laid out her thoughts. When she was finished, he said, "Chief Webber needs to hear this."

"I'm not sure if I'm connecting all the pieces correctly."

"Me neither, but the police can take it from here." He smiled wryly. "And they'll see I'm truly cooperating with them. So can I call him?"

"Go ahead," she said, taking a deep breath. She *had* promised the police chief to stay out of the investigation, and she was glad to let Neil pass along the information while she got back to looking for the truth about Adam and Barbara.

CHAPTER TWENTY

Sarah spent the rest of the morning at the historical society. She finished the 1860 census and had added a few more names to the ones she'd already written. Before heading home, she went to Liam's to satisfy her craving for a spiced chai tea. Murphy greeted her enthusiastically, and Liam called a hello from where he was carrying dirty dishes into the kitchen.

She went to the café's counter. The breakfast regulars were gone, and the lunch crowd hadn't arrived yet.

Why had Bob changed from a dependable plumber to an erratic one? And if he needed money, all he had to do was finish some of the jobs he'd left half done.

Sarah was so lost in thought she jumped when she heard, "I couldn't think of a more charming sight than a charming lady."

"Liam!" Her laugh was shaky. "You scared a year off my life sneaking up on me."

He scolded her in a teasing tone. "First, no Connolly ever sneaks. We do our mischief for the whole world to see. And secondly, this old face might be a bit battered, but it shouldn't be that frightening. What can I get for you today?"

"Whatever soup you have and a cup of spiced chai. To go." She should have guessed Liam would lift her spirits. He was ever the genial host, wanting everyone to enjoy themselves while under his roof.

The bell on the counter in the bookstore chimed. "Let me ring up that customer, if you don't mind. He arrived before you did."

"Go ahead."

He called to Karen to fill Sarah's order, and then rushed to the other side of his store. He greeted several people coming in to look around. He focused his attention on the bookstore customer, who was smiling happily as he left the bookstore. Sarah couldn't imagine anyone being in a bad mood around Liam.

When Karen brought over her soup — a fragrant tomato and basil — and her cup of tea with whipped cream on top as her sweet tooth loved it, she put tops on each container. "You picked a good time to come in. We were crazy busy at breakfast because there's a big craft fair in Pittsfield today. We had a line out the door until about a half hour ago."

"It's a good thing you're working today."

Karen nodded. "Otherwise Liam wouldn't have any help but Murphy. Can't say he's a tremendous amount of help other than getting rid of excess kibble." She gestured toward the dog sitting at the very edge of the bookstore, too well trained to come into the café. "I don't know what Liam's going to do next weekend when I'm at college."

"I didn't know you were going to college."

Putting the two containers in a white bag with black spots and the café's name, Karen said, "I'm in a program at UMass in Boston. I'm studying interior design and decoration. When I have a spare moment, which isn't very often, I visit furniture and antiques stores. I check out what's being sold and what's popular, so I can keep up with the trends. Maggie has been patient with all my questions."

"That's wonderful!" Sarah was glad to know that Karen had a good reason for the questions she'd been asking Maggie. Sarah paid for her lunch and added, "And you're lucky that Liam can give you the time off."

"I promised I'd be here when the leaf-peepers descend on us." She pretended to wipe sweat from her forehead with the back of her hand. "He doesn't mind being the chief cook, bottle-washer, kibble-fetcher, and clerk, but he doesn't like being the *only* one."

After parking in front of Jason and Maggie's house, Sarah got out. She picked her quilting bag up off the passenger seat. She probably wouldn't get much work done while babysitting the twins, but she'd brought the wall hanging along just in case.

Leaves twirled in abstract dances along the sidewalk, and each gust of wind smelled of rain. The yard was a crazy quilt of scattered leaves. Twilight had faded the bright colors into grays, but that didn't lessen the satisfying crunch beneath her feet.

Maggie threw open the door. She was a silhouette against the lamplight which flowed out to draw Sarah inside.

"Dave's been working on the front hall circuit," Maggie said. "Don't worry. The TV works. I wouldn't ask you to babysit if the TV was kaput."

"I'm sure I could find something for us to do." Sarah shifted her bag from one hand to the other as she slipped off her red windbreaker.

"I don't doubt that. Let me hang up your coat." Maggie took it. "Is it getting colder?"

"Cooler. Of course, you've got that thin Southern California blood, so you may think it's cold."

"Don't remind me. Just the mention of winter gives me the shakes." She hung Sarah's coat in the hall closet.

The twins and Jason were waiting in the parlor. Sarah loved the hugs and kisses. She knew she'd never take them for granted. Setting her bag on the sofa, she turned and saw Maggie clearly for the first time.

"Look at you!" Sarah said. "All dressed up fancy."

Maggie turned slowly to show off her sleek black dress and upswept hair. Sparkling earrings dangled toward her pearl necklace. "We want to wow them at the Old Mill Tavern."

"You'll turn every head."

"Especially mine," Jason said as he helped Maggie with her coat. "But then you always do."

"Ewww," groaned the twins in unison.

Sarah said, "Someday you'll want a gentleman to say something sweet like that to you."

"Not in this lifetime," Audrey said as Amy repeated, "Ewww."

"I think your father is adorable," Maggie said before giving Jason a kiss on the cheek.

265

With a laugh, she pulled out a tissue and wiped lipstick away. "And did he tell you why we're celebrating tonight, Sarah? He got his first client this week!"

Sarah knew her eyes were sparkling with pride. "That's wonderful. Congratulations, Jason."

"Thanks, Mom." He gave her a wide grin. "Maggie's doing well with her store. I figured it was time I show her she's not the only one who can be successful in Maple Hill."

They continued to banter as they went into the foyer. Jason made sure he had his golf umbrella in case it was raining when they came home.

Sarah held the door for them. As they went out on the porch, she said, "Have a wonderful time."

"Don't forget!" said Audrey. "Bring us home a doggie bag!"

"A *dessert* doggie bag," Amy said.

"A *chocolate* dessert doggie bag," Audrey said, as always wanting the last word.

Closing the door, Sarah said, "Let them order appetizers before you lay claim to their desserts!"

"Grandma," Amy asked, "will you be our guinea pig?"

"For what?"

"Mrs. Jefferson wants us to practice our presentations. Mom and Dad have already seen them twice. Will you watch?"

"Sure."

Amy ran toward the stairs, but turned when her twin didn't move.

"C'mon, Audrey," Amy said. "You've been complaining that you haven't had enough practice."

"*I've* had practice, but Tracy hasn't. She keeps coming up with excuses why she can't come over to work on what's supposed to be *our* project."

Amy's hands clenched in frustration. "Maybe if you went to Tracy's house —"

"She doesn't want me there either." Audrey clamped her folded arms in front of her. "She'd rather get an F than work with me. She's the meanest person I've ever met."

Amy looked to Sarah for help.

Sarah said, "I'd like to see *your* part of it. I'll see your partner's share at the open house."

"Don't remind me," Audrey said. She clenched her jaw and tears started welling in her eyes.

Sarah steered her granddaughter to sit beside her on the couch. She didn't say anything as she smoothed Audrey's hair away from her damp face. Instead, she let Audrey release her frustration and hurt. Sarah still couldn't understand why Tracy, who had seemed so polite at the auditions, would treat Audrey as she did.

"I know you can work this out, Audrey," Sarah murmured as Amy edged back into the room.

"It's too late, Grandma."

"I don't believe that. I know you don't want to hear this, but it's important for us to learn to work with all kinds of people — those we like and those we find are difficult to work with."

Audrey raised her head. With a watery smile, she said, "You're right, Grandma. I don't want to hear that."

"Your Grandpa Gerry used to say that you have to be a friend to make a new friend. Not that he ever met a stranger." She smiled at the memory of how easily Gerry made friends. If only he could be there to tell the story himself. He would have loved getting to know his granddaughters better. "Remember when we went out to California for your birthday party? He knew everyone in the neighborhood within days. Why? Because he always greeted people and, when they talked to him, he was interested. He didn't just act interested. He *was* interested, and that urged them to open up to him. He was a friend so he could make a new friend."

"But Tracy isn't interested in me. She's made that clear."

"Are you interested in her? You're both in the play. Have you asked her opinion about how it's going?"

"No."

"Maybe you should try."

"And if she won't speak to me?"

Sarah didn't answer quickly. She wanted to give Audrey good advice. Audrey was so angry with Tracy that she couldn't imagine something good might happen if she reached out in friendship. What would Gerry suggest if he were sitting here? The answer was simple.

"All you can do," Sarah said, "is follow your Grandpa Gerry's advice. Be a friend. Don't push her, but give her a chance by being friendly when you're working on your presentation."

Audrey groaned. "Our presentation is going to be the worst one."

"I doubt that," Sarah said. "You've put a lot of work into it. You spent a whole afternoon working on it while Amy and I went to visit Grandpa William."

"And you've made great posters and slides," Amy said. "I wish ours looked half as nice."

"Why don't you experiment on this guinea pig?" Sarah gave her granddaughters gentle nudges. "I want to hear and see what you're presenting about unsung heroes."

It took several minutes to get the materials set up, chairs serving as easels for the poster boards.

"Before you start," Sarah said, "I have something I want to say to you. Just you two." She looked from one girl to the other. They were outwardly alike, but so different inside — except for their loving hearts. "I want you to know how much I appreciate how much you gave up to come here so our family can be together." She put a hand on each girl's shoulder. "Thank you."

Amy came forward and gave her a hug. A moment later, Audrey joined in. She knew the adjustment from Los Angeles to Maple Hill was far from complete, but she wanted them to know how grateful she was. She must tell Maggie and Jason the same.

"Don't squeeze the stuffing out of me," Sarah said with feigned horror. "Or is this your way of getting rid of your guinea pig?"

The girls insisted that Sarah sit in the center of the camelback sofa, where she'd have a perfect view of the laptop, around which they'd set their posters.

When Audrey offered to go first, Sarah wasn't surprised. The few posters and slides Audrey had made were beautiful. A lump rose in Sarah's throat as she heard the man on the screen speak about the sacrifices made by those who had served in the military.

The man in the daguerreotype must have made similar sacrifices along with his wife. And now they both had been forgotten. Maybe someone somewhere remembered them. She hoped so. Audrey's speech inspired her, even more, to find out why Adam was not listed on the memorial plaque.

Sarah applauded when Audrey finished, but didn't have a chance to say anything before Amy began her presentation. Sarah was pleased to hear Amy speak with almost as much confidence as her twin. Like her sister, Amy had edited the video interviews to present the best side of the hikers she and her team had spoken with.

Amy paused and smiled. "The rest of it will be done by Cole and Emma."

"Well done." Sarah clapped enthusiastically. "Both of you."

The girls bowed.

"Audrey, your visual aids are wonderful."

Audrey's smile widened even farther.

"Thanks, Grandma."

"And I don't know why you think you can't do public speaking, Amy. You're great."

"Because I'm talking to you. When I do it in front of everyone, I know — I absolutely know — my mouth won't work."

"Then do the presentation just for me."

"Grandma, there are going to be lots of people there."

Sarah spread out her hands. "All you have to do is look right at me. Don't look at anyone else. Just me. Do you think you can do that?"

"I can try."

"Of course you can." Sarah got up to help the girls gather their posters in careful stacks. "If either of you needs to practice again, let me know."

"You'll be bored, Grandma, if you keep hearing us do it over and over," Audrey said.

"I promise I won't fall asleep in the front row, if that's what you're worried about. And if I do fall asleep, I won't snore."

"Grandma!" the girls said together, and they laughed.

"How about some warm cider and a movie, girls?"

When they agreed, Sarah walked to the kitchen as her granddaughters toted their project materials upstairs. This evening, she wouldn't be thinking of the mystery. This evening, she would enjoy her granddaughters' company. Having them in Maple Hill was the answer to her prayers. She must hold on to her faith that God had blessed her with her family being near, and he would bless her again.

"Lord, I know I need to remember that the world unfolds to your timetable, not mine," she said with a laugh as she took the cider out of the refrigerator. "Thank you for helping me remember that."

Staring at the computer screen was worthless, but Sarah was out of ideas. She'd spent the past hour since she'd gotten home going around in circles. She'd visited dozens of Web sites in the futile search to find Adam's unit. And still no answer from the college professor.

She looked at the photo she'd propped against her printer. Adam and Barbara stared out at her, so somber. She wondered how long it had been before Adam had left to fight. Had he come back? Had he died in battle and was that why she wasn't making any progress? Then why wasn't his name on the memorial rock on the green? She hoped Adam and Barbara had found plenty of reasons to smile on the day they married.

Married . . .

Their marriage would have been registered with the town clerk. She couldn't believe she hadn't thought of it before. She typed in her search. She clicked on the first site listed. Again, without a surname, she couldn't get far. Going down the site's links, she tried one for birth, marriage, and death records. It took her to a genealogical site. The historical society had access to an in-depth genealogical site, but his might have some basic information.

She pulled out the names she'd found in the censuses. She knew the year was 1861 and the state was Massachusetts. She selected the first Barbara and typed in her first and last names. Clicking the search button, she held her breath.

No match with an Adam.

Going back to the previous page, she did the same with the next name. She kept going until she reached the next-to-last name: Barbara Vanderberg.

She gasped as the new page loaded. There at the top were Barbara Vanderberg and Adam Hazzard, married June 8, 1861, in Maple Hill, Massachusetts. Now she had a name. She googled it, and a page popped up. It looked decidedly amateur, but was full of historical information about military history. She found Adam Hazzard listed as a member of the 15th Regiment Infantry. The unit had been mustered in on June 12, 1861, in Worcester. The men fought in many battles, including Gettysburg. The unit was mustered out after the battle at Petersburg, Virginia, in 1864.

"And then did you come back to Maple Hill, Adam?" she asked.

Looking back at her list, she found Adam Hazzard's name among the names she'd found on the 1860 census. After it was his age — twenty years old — and his occupation — cobbler. She couldn't help wondering where his shop had been in Maple Hill.

She looked up his address and saw no one else listed under there. He must have owned a home before he married Barbara. 307 County Street.

Why did that address sound familiar? She typed it into her computer. Her eyes widened when she saw the result. 307 County Street was the Kirschners' address! Had they been robbed because of a connection to Adam and Barbara Hazzard?

She reached for the phone. Chief Webber needed to know this immediately.

CHAPTER TWENTY-ONE

As Sarah entered the sanctuary of the Bridge Street Church with her family, she left her frustrations outside. She had come to listen to the sermon and to thank God for guiding her to unexpected answers last night.

Lord, she prayed as she walked beside Audrey along the red carpeted aisle on the left side of the sanctuary, *thank you for your guidance. Now I need to figure out how, if the daguerreotype is connected to the Kirschners and the robbery, Peg fits in. Help me to be patient and run the race I've been given.*

"Right here," Audrey said, stopping and tugging on Sarah's hand. She opened the door of the box pew and stepped in. "This is perfect."

"But we usually sit closer to the front."

"Let's try sitting here. Just for this week."

Amy held back as Jason and Maggie took a seat beside Audrey. She lowered her voice to a whisper. "She doesn't want to have to speak to Zoe."

Sarah looked toward the front of the sanctuary. She recognized Zoe from the drama auditions. The girl sat with her family in the second row of pews.

"Why would I want to talk to *her?*" Audrey said, keeping her voice to a whisper.

"All right," Maggie said. "Enough of that. Don't forget where you are. This is our Lord's house, and we learn here to do unto others as we would have them do unto us."

Audrey sighed. "I know. I'm sorry. It's just . . ." Tears bubbled into her blue eyes.

"We understand." Sarah sat next to Amy on the red cushion that matched the carpet. "Don't forget that, Audrey. Your mother and your father and I have faced challenging people, and we may again. Follow your heart, and heed what it tells you."

Audrey blinked fast to keep the tears from falling. Jason put his arm out, and Audrey snuggled against him. Her twin picked up a hymnal and began paging through it, obviously hoping nobody would notice them.

Sarah gave Amy a quick squeeze. Amy kept her head down, her gaze on the hymnal, but now she wore the hint of a smile.

She looked around the church. There were the Kirschners, and she was glad to see

Martha and Ernie taking their usual pew. Some of Martha's grandchildren were with their parents. She smiled when she recognized two more people coming into the sanctuary. She stood and went to the rear of the church.

"Liz, Dave," she said, smiling, "I'm glad to see you here. Why don't you come and sit near us?"

"Thank you!" Liz's voice was filled with gratitude. She wore a blouse with tiny robins embroidered on the collar.

"Did you sew those birds?"

Liz nodded while Dave smiled. It was the first time Sarah had seen him in a coat and tie, and he looked very different from the guy in jeans with plaster dust coating his hair.

"You do lovely work," Sarah said. "You're going to have no problem quilting."

"I hope I can live up to your expectations."

"How are you, Dave? Busy as always?"

"I've got another week to finish up the wiring at Jason's house. After that —"

Liz hushed him, saying, "This isn't the place, Dave. Let's enjoy the service."

Sarah sensed the anxiety between the couple, but she said nothing as Dave put an attentive hand under his wife's elbow. They walked to the pew behind where Jason's family sat.

Jason stretched out his hand and shook Dave's. "Good to see you."

Liz shifted to get more comfortable on the pew. "I'm Liz, by the way."

Introductions were finished just as the organist played the first notes of the processional. Sarah smiled when she noticed the twins both sneaking looks at Liz's belly each time they stood to sing a hymn.

Pastor John's sermon focused on a verse from Romans about forgiveness. "Let us not therefore judge one another any more: but judge this rather, that no man put a stumbling block or an occasion to fall in his brother's way," he said, looking out over the congregation with his stern, loving green eyes.

It was an apt lesson. Pastor John thanked God for keeping them safe. He asked for guidance for the police in their investigation. Lastly, he prayed that the thief would see the mistake he had made and turn back to God. Sarah still found it difficult to pray for the thief, especially since the robbery at Martha's house. She bowed her head and murmured a prayer for her heart to be opened to allow forgiveness for others, even the thief.

When the final hymn was sung and the benediction given, Sarah realized she hadn't been the only one thinking about the break-in at the Maplethorpes' house. Many in the congregation were talking about it and offering Ernie and Martha condolences.

"Is that the couple who were robbed?" asked Liz. "What a shame! They look like nice people."

"They are," Sarah said, "and I happen to know that they're looking for a handyman. If you want, I'd be glad to introduce you, Dave."

Liz asked, "Will they think I'm rude if I sit here and wait?" She put her hand on her stomach. "He's trying out for the Olympic gymnastic team today."

"Of course not. Martha's had four children, and she's got nine grandchildren with another on the way. She'll understand."

"Good." Liz smiled at the twins. "I'll talk with Maggie and these girls, who've been giving me the eye. So, tell me, what's it like being a twin?"

Sarah smiled as she walked with Dave toward where the Maplethorpes stood with the Kirschners in the vestibule, comparing their experiences. When she remarked how good Liz was with children, Dave couldn't hide his pride in his wife. She wondered if these two young people realized how blessed they were to have each other. She hoped they did. There had been times when she and Gerry had been at odds, but the reasons why had faded. What brought her joy was remembering the blessings they'd shared: a home, healthy children, darling grandchildren, and a love that outlasted his passing.

They had to wait a few minutes before the crowd around Martha and Ernie thinned. Dave greeted the Kirschners. Dottie smiled and replied, but Arnold mumbled something under his breath and turned away. Dave's brow furrowed in a frown.

What was that about? Sarah wondered.

"Arnold, Dottie," she said. "Can I speak with you before you leave?"

Dottie asked, "How about outside?"

"I'll be there in a minute or two."

Dottie nodded, and then was drawn back into the conversation with her husband and other parishioners.

Sarah introduced Dave to the Maplethorpes.

Ernie said, "So you're Dave. I've heard great things about you. Not only do you do good work, but you also show up on time."

"I try, sir."

"Jason has been singing your praises."

"I'm glad to hear that."

"If you want a break from chasing wires through his house, we need to have our picture window replaced. We've got a replacement window on order, and it'll be a few days before it's in. But in the meantime, we could use your plumbing skills. We got left in the lurch by the last guy we hired. Our kitchen sink is out of commission, and my poor wife is slowly being driven mad by the bathroom sink dripping."

Dave grinned. "I understand, sir. I could come over tomorrow morning if you don't mind it's early."

"The earlier the better," Martha said. "Ernie's not exaggerating how irritating that drip is."

"I'll be there around seven thirty." He pulled a pad out from beneath his coat. "Give me your address and phone number. If I get delayed, I'll let you know."

Sarah took the time while Ernie and Dave traded numbers to ask Martha how she was doing.

"Better now that I don't have half the Maple Hill police force in my living room." Martha smiled to soften her words. "I appreciate their hard work, but I was beginning to wonder if I'd ever be able to get my furniture on its feet. It took me hours to untangle the yarn and wind each color onto its proper ball. Thank heavens, Peg stopped by to check on Ernie. We had a nice long talk. A very long talk." Martha seemed about to add more, but didn't.

"Ernie looks good today," Sarah said.

"Doesn't he?"

"Any word yet from the police?"

"Nothing, but I'm not sure they'll have anything to tell us before they capture the thief." Martha lowered her voice. "How are you doing with your own investigation?"

Sarah took her friend's arm and drew her to one side. Quickly she outlined what she'd discovered last night.

"That's amazing!" Martha chuckled. "You're amazing. You don't give up until you get the answer. Have you told the Kirschners yet?"

"They're next. I left a message for Chief Webber last night, so he may have already contacted them. I didn't want to call you or Dottie and Arnold because it was so late."

"I hope that this will help catch the thief."

Sarah gave her friend a smile. "I know you do." She walked back to where Maggie and Liz were involved in an animated conversation, still sitting in the pews.

Both women were laughing. Sarah's smile

broadened. She should have invited Liz to visit the store and meet Maggie. But God had found a way to bring them together in his house.

Picking up her purse, Sarah said, "I'll meet you outside. OK?"

"We'll be along as soon as Dave and Jason get back," Maggie said. "The girls are already outside. Amy heard someone has a soccer ball out there. She can't resist the chance to kick it around."

The vestibule was almost empty as Sarah passed through on her way out to the broad steps along the front of the church. It was a perfect autumn day. The sky was a breathtaking blue, and mums splashed color along the driveway and parking lot. On the grass, several kids had faced off in an impromptu game. Their happy shouts brightened the day further.

"Sarah!" called Dottie. "Over here."

Sarah went over where she and Arnold stood at the edge of the parking lot. "Thanks for waiting. I've got something I can't wait to tell you."

"I'm sorry I couldn't talk yesterday," Arnold said. "Dottie would have shot me if she came home to find paint all over the kitchen floor." He grinned at his wife. "What's up?"

"Did Chief Webber call you?"

Arnold and Dottie exchanged a glance. Dottie said, "No. Why?"

Sarah took the photo out of her purse. Handing it to Dottie, she said, "This is a picture of the daguerreotype that was found with the stolen antiques up on Mount Greylock. I don't know if you got a good look at it at the police station."

"Not really."

"I've been trying to find out about the couple. Last night, I got the break I'd been hoping for. Their names are Adam and Barbara Hazzard. They were married in June 1861 before Adam went to fight in the Civil War. The most interesting fact I uncovered —"

She jumped aside as the soccer players ran past. She smiled to see Amy in the midst of the game.

"Watch out!" called Jason as the players almost ran down Liz and Maggie.

The kids shouted their apologies, but kept chasing the ball and each other.

"You were saying . . ." Arnold said.

Sarah smiled at the Kirschners. "The most amazing fact I uncovered was that Adam Hazzard used to live in your house."

"That's very interesting," he said. "But what does this have to do with Chief Webber calling us?"

"Don't you see? The daguerreotype was found with the stolen antiques. It could be the connection the police have been looking for. The Hazzards lived in your house, and you were robbed."

Arnold frowned. "But what about the other victims? How does this connect to them?"

"I haven't worked that out, but maybe Chief Webber has."

Dottie looked up from the photo. "Arnold, you've collected all those antiques. Is there anything you've bought that could help the police get to the bottom of this?"

"I'll look," he said. "I'm sure I can find something."

"Will you let me know what you find?" Sarah asked.

"Of course," Dottie said. "Why don't you drop by tomorrow?"

"What time?"

"How about in the afternoon?" Dottie glanced at her husband. "We'll need that long to sort through everything."

Sarah agreed. She'd use the time in the morning to go to the historical society and look at the 1870 census. This time she'd search specifically for the County Street address and see what else she could find out about the Hazzards.

Dottie gave Sarah the photo. "Arnold, we'd better get home. You've got a lot of stuff to look through."

As the Kirschners headed toward their car, Sarah turned to see Dave watching with another frown. She wondered again why.

Suddenly he yelled, "Duck!" She did. The soccer ball soared past her, hit the parking lot, and bounced into Dave's truck. It smashed into the tarp several times as it ricocheted under the cap. Papers exploded out.

Two boys ran toward the truck.

"Stay away from the truck!" Dave shouted.

The boys paused. "We just want to get our ball."

"I'll get it." He ran over, reached in, and pulled out the soccer ball. "You need to be more careful where you kick this. If you've broken anything . . ."

They began to scoop up the large square pieces of paper.

"Leave it!" Dave said. "I'll take care of it."

The boys tried to apologize, but he ignored them as he bent to gather up the papers. As the kids ran past Sarah, she saw they were struggling not to cry.

Liz must have noticed their expressions too, because she said, "I'll talk to him." She took a step, and then put her hand against her side. "That was a really big kick."

Sarah put her hand under Liz's elbow. "Let me help you."

Maggie did the same on the other side. They slowly walked Liz over to the truck. By the time they reached it, Dave had shoved all the papers into the back.

"Dave, you should apologize to those kids." Liz's voice was weak. "They didn't do it on purpose."

The anger drained from his face, revealing lines Sarah hadn't noticed before. "You're right. I overreacted. I just didn't want anything to get broken." He looked at Sarah and her family. "I'm sorry."

"It's OK," Jason said.

"Liz, are you OK?" Dave asked.

"I'm fine. Tell your son to stop doing somersaults."

Maggie said, "Make her take it easy when you get home."

"I will." Dave helped Liz into the truck.

She rolled down the window. "Sarah, any chance you'll have time on Tuesday to give me a quilting lesson?"

"I'll call you tomorrow evening," Sarah said. "If you're up to it, we'll make a date."

"That sounds wonderful." She relaxed back against the seat and closed the window as Dave got behind the wheel.

The Harts stood to one side as he drove out of the parking lot. He paused in the driveway and called to the kids.

Sarah couldn't hear what he said. The kids waved as the Diamonds left, so he must have squared it with them. When Jason called to the girls, both Amy and Audrey were smiling as they ran over to get into the car.

Jason opened his door. "Coming over for the football game, Mom?"

"I wouldn't miss it for the world. Save me a seat for the game."

"Right on the fifty-yard line." He winked. It reminded her of his father.

She stepped away as he started the car and backed it up. When he drove forward, a piece of paper fluttered out from under the car. It was the size of the ones from Dave's truck. He must not have seen it. She gasped when she picked it up. It wasn't paper. It was gauze. She flipped it over and stared at the white plastic on the back.

It was identical to the hospital-bed pads she'd seen in the cellar on Mount Greylock. Why did Dave have hospital supplies in his truck?

She thought of his reaction when the kids reached in to get the ball. He'd been worried that something would be broken. The things under the tarp that jutted at odd angles?

Not odd angles if they were chair legs, she thought. The Poplawskis' chairs hadn't been recovered. What if they'd been in the back of Dave's truck all along?

Her stomach twisted. Could Dave be the thief?

CHAPTER TWENTY-TWO

"Go Pats!" shouted the girls, jumping to their feet as the Patriots scored a touchdown after an interception.

"Whoa!" Maggie said as she put her hand on the pizza box. "Watch out. You almost knocked over Grandma's soda."

Sarah blinked. Amy and Audrey were high-fiving, and Sarah glanced at the TV in time for the instant replay. She wasn't paying attention to the game. Over and over, she replayed the memory of Dave's reaction when he saw the boys running toward his truck. She'd thought at the time he was angry. Now she wondered if she'd heard panic in his voice.

Dave? Dave a thief? She didn't want to believe it, but after what she'd witnessed, she had to consider him a suspect. Had he offered to help her find out about Adam simply to divert suspicion away from himself? What connection did he have with the victims? Or had the robberies been random, simply crimes of opportunity? He'd been out of work for a while. Liz had mentioned that Jason and Maggie had offered him his first steady work since the Diamonds moved to Maple Hill last year. Also, Liz had given up her job when Dave left the army. With a baby on the way, had Dave become so desperate that he stole from his neighbors?

She remembered Liz saying he had been an Eagle Scout, and Dave had been so fervent talking about helping vets. She couldn't let those good deeds distract her. After all, Peg was on her suspects list, and the visiting nurse's most suspicious act had been donating money to a worthwhile charity.

The girls sat back on the floor. They didn't move when the doorbell rang, though usually they rushed to the door. All their attention was riveted on the game.

Jason laughed. "I'll get it." He went out into the foyer.

Sarah stiffened when she heard Jason say, "Hi, Dave."

Maggie said quietly, "I hope he's not planning to work now. If the power goes out and the game goes off —" She rolled her eyes.

Knowing that Maggie was joking, Sarah tried to laugh, but it had a hollow, fake sound. She stood and went to the parlor door as Dave stepped in. He glanced at her, and then lowered his eyes.

A pulse of dismay surged through her. Gerry had called that "a hangdog expression," a look both Jason and his sister had displayed whenever they were caught attempting to hide some misdeed. Now, she suspected, Dave was.

"I need to get a tool upstairs for the job over at the Maplethorpes' tomorrow morning," Dave said. "I figured it'd be better to come over now than in the morning."

"Sure," Jason said. "But you're missing the game."

Dave looked at the TV. "How are the Pats doing?"

"They're ahead by a touchdown."

Maggie came out into the foyer as Dave went to the stairs. "How's Liz? She looked pretty peaked when you left church."

"She took a nap," he said with his foot on the first step. "She's doing better. In fact, she drove over here with me because she wanted some fresh air."

"She's here?" Sarah asked. "While you go upstairs, I'm going to run out and find out what sewing needles she has. That way I'll know what to bring over for the quilting lesson on Tuesday."

Dave hesitated, but Jason started asking questions about the wiring in the back bedroom. Sarah went out before Dave could give her some excuse not to go to the truck.

Liz opened the door and climbed out. She stood in front of the cab's side window. "Hi, Sarah!"

"You didn't need to get out," Sarah said. Now she wouldn't be able to look into the back without elbowing Liz aside. Was Liz in on the robberies too? Could she want to prevent anyone from seeing into the back?

"I get really uncomfortable if I don't keep moving around. Oh!" Liz stood straighter. "That was a strong kick. I'm looking forward to your coming over on Tuesday, Sarah."

"I love introducing people to quilting." She asked Liz about what sewing supplies she had. Trying not to be too obvious, she tried to steal a look into the back of the truck. All she could see was the blue tarp.

"Anything else I'll need?" Liz asked.

Sarah looked back at Liz. She hadn't heard a word the young woman said. "I'll bring along a few basics, just in case."

"I can't wait to get started." She smiled. "Hi, Maggie!"

Coming down the front steps, Maggie asked, "Why don't you come in? The guys are going to be a few minutes. Jason has about a hundred questions he's been saving up."

"Thanks. That —" Her eyes widened. "Oh!" She flushed, and then said through clenched teeth, "He won't stop kicking today."

Sarah exchanged a quick glance with Maggie, who asked, "How long ago was the last kick, Liz?"

"I don't know."

"About two minutes," Sarah said.

"I think he's trying to kick his way out," Liz said.

"I think you're right that he's ready to escape," Maggie said. "How long have you been feeling these strong kicks?"

"Since early this morning."

"That sounds like labor pains to me." Maggie ran back to the house, opening the door and shouting Jason's name and Dave's.

"I can't be in labor," Liz gasped. "It feels like he's kicking. Not —" Her face twisted with pain. "OK. That was a contraction."

Amy ran out onto the porch. "What's going on?"

"Amy," Maggie said, "go and get Dave and your father."

"Audrey went to get them. Is the baby coming?" Amy asked.

Maggie shooed her away from the truck. Amy ran across the yard and started down the street.

Sarah helped Liz sit on the running board. "Breathe fast and shallow. It'll help."

Dave burst through the door. All color washed from his face as he saw Sarah by the truck. His fearful eyes focused on the back. Did he think she'd been snooping in it and had found the stolen chairs?

Sarah pushed that thought aside. They needed to focus on Liz now.

"Call Liz's obstetrician!" Maggie said. "Now!"

Dave blinked several times, and then flipped open his cell. He pressed a single button and held the phone to his ear. His face got even paler.

"What's going on?" Jason asked as he came outside followed by Audrey.

As Maggie sent Audrey back inside, Sarah worked with Liz on her breathing. The contraction passed, and Liz slumped back against the truck's door.

"How could I miss that these were contractions?" Liz asked.

"It's your first baby. You'll know better next time."

Dave closed his phone and put his hand on Liz's shoulder. "The doctor will meet us at the birthing center in North Adams."

"All right," Liz said weakly. "That sounds good."

"Anything I can do to help?" asked a calm voice. Sarah turned to see Amy and Peg Girard, who was holding a black bag. "Amy ran down the block and told me someone is having a baby." She smiled at Liz. "From the looks of things, I'd guess it's you."

Liz smiled back.

Peg took Liz's pulse and blood pressure. She sent Amy inside to collect some blankets and asked about transportation to the hospital.

"I'll get the Tahoe and bring it around," Jason said.

Liz started to stand, but then bent with the beginning of another contraction.

With his arm around her, Dave said, "My truck's right here. We can —"

Jason interrupted. "Nonsense. That baby is coming quickly. Liz needs to lie down and have a breathing coach. You can't do that and drive at the same time."

"He's right, Dave," Liz said breathlessly. "Besides there's no room for me in the back of the truck. It's full with those chairs you found —"

"I didn't mean you should ride in the

back," Dave said. His face lost all color again.

Chairs? Did that mean they were the stolen chairs? Or had Dave told Liz he'd picked up the chairs out of someone's trash? Sarah wanted to ask Liz, but this wasn't the time. They needed to get Liz safely to the hospital.

"I know," Liz said. "I'm teasing you."

It was quickly arranged. Maggie would drive the Diamonds and Peg in the Tahoe. Jason would follow in Dave's truck. Amy and Audrey came out with two armloads of blankets, and soon Liz was wrapped in them on the backseat.

Jason took Dave's keys, got into the truck, and turned it around to lead the way to North Adams. Maggie slipped behind the wheel of the Tahoe as Peg opened the passenger side door.

Peg turned to Sarah. "Mrs. Hart, will you be at home tomorrow morning?"

"Yes," Sarah said, startled.

"Can I call you around eight?"

"Of course." Sarah stepped back as Peg climbed up into the Tahoe. She wanted to ask why Peg had changed her mind, but again that would have to wait.

Sarah put an arm around Audrey's shoulders and smiled at Amy. "We might as well go back inside. Your parents won't be back for at least a half hour. Probably closer to an hour, because they'll want to make sure Dave and Liz are set before they leave."

"Is the baby really about to be born?" whispered Audrey. Awe and a bit of fear shone in her eyes.

"Yes." Sarah gave her granddaughter's shoulders a gentle squeeze. "We need to pray that the baby waits until they get to the birthing center. Thank goodness Peg is going with them."

"Will Liz be OK?" asked Amy as they went into the house.

Sarah smiled as she took each one by the hand. "Shall we ask for God's blessing upon them?"

The girls clasped each other's hands to complete the circle. Sarah asked for God to watch over Maggie while she drove and for everything to go smoothly at the hospital. Amy prayed for God's blessing on the doctor and nurses and the rest of the hospital staff. Audrey completed the prayer circle by asking that Liz and the baby come home soon.

Sarah said, "Let's go and watch the game. You know your father will want a play-by-play report when he gets home."

As the girls went into the parlor, Sarah

hung back. She looked out at the street where Dave's truck had been parked. She couldn't forget his expression when he burst out of the house and stared in despair at the back of the truck. That, along with him interrupting Liz when she mentioned what was under the tarp, confirmed what she'd guessed. The odd shapes were chairs, but were they the stolen chairs? She needed to find out.

CHAPTER TWENTY-THREE

The phone rang at exactly eight the next morning. Sarah picked it up before the second ring. It wasn't Peg. It was Martha.

"Sarah, can we come over?"

"You and Ernie?"

"No, me and Peg."

Sarah agreed. Questions buzzed through her head. Ten minutes later, Sarah welcomed Martha and Peg into her house. She led them into the parlor. No one spoke as Martha and Peg sat on the sofa and Sarah chose the rocking chair.

Martha broke the silence. "Sarah, first things first. Have you heard if Liz had her baby?"

"Dave called us last evening," Sarah said. "David Diamond Jr. was born only an hour after they got to the hospital. All of them are doing fine. They should be coming home this afternoon."

Peg's strained face softened. "I'm glad to

hear that."

"Me too." Martha paused and then said, "Sarah, I talked Peg into talking to you. I know you've considered her a suspect since you saw that VNA box on Mount Greylock."

"How did you know?"

"I know you." Martha smiled for a moment. "And when I mentioned Peg's donation to the hospice, you got all quiet. That means you were thinking hard."

"You do know me."

"But you're wrong about Peg. She didn't have anything to do with the robberies. I know because she told me the truth about where the money for the donation came from." She looked at Peg. "Go ahead."

"I want to say I'm sorry," Peg said. "I've been rude to you. I thought you were another busybody trying to poke her nose into my business. Then Martha told me how you came over to be with them after the robbery at their house. They said how nice you were."

"Martha told me the same thing about you."

"But I haven't been very nice to you." Peg sighed. "I hope you'll understand why when I explain. I never thought giving away that

302

money would create more problems for me."

"More?"

Peg clasped her hands in her lap. "A patient gave me a lottery ticket as a gift. A winning ticket, I found out, worth more than $100,000 after taxes. I tried to give it back, but he said if I didn't want the money, I should donate it somewhere. That's what I did."

"I don't understand why you'd want to keep that secret," Sarah said. "Both you and the person who gave you the ticket did a wonderful thing."

"That's what I told her too," Martha said.

"Except," Peg said, "as a visiting nurse, I'm not supposed to take gifts from my clients. Doing so could cost me my job. I didn't realize he'd given me anything other than a card until I got home and opened it. That's when I found the lottery ticket. I should have returned it to him right away, but curiosity got the better of me, and I scratched off the numbers. I figured it probably wasn't worth anything, but it was. When I realized that, I tried to return it, but he wouldn't accept it."

"Even when he knew you could lose your job?"

"That's when he suggested I give the

303

money away. It seemed like a good idea. I decided to donate the money anonymously to protect my job, and the hospice director agreed. But someone, and I don't know who, revealed that the money had come from me. Then everyone started asking questions. I hoped if I ignored the questions, they'd stop, but they haven't." She sighed. "I understand people being curious. If I hadn't been curious about the ticket, I wouldn't be in this predicament."

Sarah hesitated, and then asked, "So why are you telling me now?"

"Martha asked me to. She knows how much you want to find the person who stole from your daughter-in-law, and she didn't want you distracted by suspecting me." Peg looked at Martha. "I didn't plan to tell her, but we got to talking, and she's so easy to talk to, it just came out. I asked her to keep it a secret."

"If Martha promised that, she wouldn't tell anyone." Sarah smiled. "Not even me."

"Then she asked me to tell you the truth."

"I told her," Martha said, "that I'd trust you with anything. I told her that she could too, so we're here to put our heads together to help Peg figure out what to do."

"Who else have you told?" Sarah asked.

Peg said, "Other than you and Martha, no one."

"Not even Chief Webber?"

She shook her head. "I was afraid he'd contact the VNA and I'd lose my job. My job is everything to me, Mrs. Hart. I'm a good nurse, and I love working with my clients."

"But you need to be honest with him. Martha's right. Suspecting you needlessly is a distraction. Chief Webber should be focusing on the real suspects." She stood. "If you'd like, Martha and I will go with you when you tell him. He may not have to tell your employer at all."

Martha got up too. "C'mon, Peg. It's the right thing to do."

Peg nodded. "All right. Let's go. I'm tired of being paranoid."

In his tiny office in a rear corner of the police station, Chief Webber sat behind a desk stacked high with folders and loose pages. He was a big man, but the pile was bigger. Tacked to the bulletin boards were more papers.

When Sarah looked into his office, her first impression was that a wastebasket had exploded. Then she saw there was a method to the chaos. Everything was divided into three parts — wall, desk, and floor.

She knocked on the open door, and Chief Webber raised his head. As he put down his pen, he asked, "Can I hope you've brought me the answer to the three antiques robberies?"

"Hey, you're the one who made me promise not to stick my nose into your investigation." She stepped in, followed by Martha and Peg. "Can we talk to you?"

"Sure. Come in. Mrs. Maplethorpe, did you get my message?"

Martha shook her head.

"We've made an arrest in your break-in."

"That's wonderful! Who did you arrest?"

"Bob Herron."

Sarah drew in her breath sharply. The call from Neil's office had alerted the police, and now they'd arrested Bob.

"Wait a minute," Martha said. "Our house was broken into. We gave Bob a key, so he could come in whenever he had a chance. Why did he break our big window?"

"That gave him the perfect alibi," Chief Webber said. "By breaking the window, he made it look like someone else did it. He thought having a key would keep him free from suspicion."

"We trusted him, and he turned around and robbed us. If he needed money, all he

306

had to do was finish up our plumbing job, and we'd have paid him lickety-split."

ChiefWebber said, "Martha, I may be asking you and Ernie to come in to make an additional statement. If any of the stolen items are recovered, you'll need to identify yours. Don't expect that to happen. You were not his only victims, and most of the items now reported missing are computer or video games, MP3 players, and other things that people would think they'd mislaid, never suspecting they'd been stolen. They're easily fenced."

"Then his trips down to Springfield weren't to get parts," Sarah mused, "as he told his wife. Was he selling the stolen items there?" That would explain why he didn't have receipts to give to Neil.

"We will make all efforts," Chief Webber said, avoiding her question, "to recover your items, but I can't make any promises."

Martha's smile returned. "I'm grateful nothing that truly matters was taken. If I'd lost my grandchildren's baby pictures, I'd be heartbroken. As it is, Ernie has already bought a new flat-screen TV. He couldn't miss baseball this close to the playoffs."

"You've handled this well." Sarah hugged her friend. "I don't know of anyone else who would have dealt with it so well."

"I would have been a basket case," Peg said with a relieved laugh. "I'm glad he was caught. Now we should be able to sleep better."

"Don't stop locking your doors," Chief Webber said. "Bob didn't have any antiques with him, and he says he didn't steal them. He admitted to other thefts, including some where the victims never even reported any missing items."

Martha shuddered. "That means the antiques thief is still out there."

Sarah looked away. Should she tell the police chief about her suspicions of Dave? So far, everything was circumstantial, but she hadn't had much more than that when she spoke to Neil and he called the police to investigate Bob. But Liz had said the chairs had been picked up out of the trash.

"So what can I do for you ladies?" Chief Webber donned his professional cop face. Wary, but curious.

Peg stepped forward. "I need to talk to you. There's some information that I should have told you when you questioned me."

He motioned to the chair in front of his desk. "If the others will excuse us —"

"No — !" Peg sat and clenched her hands tightly. "Please, can they stay? I'd really like them to stay."

"All right." He looked from Sarah to Martha. "I know you've kept quiet throughout this investigation, but I have to ask you again not to say anything to anyone — including family — about what Mrs. Girard may say."

"I understand," Sarah and Martha said at the same time.

He sat on the corner of his desk. "Go ahead, Mrs. Girard. What else do you think I should know?"

Peg repeated what she'd told Sarah a short time before. Chief Webber listened without comment. As soon as she finished, she asked, "Do you need to tell my boss what I told you?"

"No, because while you may have violated your company's policy, you haven't broken any law."

Putting her fingers to her lips, Peg blinked back tears. "Thank you."

"I appreciate your being honest with me, Mrs. Girard," he said. "May we contact you if we have further questions?"

"Certainly." She stood. "Thank you. Thank all of you." She took Martha's hand and squeezed it. "I'll see you and Ernie this afternoon."

"And Ernie's new TV. He can't wait to show it off to you," Martha said. Her eyes widened. "I've got to go and tell Ernie that our thief has been caught!"

CHAPTER TWENTY-FOUR

When Sarah entered the historical society, Irene was giving a tour to a group of eager third graders from Nathaniel Bradford Elementary School, their teacher, and their parent chaperones. Irene's charm bracelet jangled to emphasize her enthusiastic explanations of the artifacts. Sarah gave a quick wave, took the tray of microfilm reels from behind the counter, and went into the back room. She closed the door, not wanting curiosity about what she was doing to disrupt Irene's tour and not wanting sixteen pairs of eyes watching over her shoulder.

Sarah didn't even bother to take off her coat. She picked up the reels from the 1870 census. Paging through them, she found the listing for 307 County Street. A family named Ney lived there. Had Adam and Barbara moved somewhere else after they married? She scanned through the pages, but reached the end without finding Adam and

Barbara Hazzard. There were other Hazzards, but none named Barbara or Adam.
She checked for Vanderberg too, and found
no one listed by that name. She groaned in
dismay. She'd thought the rest of the information would be easy to find now.

Adam and Barbara Hazzard no longer
lived in Maple Hill in 1870. Did that matter? She'd found their names and the connection to the Kirschners' house. Maybe
Arnold would have something to help her.

Pushing back her chair, she removed the
reel and carefully put it in its box. She wrote
a quick note thanking Irene and letting her
know that she was done with the reels. She
put the tray of microfilm behind the counter
while Irene answered questions from the
children. Irene glanced at her, her brows
raised, and Sarah mouthed, "Thanks!"
before she slipped out the door.

Dottie answered the door when Sarah rang
the bell. She wore an apron and a kerchief
over her hair. Carrying a mop which she
leaned against the staircase banister, she
said, "Sarah, come in. Excuse how I look.
Once Arnold started digging around in
everything, I saw all the dust and decided
to do some fall cleaning. I look a fright."

"You look fine." Sarah stepped into the

house, which was one of the oldest in Maple Hill. Unlike her Victorian with its soaring ceilings and tall windows, the Kirschners' house had low beams and tiny windows set in thick walls. She squinted through the dim light. Nothing in the foyer was the same as when she'd last visited a couple of years ago when Dottie hosted a church committee meeting.

Instead of the white furniture and the family photos and pleasant pictures, the foyer now was crowded with a settle that almost reached the ceiling. Primitive paintings of stiff people in uncomfortable-looking clothes hung on the wall. The carpet had been torn off the stairs, and the steps painted a simple white.

"I warned you," Dottie said. "Arnold is redecorating the whole place. I tried to get him to leave at least the seascape painting we bought on our last trip to the Cape, but he was insistent." She smiled. "I sneaked it out of the barn and into the guest room upstairs."

Sarah saw the living room had undergone as drastic a change. "Is that the infamous rocking horse?" she asked with a smile when she saw the toy by the stone hearth. Faded red stars danced along the horse's back.

"Don't get me started! Did I tell you that

he spent more for that thing than he did for our first car?" Dottie shook her head, but then chuckled. "That's enough of my complaining. How about a cup of tea? I could use a break from cleaning, and Arnold hasn't moved my stove out yet."

"A cup would be nice." Sarah shivered as she shrugged off her coat. "It's getting too cold too fast."

The kitchen was cozy but tiny. The thick beams overhead were the perfect complement for the logs that made up two walls. Unlike in the rest of the house, they hadn't been covered with plaster. With two small windows, the kitchen was dark. Shadows clung to every corner.

When Dottie went to put the kettle on, Sarah sat on a stool by the kitchen counter. "Is Arnold around?" Sarah asked.

"Out in the barn. He's probably checking to make sure I haven't moved anymore of his precious pieces out there. Arnold can't wait to get the cameo home and put it up in a place of honor on the dining room mantel. Why would he want to put a piece of jewelry in the dining room?"

"I hope he can dig up something for me on the Hazzards," Sarah said.

"Everyone seems interested in the Hazzards lately." Dottie took cups out of her pine cupboards.

"Everyone?"

Dottie put the cups on the counter. "OK, I'm exaggerating. You showed us that picture. Chief Webber asked us about the daguerreotype, though we didn't know the people were Hazzards then. Arnold mentioned someone else asking about them, but I can't remember who it was."

"Could it have been Dave Diamond?" she asked.

"Could have been. He and Dave went hiking up on Mount Greylock several times in the spring. You know, Arnold knows the trails like the back of his hand after years of working up there."

Sarah asked, "Are he and Dave still friends?"

"Why do you ask?"

"Arnold acted like he was trying to avoid Dave at church."

Dottie's eyes dimmed. "I'm not sure what happened. Last spring, Dave spent a lot of time with Arnold. Dave is interested in helping vets."

"I know."

"I think Dave was hoping to get Arnold interested in helping vets too, because Arnold worked for the state and might know people who could help." She poured hot water into the cups. "I could have told Dave he was wasting his time. The only thing Arnold's interested in is this house."

"When was the last time Dave was here?"

"A couple of weeks ago. He and Arnold were out in the barn. I couldn't hear what they were saying, but it looked like they were quarreling." She put the kettle back on the stove. "When I asked him, Arnold said he didn't want to talk about it."

"Talk about what?" asked Arnold as he came in the back door along with a whoosh of cold air. He tossed his work coat onto a chair in the dusky corner.

"Hi, Arnold," Sarah said with a smile. "Have you found anything else about the Hazzards?"

He shook his head. "Not yet. Give me a few more days."

"All right. If you find anything, will you let me know right away? I discovered the Hazzards left Maple Hill sometime between 1861 and 1870."

His eyes narrowed. "How did you find that out?"

She explained about the census records.

"That's very interesting," he said, leaning one hand on the counter. "I had no idea that information was out there."

"But you don't act surprised."

"Way back in my family line, there are some Hazzards. My great-great-grandmother was a Hazzard. She lived in this house as her descendants have down to me."

Sarah considered this, and then said, "So maybe your great-great-grandmother and her husband bought this house from Adam and Barbara Hazzard when they left Maple Hill."

"It's possible." He looked at his wife. "Dottie, did you forget we were driving over to Pittsfield tonight? We should be going."

"Don't be rude, Arnold. Sarah hasn't even tasted her tea."

"But I want to get to the store before someone else buys that cider jug."

Dottie raised her hands and shrugged. "See what I mean, Sarah?"

Sarah decided she would be wise not to take sides in this discussion. She gave them a quick smile, pulled on her coat, and left.

It was not another dead end, she told herself as she got into her car. Maybe not, but it sure felt like one.

The next afternoon, Sarah clicked the send icon on the e-mail she'd written to Dr. Treadwell. The college professor had answered her e-mail with an apology for taking so long to get back to her. He agreed to look at the photo of the daguerreotype. She thanked him and was sending him the photo. Maybe he could tell her something she hadn't already discovered.

Her cell phone rang. Sarah answered and heard Maggie's voice.

"Hi, Sarah," Maggie said. "I know I said I wasn't going to do this again so soon, but could you go over to the house so you'll be there when the girls get home from school? I've got to stay late this afternoon for an out-of-town customer, and Jason can't get away either. And Dave won't be there. He's taking a few days off to spend with Liz and the baby."

"Of course, I'll go over."

Maggie's smile came through in her words. "Thanks! You're a lifesaver, and I promise I won't keep asking. Jason and I talked last night, and he's agreed it's time for me to start looking for an assistant."

"That's great news."

"It will mean more time with the girls and some time for myself. I've been flying off the handle too easily lately. Too stressed. I'm sorry if I've said anything that hurt you."

"Thank you, Maggie. And I'm sorry if I gave you reason to fly off the handle."

Sarah felt so much better when she hung up the phone. There were still many little details to iron out between her and Maggie, but she was hopeful that they would be able to. She folded her half-basted wall hanging and set it on her machine. She took her bag, went out, and locked the door. She couldn't wait to stop locking the door because that would mean the robberies had been solved. She hoped Chief Webber's investigation hadn't stagnated like hers had.

When she parked in front of her son's house minutes later, it almost seemed odd that Dave's truck wasn't there. He'd been here so much recently. Letting herself into the house, Sarah went out to the kitchen. It was a chilly day. She'd make up some cocoa for the girls.

"We're home!" came a shout from the foyer as she heated enough milk for three cups.

Turning off the stove, Sarah moved the pot onto another burner. She went out into the hall. She halted and stared. Two girls stood there. Not Audrey and Amy, but Audrey and Tracy Witherspoon.

Hoping the girls hadn't noticed her double take, Sarah said, "Hi! Audrey, your mother is going to be late, so she asked me to come over."

"I know. She called us." She held up her cell. "Amy's gone over to the Rosenthals' to work on their project, and Tracy and I thought we'd work here. Is that OK?"

"Of course. I'm just starting some cocoa, so why don't you work in the dining room?"

"I'll get our posters," Audrey said.

Tracy asked, "Can I use your bathroom?"

"It's right past the stairs, second door on the left," Audrey said. "The light is on a pull chain."

The two girls hurried away, and Sarah went into the kitchen. Only when she was sure the girls couldn't hear did she laugh and think, *Lord, your wonders never cease.*

She poured cocoa into the milk and stirred it. Once it was ready, she filled three cups. She took some cookies out of the jar that Maggie kept full and put them on a plate. When she was about to carry them into the dining room, she hesitated. She didn't want the girls to bump into the cups and spill cocoa on their work.

Audrey came into the dining room with her arms full of poster board and markers. She put them on the table. Then, seeing the cookies and cocoa, she said, "Yummy!"

"I'll leave them on the counter. You two can get them when you're ready."

"Thanks, Grandma." She toyed with the

edge of a poster. "And thanks for being cool with Tracy coming over. If you'd freaked, she might have too. I wasn't sure she would agree when I asked her to come here."

"*You* asked her? What made you change your mind?"

Audrey leaned forward on a chair, folding her arms on top. "I thought about what you said about Grandpa Gerry, how he believed you've got to be a friend to make a friend. He must have been a pretty smart guy."

"He was." She realized that the twins still could get to know their grandfather better. They could learn about him through her.

"So I asked Tracy to come over."

"But hadn't you tried that before?"

Audrey scuffed one toe against the floor. "I mean, I *did* ask twice, but when she gave me excuses why she couldn't, I assumed she was snubbing me. She wasn't. She really couldn't come then. She could today."

"I'm glad."

Audrey turned as Tracy came back into the room. "Let's get to work."

Sarah murmured a prayer of thanks. Audrey and Tracy weren't yet friends, but maybe they would be someday. Even if they never became friendly, they had learned a valuable lesson about working together.

Picking up her cup of cocoa, she had

taken only one delicious sip before Audrey rushed into the kitchen.

"Look, Grandma!" She held up her phone.

Sarah grasped her wrist so she could see the screen. "All I see is one text message that says 'Bring your grandmother too.' Where are you planning to take me?"

"To Liz's house. She wants us to come over and see the baby tomorrow after school. You too. Can we go?"

"If your mother says it's OK, then yes."

"Will you come too?"

Sarah nodded. Maggie had said Dave was taking a few days off to be home with his wife and child. This might be Sarah's best chance to get a good look in the back of his truck.

CHAPTER TWENTY-FIVE

Sarah's hopes of discovering what was beneath the tarp were dashed as soon as she stopped in front of the neat Victorian cottage where the Diamonds lived. Dave's truck was nowhere in sight. A gravel drive led around to the back of the house. Maybe the truck was there, but what excuse could she devise to go out and look in the backyard?

The girls chattered like two excited squirrels. They were carrying small packages — gifts they'd picked up at the mall last night for the baby.

When Sarah rang the doorbell, she was surprised how quickly the door opened and Liz invited them in. The young mother must have been watching for them.

"I'm very glad you were able to come this afternoon," Liz said as she hung their jackets on the newel post at the bottom of the stairs. "I hope you don't mind my leaving them there. The closet door sticks something awful, and Dave hasn't had a chance to fix it." She laughed. "The handyman's house is always the last one to get fixed."

"For the same reason the cobbler's children have no shoes." Sarah made an effort to smile. It was tough. "Where's Dave?"

"At the grocery store. He should be back soon."

When the girls held out the packages, she asked, "For the baby?"

They nodded, grinning.

Liz opened the packages to find a New England Patriots bib and tiny blue socks with flags on them. The girls had each picked out one of the gifts. "These are adorable. Thank you so much." She hugged each of the girls, and then edged aside so they could go into the front room.

After one look around the cozy living room, Sarah knew, under other circumstances that she could have felt at home very quickly. No two pieces of furniture matched. Small tables and bookcases were painted in bright colors, and tan slipcovers hid any flaws on the sofa and an overstuffed chair. Light blue walls flanked the fieldstone fireplace, which took up one whole end of the room.

"What a charming home you have," said Sarah.

"I call it eclectic, but Dave calls it trashy chic." She smiled. "Because most of our furniture are pieces we found in the trash."

By the sofa, a wooden cradle with hand-turned spindles had been painted with bright blue bears. A tiny bundle in it slept soundly.

Amy and Audrey knelt by the cradle. "Ooooo!" cried the girls in unison.

"Shhh!" Sarah put a finger to each girl's lips. "Let's not wake him."

They nodded, but didn't take their eyes from the baby.

"He's a beautiful boy," Sarah whispered.

"Thank you." Liz beamed with delight. "I think so, but I've got to admit I'm a bit prejudiced."

"The cradle is beautiful too. Did you paint it?"

"Yes. I wanted the cradle and the quilt to match." She chuckled. "I didn't get the quilt done in time, but Dave finished the cradle."

Sarah ran her fingertips along the cradle, being careful not to rock it. "Do you mean that *this* is another of Dave's trash finds?"

"Can you believe it?" She ran her fingers along the top, taking care not to rock it. "It had fallen to pieces. He rebuilt it. Maggie said he shouldn't have stripped it, because the antique value is decreased when the original finish is gone. But I don't care. It's going to be an heirloom."

"The quilt would have been the perfect size for the cradle."

"I thought I might turn the quilt into a wall hanging instead."

"What a wonderful idea! And I would be happy to help you, if you'd like." Sarah was glad for a reason to smile.

Liz motioned for Sarah to sit. A few minutes later, much to the twins' delight, little David woke with a mewling cry. The girls had to wait patiently while Liz nursed the baby. Then they giggled when Liz asked if they wanted to hold him.

"Support his head like your mother showed you," Sarah said as Liz sat between the girls and placed the baby in Amy's arms.

Sarah sat on the rocker while Amy gazed down at David. For the first time, Sarah imagined herself as a *great* grandmother. It would be years before the twins would start families of their own, but Amy had such a loving expression. Babies were a blessing in many ways.

Audrey touched the baby's little fingers that were clenched in fists and oohed and aahed over his tiny fingernails. When Liz unwrapped the blanket to let them see his toes, the oohs and aahs began again.

Then Amy said, "Um, I think he needs to be changed."

Liz looked flustered as she took David from Amy, and Sarah asked what she needed.

"Baby wipes," she answered.

"Where are they?"

"Upstairs in the nursery."

"Let me go up and get them. I know you want to keep a close eye on everyone."

Liz gave her a grateful smile. "The nursery's on the right at the top of the stairs. The wipes are on the dresser."

"I'll find them. You sit."

"No." Liz looked from Audrey to Amy. "I think I'll show my future babysitters how to change a diaper."

"We know how to do that," Audrey said. "They taught us in our babysitting course."

"With a real baby?"

The girls exchanged glances, and then Amy replied, "Dolls."

"Then it's time for you to watch how it's done with a real baby and a real dirty diaper."

The twins shared another anxious glance. They wanted to prove they could handle babysitting, but they clearly wished they could have started with giving him a bottle or tying on a bib.

As she turned to go, Sarah said, "Girls, remember that he isn't a toy."

"Grandma!"

As she climbed the stairs, Sarah let her laugh ring out. Amy and Audrey were at an age where they baffled their parents at times and tested Maggie's and Jason's patience, but Sarah enjoyed their swings from responsible young adults to silly kids.

The baby wipes were where Liz had said. The sounds of the girls laughing rose up the stairs. Sarah reached for the banister to head back down, but halted when her eye was caught by a bright gold frame. It looked oddly like the frame around the daguerreotype.

She looked at what it held. It must have been the newspaper page Liz and Dave had found behind a mirror and had framed — *The Maple Hill Monitor,* dated Wednesday, September 25, 1867.

Curious, she scanned the articles. The weather forecast and ads for local stores were in the column farthest to the left. News filled the other three columns. The two center columns contained articles about the call to impeach the president, Andrew Johnson, but the other column focused on

328

local news. That interested her most.

She smiled when she read about how the mill was undergoing repairs and a covered footbridge was being built at the end of what would become known as Bridge Street. The last article was in the bottom right-hand corner. It was headlined:

Auction to be held at Hazzard Farm
Saturday, September 28, 1867
10 A.M.

"Whoa," she said, bending closer to read the tiny print. Her heart pounded like a hammer on a metal drum.

Only a tantalizingly short portion of the article had survived, because, like the other articles, it continued on an inside page. Still, it was enough to let her know she'd found a vital clue. The auction was to be held to raise money to help clear Adam Hazzard's name. Clear it from what? Maybe the answer was in the rest of the article. The historical society had the archives, but they would be closed tomorrow. It should be in the archives at the library, though.

She could go there and read it when the library opened tomorrow morning, but it would only be to confirm her saddest suspicion: Dave had known about the Hazzards already. Something had happened to besmirch Adam Hazzard's name. Adam Hazzard, a Civil War veteran, needed to regain his reputation.

It was just the sort of cause that Dave embraced, but she couldn't help wondering if he might have gone too far this time.

The library appeared deserted when Sarah arrived shortly after the doors opened the next morning. She hoped the newspaper would be the breakthrough she needed. Dr. Treadwell, the college professor, had finally sent her a long e-mail with information on Adam's unit. It hadn't included anything she hadn't already seen online.

Spencer smiled as he stepped out from between the tall shelves with an armload of books. "How's it going, Sarah?" He set the books on the circulation desk. "I heard you and Neil helped the cops nab a thief."

"Neil should get the credit. He's the one who called them."

"What can I do for you today? Do you want to look at the Maple Hill history again?"

"Actually, can I have the key to the archive room?"

He took a metal box from a drawer behind the desk. Opening it, he fished around inside and then lifted out a small key. From it hung a round tab with Miss Carpenter's scrawl: *Special Collections.* "Here you go."

Sarah picked up the key. "I'll return this when I'm done."

"What are you planning to look at in the archives?"

"Bound newspapers."

"Enjoy using them while you can." He put the key box in its drawer. "The library trustees are worried about the deteriorating condition of those newspapers. I'm working on a grant to have them scanned before we lose them completely. But if the grant doesn't come through, the trustees may arrange for them to be put somewhere else to protect them."

"But then the public couldn't use them."

He nodded. "And there's the problem. Do we save them for future generations while we deny current patrons?"

"Too big a question for me." She stepped away from the desk. "At least until I answer a few of my own."

"Knock yourself out." He grinned. "Not literally. If you need help getting volumes down, give a yell. Good researching."

"Thanks."

As she climbed to the second floor, the library's quiet wrapped itself around Sarah. Her footsteps sounded extra loud on the wood floor as she walked past more bookcases and carousels holding DVDs. The Special Collections door was in the rear right corner. Sounds of Spencer reshelving books faded as she walked toward it.

She opened the door and stepped inside the windowless room. The motion-control lights flickered on to reveal a library within the library. The room smelled of time, a mixture of lingering heat from summer and book dust.

Putting the key on the lone table between three rows of bookcases and the copier, she looked for bound copies of *The Maple Hill Monitor.* The dark green books were shelved chronologically . . . except for the 1867 volume. Where was it? Had it been tampered with — or stolen?

Calm down, she told herself, when she saw 1867 between the volumes for 1876 and 1878. She drew the heavy book off the shelf. She set the 1867 book on the table. Then she sat and carefully opened the book. More scents of dust and decomposing paper rose out of it. She hoped the library would get the grant to scan these pages before the newspapers fell apart completely.

Putting on her glasses, she thumbed through to September, turning each individual page with care. They crackled a warning, and she forced herself to slow down.

She didn't want to damage the pages in her zeal to get to the truth.

She smiled when she saw the front page of the September 25, 1867 issue. Her fingers trembled with anticipation as she turned that page and the next one so she could see the last page of the issue.

There!

There was the rest of the article.

The auction will include many items of interest to residents of Maple Hill and the surrounding villages. Those wishing to bid are invited to arrive an hour early to view the lots. Farm equipment will be available for viewing in the barn. Household goods will be available for viewing on the front porch or inside the house. Among the household items that will be put up for bid are:

Furniture including a bedstead, a round oak dining room table. Cranberry glass including a lamp and two serving bowls. Cast iron kitchenware including a kettle, a dutch oven, and utensils. Short case wall clock. Boot scrapers. Personal items including ladies' silk fans (one white, one black) and silver-framed dressing table set (mirror, comb, brush, containers). Children's toys including books and dolls and a toy rocking horse.

The full list of items to come under the ham-

"Oh, my!" Sarah said as she continued to read. The items' descriptions took two columns. They were so specific that she recognized the book of poetry as well as Maggie's clock and Arnold's cameo. She had found the connection between the Hazzards and the robberies. Every stolen item had been sold at that auction.

She went to the first page and began to read the article again. She stared at the sentence that stated the Hazzards were selling everything they owned to raise money to clear Adam's name. She turned to the last page again and read the rest of the sentence. The auction was to raise money to get Adam the honorable discharge he deserved rather than the dishonorable one he had received.

"Oh, my!" she whispered again as she pushed back from the table.

Dave must be the thief. He was the only person in Maple Hill who would care about helping Adam Hazzard. Everyone else had forgotten about him. With the description of the items auctioned off back in 1867, it would have been easy to know which items to take. But why? To reclaim everything that was once Adam Hazzard's? That didn't make sense. What purpose could that serve?

Carrying the volume to the copier, Sarah dropped coins into the slot and placed the book on the flat glass bed. She made two copies of the full article, and then closed the book and put it in the proper place on the shelf.

She took the copies out of the tray and reread them. She had hoped she was wrong, but now she knew she wasn't. Who else in Maple Hill would care about the Hazzards and all they'd lost when they left town under a cloud of shame?

CHAPTER TWENTY-SIX

Sarah returned the archive room key to Spencer and then left the library. She walked across the parking lot, holding the copies tightly to prevent the fall breeze from stealing them.

Minutes later, Sarah stopped her car in front of Dave and Liz's house. Dave's truck was parked in the driveway. He appeared around it, wiping his hands on a greasy rag, as she got out of her car.

He froze when he saw her. She walked over to him and held out the pages. His brow furrowed as he took them. He glanced at them, and his face turned gray.

"Maybe we should find some quiet place to talk," she said. She aimed a meaningful glance at the house and added, "Just you and me."

He nodded. "Where do you want to talk?"

"Wherever it's comfortable for you."

"You don't have to be so nice, Sarah. I'm

actually glad to be able to talk about this. It's been eating me up inside." He held the pages as tightly as if they were a lifeline. As they sat on the front steps, he said, "You know all about it now, I guess."

"About Adam Hazzard? Yes. About you?" She sighed. "Yes, even though I keep hoping I'm wrong."

"You're right. About both of us. I should have been honest with you right from the beginning."

"That you're trying to help Adam Hazzard?"

"First Sergeant Adam Hazzard was accused of deserting after the Battle of Petersburg in Virginia. Many men on both sides of the battle fled when the Union Army detonated the bomb that created the great crater in the battlefield. But, according to the letters he and others wrote to clear his name, Adam Hazzard did not."

"I thought they shot deserters." Sarah shivered at her own words.

"There were enough people who believed he hadn't deserted his post. He had witnesses, but he couldn't get a hearing. The government officials were too busy with trying to impeach the president and to rebuild the country to worry about one misjudged army sergeant."

"So that's why the Hazzards had an auction in September 1867. They were selling everything they owned, including a cranberry lamp, that copy of *Leaves of Grass,* and a now battered oak clock. A familiar list." She tapped the pages she'd given him. "But the daguerreotype wasn't on it, and it wasn't stolen either."

"When I learned about Sergeant Hazzard, I was able to contact a couple of his descendants who had the picture. I told them I was trying to clear his name. They sent me the daguerreotype, along with copies of all the correspondence they had about Sergeant Hazzard's efforts to clear his name. I carried the picture with me as a constant reminder of why I was doing what I did." He sighed. "Then I lost it. I was shocked when you told me the police had it."

"Why? You knew Martha and I had found the antiques up on Mount Greylock. I know you've hiked a lot up there, so it was an obvious place for you to hide the antiques you'd stolen."

He stared at her, open-mouthed.

"Don't you have the Poplawskis' missing chairs under the tarp in the back of your truck?"

"Y-y-yes," he stammered. "I mean, I think so. I'm not sure."

"How can you not be sure? If you took the chairs when you took the other items from their barn —"

"Sarah," he said, grasping her hand and meeting her eyes for the first time since she'd given him the photocopies. "I'm not a thief. I didn't take any of those antiques."

"But you said you have the missing chairs in your truck."

"They *may* be the missing chairs. I picked them up off the curb early on the morning after the robberies. Then I heard what had been taken, and I didn't know what to do with the chairs. I was afraid if I went to the police, they'd think I was the thief."

Sarah stared at him. Every clue had pointed to him. He had wanted to draw attention to the injustice done to Sergeant Hazzard. He'd hiked Mount Greylock. He had been acting like a man with a terrible secret.

At that thought, she asked, "If you didn't steal the antiques, why have you been acting so guilty? You've gone out of your way not to talk to me."

"I felt bad that I wasn't helping you find out more about Sergeant Hazzard and his wife. I'd seen how eager you were to learn about them. You didn't know about 'the wrong done to them.' I wanted to help you, but if I'd said anything —"

"I might have believed you were the thief and gone to the police."

"And then I'd have been caught with what might be stolen chairs in my truck. I could have been arrested, and what would that have done to Liz? As well, any chance I had to help Sergeant Hazzard would be gone. You believed I was a thief, and you know me."

Sarah sighed. "Maybe, if we work together, we can come up with a way to let people know about Sergeant Hazzard. In the meantime, you need to turn the chairs over to Chief Webber and tell him where you picked them up. That might be a clue to the real thief." She put her hand on his arm. "I'll go with you, if you'd like. We can get Pastor John too."

"So you believe me?"

"Yes."

Tears glistened in his eyes. "Thank you, Sarah. It's nice to know I've got a real friend in Maple Hill."

"A friend who thought you were capable of stealing from your neighbors. I'm so glad you're not the thief." She sighed. "Now I've got to look at the clues all over again and see if I can figure out who else might have had a reason to take those antiques."

"I wish I could help, but I don't have any ideas."

"Where *did* you find the chairs?"

"On County Street, two or three blocks out."

Sarah looked from him to her copy of the newspaper article. Her eyes were caught by one particular description among the children's toys. A rocking horse with red stars on its back. She knew where that toy was now. She'd seen it just two days ago. On County Street. Her stomach tightened into knots, but Gerry's voice whispered in her head. It reminded her that it was better to face her problems head on rather than waiting and worrying.

She stood. "Dave, I think it'd be better if you stay here until I get back."

"Where are you going?" he asked, astonished. "I thought we were going to call the police and get this cleared up."

She glanced at her watch. The Kirschners went to Liam's every morning. She might not be too late. "We will . . . when I get back. Don't go anywhere. Promise me that."

"I won't, but, Sarah, where are you going?"

"To get to the bottom of this. I'll be back as soon as I can. Trust me on this."

He nodded, even though she could almost

341

see the questions whirling through his head.

Sarah went to her car and headed back to town. She drove the speed limit, but her thoughts were going at light speed. She found a parking space and hurried to The Spotted Dog.

When she opened the door, she looked toward the café. At one table, Dottie and Arnold Kirschner were eating breakfast as they did most mornings. Dottie waved, but Arnold didn't look up. Three other tables were filled, including one where Chief Webber and two of his officers were enjoying coffee and Liam's cranberry scones.

Liam smiled at Sarah. "It looks like someone needs to satisfy a chai latte craving this morning."

Sarah didn't answer as she walked into the café. She went to where the Kirschners sat.

"Good morning." Her voice quavered, but she couldn't help that. "Mind if I join you?"

"Please do." Dottie added, "Arnold, move that ratty old coat of yours so Sarah can sit down."

He drew his coat off the chair and onto his lap before Sarah could get more than a quick look at it, but that quick look was enough. It was a dark green work coat like he would have worn while working for the state up on Mount Greylock.

"How's the antique buying going, Arnold?" Sarah asked. "Maggie told me you'd given her a whole shopping list of things you're looking for. She mentioned you were particularly interested in a cranberry bowl. Have you found one you like yet?"

"It's going slow." He stirred more sugar into his cup.

"I've got a list of my own." She set the copied pages from the newspaper on the table by his plate. "But I suspect you've already seen it."

He took one look at it, and his face went as pale as Dave's had. "Where did you get this? Did Diamond give it to you too?"

"No. I got it from the library," she answered, her voice growing steadier. "Where Dave also found it." She saw bafflement on Dottie's face and wished there were a way to ease this for her friend. Sarah turned her attention back to Arnold. "He must have mentioned the article to you when he came over to ask you about the Hazzards."

Arnold, for once, was silent. He kept staring at the pages.

"So you befriended him, pretending you had information you didn't, until he gave you a copy of the items sold at the Hazzard auction. Then you decided to get those

343

antiques for yourself. You bought some, and then when others weren't for sale or you couldn't afford the price, like with the clock you stole from Maggie after losing out at the fundraiser for the school newspaper, you took them."

"But we were robbed too!" Arnold cried. "How can you accuse me of being the thief when *we* were robbed?"

Sarah heard chairs scraping behind her and guessed Arnold's raised voice had gotten Chief Webber's attention.

"But you were robbed last," Sarah said. "Once you heard that the other robberies had been reported, you reported one too, to throw suspicion off yourself. And who else knows Mount Greylock like you do? Only someone who worked up there all those years would know about a storage cellar where he could stash the antiques until he could sneak them into his house. Did you think you'd shift suspicion to Peg Girard by using the hospital bed pads she must have given you after your surgery, or were you thinking only of keeping the antiques from damage?"

"This is nonsense. I won't listen to another minute of it." He pushed back his chair. "C'mon, Dottie. We're leaving."

Dottie's face was gray with shock.

344

"The chairs that belonged to the Poplaw-skis confused me," Sarah said. "Why weren't they with the other stolen antiques? Why did you put them out with one of your neighbors' trash?"

Arnold's fingers closed into fists on the table. "You're making wild accusations."

"I could think of only one reason. You didn't want the chairs after you stole them. You made a mistake thinking they had belonged to the Hazzards, but they hadn't. Those two chairs weren't your first mistake, were they, Arnold? You told Maggie you wanted to sell her your other mistakes, but you didn't dare take the chairs in once the other antiques were discovered."

Now his face was as ashen as Dottie's.

"The daguerreotype was a puzzle too," Sarah said. "But I've just learned that it was Dave's. He lost it. That's why he was shocked to see a copy of the picture I took of it. Arnold, you must have found it and had it with you when you hid the stolen antiques up on Mount Greylock because you couldn't put them in your house until everyone gave up looking for them. But then you lost the daguerreotype too, Arnold. Were you looking for it when you were caught on video in your green coat at the peak?"

Dottie grabbed Sarah's arm. "Stop it! Arnold wouldn't do anything like that. Tell her, Arnold! Tell her you didn't steal those antiques." When he didn't reply, she gasped, "You didn't, did you?"

"They are mine!" Arnold exploded. "My family never should have let that coward Adam Hazzard sell our things. It would have been better if he'd never come back to Maple Hill."

Dottie moaned and covered her face with her hands.

"Don't you see?" He pushed back his chair and stood. "The antiques belong to me and my family! Not to a deserter who shamed our family and then sold everything we owned! Once I get the antiques back where they belong, it'll be like it was supposed to be."

Silence clamped on the café.

Chief Webber put a hand on Arnold's shoulder. "Why don't we take this discussion down to the police station and let Liam's other customers get back to their coffee?"

Arnold seemed to shrink before Sarah's eyes as all his bravado faded. Beside her, Dottie wept. It was clear that her husband needed help, and Sarah prayed that he would find someone who could help him.

When another officer offered to help Dottie to her feet, she let him.

Sarah watched the police lead the Kirschners out of the café. Standing, she nodded to Liam when he asked if she was OK. She had to get back and let Dave know what had happened; then together they'd take the chairs to Chief Webber. She knew the Kirschners had a hard road ahead of them. But she'd be behind them every step of the way.

EPILOGUE

The open house night at Hawthorne Middle School was unseasonably hot and humid. The doors of the gym had been left open to channel through any breath of air. Lightning flickered across the mountains.

In the gym, the bleachers had been pulled out. The center of the floor was filled with chairs for proud parents and other family members.

The crowded gym burst into polite applause at the end of each presentation on unsung heroes. Every time a new group of children stepped onto the stage, different parents stood and aimed their video cameras. Amy's team had been one of the first, and Amy had spoken directly and calmly to Sarah, who sat in the front row. When her team's presentation was over, Amy hadn't returned to sit with her parents as the other students did.

Sarah sat with Jason and Maggie on one

side and the Diamonds on the other. Both Liz and Dave had been hesitant about coming tonight. When Martha offered to babysit, Liz and Dave had agreed to attend.

Dave had smiled and joked with Jason before the presentations began. Since Dave had turned the chairs over to Chief Webber, he had been a new man. The tension that had weighed down his shoulders was gone, and his eyes had taken on a mischievous twinkle.

The Poplawskis had been pleased to get their chairs back. The chairs were heirlooms from Mrs. Poplawski's family. Arnold wasn't cooperating with the police, but the pieces seemed to be coming together.

"Audrey's up next," whispered Jason. He turned on the video camera.

Audrey began her and Tracy's presentation on the Veterans War Memorial Tower. They ended with the video of the veteran who spoke of the sacrifices made by military men and women and their families. Dave wasn't the only one who wiped away a tear.

The applause was enthusiastic when they finished. Audrey remained on stage as her teacher, Mrs. Jefferson, came out to the microphone.

"I want to thank you for coming tonight to see our students' hard work." More applause followed her words. She raised her hands as people started to stand. "We have one more, very special presentation tonight. The students involved asked if they could do this in addition to their other projects. They have had only a few days to prepare and have worked very hard. Please give your attention to Amy and Audrey Hart."

There was a rustle through the gym as the twins walked back to the center of the stage.

"Tonight," Audrey said, her voice even and clear, "we have been introducing you to unsung heroes, past and present."

"But there is one more unsung hero who has been waiting 150 years for his story to be told." Amy tapped a key on the computer connected to the screen.

The image from the daguerreotype of Adam and Barbara Hazzard appeared on the screen. Beside her, Sarah heard Dave draw in a quick breath. He looked at her, and she nodded. As a slow grin inched across his face, she knew he understood that *this* was what she'd come up with to remind folks in Maple Hill about the injustice done to Adam Hazzard.

"Allow us to introduce you to Sergeant Adam Hazzard and his wife, Barbara," Audrey said. "They lived in Maple Hill 150 years ago. Sergeant Hazzard served in the

Union Army with the 15th Infantry Regiment during the Civil War."

"But if you go to the memorial stone on the green," Amy picked up the story with a confidence that delighted Sarah, "you won't find Sergeant Hazzard's name on the plaque. Why?"

It was Audrey's turn. "Because he was falsely accused of desertion." The picture on the screen changed to a photograph of the battlefield in Petersburg, Virginia, showing the crater left after the Union bomb had exploded. "He survived the war, but was accused of desertion. To raise money to try to clear his name of that horrible blemish, he and his wife were forced in 1867 to sell everything they owned. They sold everything in an auction. Their furniture, their few pieces of jewelry, even their children's toys. They probably didn't have much more than the clothes on their backs when they left Maple Hill on a quest to gain a hero the recognition he deserved."

"They must have failed because Sergeant Hazzard's service record was never changed," Amy said, "and eventually they were forgotten in Maple Hill."

"Until Maple Hill resident Dave Diamond discovered the truth and set out to help Sergeant Hazzard as he has helped other veterans," Audrey said. "What truth did Dave uncover? He searched through military archives and private correspondence between Sergeant Hazzard and members of his unit. The truth was there. At Petersburg, the Union troops dug a mine beneath Confederate fortifications and filled it with gunpowder. When the gunpowder exploded, it sent earth and stones and debris high in the air. No one could see anything more than a few inches away. Many men ran in terror, but Sergeant Hazzard held his position. That was confirmed by two of his men, but when they later died of their wounds, their testimony was disregarded."

"Others stepped forward to say he hadn't run as some men did," Amy said, "but by then a charge of desertion had been brought against Sergeant Hazzard. He escaped being hanged because of the conflicting reports, but was given a dishonorable discharge. He came home to Maple Hill, sure he'd be able to clear his name quickly."

"It didn't happen." Audrey brought up pictures of Abraham Lincoln and Andrew Johnson. "President Lincoln was assassinated, and the nation became obsessed with impeaching President Johnson. The concerns of a dishonorably discharged soldier were ignored."

There was a low rumble through the gym from the thunder outside. Everyone inside listened, rapt, to the girls.

"Until Dave decided to help, but Dave hasn't had any luck clearing Sergeant Hazzard's name either," Amy said. "He ran into the same resistance Sergeant Hazzard did. We wanted to tell you about Sergeant Hazzard's story to help make sure Sergeant Hazzard takes his rightful place with other heroes. This is what we have done to help. What will you do?" No one spoke. No one moved. Then someone began clapping, and the gym resounded with applause.

"I had no idea they'd do something this wonderful," Dave said.

"They're pretty wonderful girls." Sarah didn't try to keep her pride out of her voice.

Maggie stood and faced the audience. "I know many of you don't know me, but Amy and Audrey are my daughters, and I own Magpie's Antiques. I'd like to suggest we hold another auction to raise money for Sergeant Hazzard and his family. With the money raised, we can petition for the hearing that Sergeant Hazzard must never have gotten."

Several people shouted their agreement, and smiles appeared around the gym.

"We can easily publicize it," Maggie said,

"if we sell the items that were sold at the auction in 1867. We may not be able to find all the antiques listed in the newspaper in 1867, but I know many are still in Maple Hill. For example, I know where the short-case wall clock is." She held up a sheaf of pages. "I've got copies of the list from the newspaper for anyone who wants one. I'm sure we can add other items as well, so everyone can participate who wants to."

Sarah thought about her wall quilt. She had planned to hang it over her fireplace when it was finished. Now she would rather see it in the auctioneer's hand as it was sold.

Audrey motioned for her mother to step up on stage. Quickly a crowd gathered around her as people asked for a copy of the list and offered help. Sarah guessed that many barns and attics would be searched that night and the next.

"I want everyone to know that the pro- ceeds from the auction will be put in an ac- count at the Maple Hill Savings and Loan," Maggie said. "It will be used for Sergeant Hazzard's defense fund. A local attorney has agreed to handle the case pro bono." She smiled at Jason, who blushed as cheers met her words.

Again Maggie held up her hands for quiet. "But there will be other expenses while we work to clear Sergeant Hazzard's name, so I hope you'll help by donating what you can to the auction and bidding on the items. Any funds raised will be administered by a committee of three Maple Hill residents. First, Irene Stuart, because she knows the history of Maple Hill better than anyone else. The second member is Neil Lawton because of his financial background. The last member is the one person who knows a lot about helping veterans and has the best chance of proving that Adam Hazzard was no deserter. Someone who has helped many other veterans and never looked for any thanks. That's Dave Diamond."

Again cheers rang through the gym as Maggie stepped down off the stage. It was a sensible arrangement with the three best people for the job of clearing Sergeant Hazzard's name . . . finally.

Dave shook Sarah's hand and then Jason's. "Let me thank you because Sergeant Hazzard can't." He gulped. "Thank you for helping him and me." Jason grinned.

Liz stared at Dave in astonishment and asked, "Did you hear that? They all want to help."

"I don't know if I believe my ears." He looked at Sarah, and then gave her a big hug. "I can't believe they all want to help!"

"Most folks here really do care about one another," Sarah said with a broad smile. "Welcome to Maple Hill."

Linking her arm with her husband's, Maggie said, "Not just welcome to Maple Hill. Welcome home."

ABOUT THE AUTHOR

Jo Ann Brown has published more than 80 titles under various names. Her most recent title was the novelization for Thomas Kinkade's *Christmas Cottage* movie. Raised in a small town, she served as a US Army officer. She has lived in New England most of her life along with her husband and her three children and two very spoiled cats.